Gottfried Keller

Romeo und Julia auf dem Dorfe

Romeo and Juliet of the Village

German | English

Übersetzt von Wolf von Schierbrand

Gottfried Keller: Romeo und Julia auf dem Dorfe / Romeo and Juliet of the Village.

German | English

Übersetzt von Wolf von Schierbrand.

Entstanden 1855. Erstdruck: Braunschweig (Vieweg) 1856.

Neuausgabe
Herausgegeben von Karl-Maria Guth
Berlin 2021

Der Text dieser Ausgabe folgt:
Gottfried Keller: Sämtliche Werke in acht Bänden, Berlin: Aufbau, 1958–1961.

Umschlaggestaltung von Thomas Schultz-Overhage unter Verwendung des Bildes: Ernst Würtenberger, Sali und Vrenchen auf der Kirchweih, 1919

Gesetzt aus der Minion Pro, 11 pt

Die Sammlung Hofenberg erscheint im Verlag
Henricus - Edition Deutsche Klassik GmbH, Berlin
Herstellung: Books on Demand, Norderstedt

ISBN 978-3-7437-4201-7

Bibliografische Information der Deutschen Nationalbibliothek:
Die Deutsche Nationalbibliothek verzeichnet diese Publikation in der Deutschen Nationalbibliografie; detaillierte bibliografische Daten sind im Internet über www.dnb.de abrufbar.

Romeo und Julia auf dem Dorfe

Diese Geschichte zu erzählen würde eine müßige Nachahmung sein, wenn sie nicht auf einem wirklichen Vorfall beruhte, zum Beweise, wie tief im Menschenleben jede jener Fabeln wurzelt, auf welche die großen alten Werke gebaut sind. Die Zahl solcher Fabeln ist mäßig; aber stets treten sie in neuem Gewande wieder in die Erscheinung und zwingen alsdann die Hand, sie festzuhalten.

An dem schönen Flusse, der eine halbe Stunde entfernt an Seldwyl vorüberzieht, erhebt sich eine weitgedehnte Erdwelle und verliert sich, selber wohlbebaut, in der fruchtbaren Ebene. Fern an ihrem Fuße liegt ein Dorf, welches manche große Bauernhöfe enthält, und über die sanfte Anhöhe lagen vor Jahren drei prächtige lange Äcker weithingestreckt gleich drei riesigen Bändern nebeneinander. An einem sonnigen Septembermorgen pflügten zwei Bauern auf zweien dieser Äcker, und zwar auf jedem der beiden äußersten; der mittlere schien seit langen Jahren brach und wüst zu liegen, denn er war mit Steinen und hohem Unkraut bedeckt, und eine Welt von geflügelten Tierchen summte ungestört über ihm. Die Bauern aber, welche zu beiden Seiten hinter ihrem Pfluge gingen, waren lange knochige Männer von ungefähr vierzig Jahren und verkündeten auf den ersten Blick den sichern, gutbesorgten Bauersmann. Sie trugen kurze Kniehosen von starkem Zwillich, an dem jede Falte ihre unveränderliche Lage hatte und wie in Stein gemeißelt aussah. Wenn sie, auf ein Hindernis stoßend, den Pflug fester faßten, so zitterten die groben Hemdärmel von der leichten Erschütterung, indessen die wohlrasierten Gesichter ruhig und aufmerksam, aber ein wenig blinzelnd in den Sonnenschein vor sich hinschauten, die Furche bemaßen oder auch wohl zuweilen sich umsahen, wenn ein fernes Geräusch die Stille des Landes unterbrach. Langsam und mit einer gewissen natürlichen Zierlichkeit setzten sie einen Fuß um den andern vorwärts, und keiner sprach ein Wort, außer wenn er etwa dem Knechte, der die stattlichen Pferde antrieb, eine Anweisung gab. So glichen sie einander vollkommen in einiger Entfernung; denn sie stellten die ursprüngliche Art dieser Gegend dar, und man hätte sie auf den ersten Blick nur daran unterscheiden können, daß der eine den Zipfel seiner weißen Kappe

Romeo and Juliet of the Village

Near the fine river which flows along half an hour's distance from Seldwyla, rises in a long stretch a headland which finally, itself carefully cultivated, is lost in the fertile plain. Some distance away at the foot of this rise there lies a village, to which belong many large farms, and across the hillock itself there were, years ago, three splendid holdings, like unto as many giant ribbons, side by side. One sunny September morning two peasants were plowing on two of these vast fields, the two which stretched along the middle one. The middle one itself seemed to have lain fallow and waste for a long, long time, for it was thickly covered with stones, bowlders and tall weeds, and a multitude of winged insects were humming around and over it. The two peasants who on both sides of this huge wilderness were following their plows, were big, bony men of near forty, and at the first glance one could tell them as men of substance and well-regulated circumstances. They wore short breeches made of strong canvas, and every fold in these garments seemed to be carved out of rock. When they hit against some obstacle with their plow their coarse shirt sleeves would tremble slightly, while the closely shaved faces continued to look steadfastly into the sunlight ahead. Tranquilly they would go on accurately measuring the width of the furrow, and now and then looking around them if some unusual noise reached their ears. They would then peer attentively in the direction indicated, while all about them the country spread out measureless and peaceful. Sedately and with a certain unconscious grace they would set one foot before the other, slowly advancing, and neither of them ever spoke a word unless it was to briefly instruct the hired man who was leading the horses. Thus they resembled each other strongly from a distance; for they fitly represented the peculiar type of people of the district, and at first sight one might have distinguished them from each other only by this one fact that he on the one side wore the peaked fold of his white cap in front and the other had it hanging down his neck. But even this kept changing, since they were plowing in opposite directions; for when they arrived at the end of the new furrow

nach vorn trug, der andere aber hinten im Nacken hängen hatte. Aber das wechselte zwischen ihnen ab, indem sie in der entgegengesetzten Richtung pflügten; denn wenn sie oben auf der Höhe zusammentrafen und aneinander vorüberkamen, so schlug dem, welcher gegen den frischen Ostwind ging, die Zipfelkappe nach hinten über, während sie bei den andern, der den Wind im Rücken hatte, sich nach vorne sträubte. Es gab auch jedesmal einen mittlern Augenblick, wo die schimmernden Mützen aufrecht in der Luft schwankten und wie zwei weiße Flammen gen Himmel züngelten. So pflügten beide ruhevoll, und es war schön anzusehen in der stillen goldenen Septembergegend, wenn sie so auf der Höhe aneinander vorbeizogen, still und langsam, und sich mählich voneinander entfernten, immer weiter auseinander, bis beide wie zwei untergehende Gestirne hinter die Wölbung des Hügels hinabgingen und verschwanden, um eine gute Weile darauf wieder zu erscheinen. Wenn sie einen Stein in ihren Furchen fanden, so warfen sie denselben auf den wüsten Acker in der Mitte mit lässig kräftigem Schwunge, was aber nur selten geschah, da derselbe schon fast mit allen Steinen belastet war, welche überhaupt auf den Nachbaräckern zu finden gewesen. So war der lange Morgen zum Teil vergangen, als von dem Dorfe her ein kleines artiges Fuhrwerklein sich näherte, welches kaum zu sehen war, als es begann, die gelinde Höhe heranzukommen. Das war ein grünbemaltes Kinderwägelchen, in welchem die Kinder der beiden Pflüger, ein Knabe und ein kleines Ding von Mädchen, gemeinschaftlich den Vormittagsimbiß heranfuhren. Für jeden Teil lag ein schönes Brot, in eine Serviette gewickelt, eine Kanne Wein mit Gläsern und noch irgendein Zutätchen in dem Wagen, welches die zärtliche Bäuerin für den fleißigen Meister mitgesandt, und außerdem waren da noch verpackt allerlei seltsam gestaltete angebissene Äpfel und Birnen, welche die Kinder am Wege aufgelesen, und eine völlig nackte Puppe mit nur einem Bein und einem verschmierten Gesicht, welche wie ein Fräulein zwischen den Broten saß und sich behaglich fahren ließ. Dies Fuhrwerk hielt nach manchem Anstoß und Aufenthalt endlich auf der Höhe im Schatten eines jungen Lindengebüsches, welches da am Rande des Feldes stand, und nun konnte man die beiden Fuhrleute näher betrachten. Es war ein Junge von sieben Jahren und ein Dirnchen von fünfen,

up on high, and thus passed each other, the one who now strode against the strong east wind had his cap tip turned over until it sat in the back of the bull neck, while the second one, who had now the wind behind him, got the tip of his cap reversed. There was also a middling moment, so to speak, when both caps of shining white seemed to flare skywards like shimmering flames. Thus they plowed and plowed in restful diligence, and it was a fine sight in this still golden September weather to see them every short while passing each other on the summit of the hill, then easily and slowly drifting farther and farther apart, until both disappeared like sinking stars beyond the curve of the rise, only to reappear a bit later in precisely the same fashion. When they found a stone in their furrows they threw it on the fallow field between them, doing so leisurely and accurately, like men who have learnt by habit to gauge the correct distance. But this occurred rarely, for this waste field was apparently already loaded with about all the pebbles, bowlders and rocks to be discovered in the neighborhood. In this quiet way the long forenoon was nearly spent when there approached from the village a tiny vehicle. So small it looked at first when it began to climb up the height that it seemed a toy. And indeed, it was just that in a sense, for it was a baby carriage, painted in vivid green, in which the children of the two plowers, a sturdy little youngster and a slip of a small girl, jointly brought the lunch for their parent's delectation. For each of the two fathers there lay a fine appetizing loaf in the cart, wrapped neatly in a clean napkin, a flask of cool wine, with glasses, and some smaller tidbits as well, all of which the tender farmer's wife had sent along for the hard-working husband. But there were other things as well in the little vehicle: apples and pears which the two children had picked up on the way and out of which they had taken a bite or so, and a wholly naked doll with only one leg and a face entirely soiled and besmeared, and which sat self-satisfied in this carriage like a dainty young lady and allowed herself to be transported in this way. This small vehicle after sundry difficulties and delays at last arrived in the shade of a high growth of underbrush which luxuriated there at the edge of the big field, and now it was time to take a look at the two drivers. One was a boy of seven, the other a little girl of five, both of them sound and healthy, and else there was nothing remarkable about them except that they had very fine eyes and the girl, besides, a rather tawny complexion and curly dark hair, and the expression of her little face was ardent and trustful. The plowers meanwhile had also reached once more the top, given their horses a provender of clover, and left their plows in the half-done furrow; then as good neighbors they went to partake jointly of the tempting

beide gesund und munter, und weiter war nichts Auffälliges an ihnen, als daß beide sehr hübsche Augen hatten und das Mädchen dazu noch eine bräunliche Gesichtsfarbe und ganz krause dunkle Haare, welche ihm ein feuriges und treuherziges Ansehen gaben. Die Pflüger waren jetzt auch wieder oben angekommen, steckten den Pferden etwas Klee vor und ließen die Pflüge in der halbvollendeten Furche stehen, während sie als gute Nachbaren sich zu dem gemeinschaftlichen Imbiß begaben und sich da zuerst begrüßten; denn bislang hatten sie sich noch nicht gesprochen an diesem Tage.

Wie nun die Männer mit Behagen ihr Frühstück einnahmen und mit zufriedenem Wohlwollen den Kindern mitteilten, die nicht von der Stelle wichen, solange gegessen und getrunken wurde, ließen sie ihre Blicke in der Nähe und Ferne herumschweifen und sahen das Städtchen räucherig glänzend in seinen Bergen liegen; denn das reichlich Mittagsmahl, welches die Seldwyler alle Tage bereiteten, pflegte ein weithin scheinendes Silbergewölk über ihre Dächer emporzutragen, welches lachend an ihren Bergen hinschwebte.

»Die Lumpenhunde zu Seldwyl kochen wieder gut!« sagte Manz, der eine der Bauern, und Marti, der andere, erwiderte: »Gestern war einer bei mir wegen des Ackers hier.« – »Aus dem Bezirksrat? bei mir ist er auch gewesen!« sagte Manz. »So? und meinte wahrscheinlich auch, du solltest das Land benutzen und den Herren die Pacht zahlen?« – »Ja, bis es sich entschieden habe, wem der Acker gehöre und was mit ihm anzufangen sei. Ich habe mich aber bedankt, das verwilderte Wesen für einen andern herzustellen, und sagte, sie sollten den Acker nur verkaufen und den Ertrag aufheben, bis sich ein Eigentümer gefunden, was wohl nie geschehen wird; denn was einmal auf der Kanzlei zu Seldwyl liegt, hat da gute Weile, und überdem ist die Sache schwer zu entscheiden. Die Lumpen möchten indessen gar zu gern etwas zu naschen bekommen durch den Pachtzins, was sie freilich mit der Verkaufssumme auch tun könnten; allein wir würden uns hüten, dieselbe zu hoch hinaufzutreiben, und wir wüßten dann doch, was wir hätten und wem das Land gehört!« – »Ganz so meine ich auch und habe dem Steckleinspringer eine ähnliche Antwort gegeben!«

Sie schwiegen eine Weile, dann fing Manz wiederum an: »Schad ist es aber doch, daß der

collation, and meeting there they gave greeting, for until that moment they had not yet spoken to each other on that day.

While they ate, slowly but with a keen appetite, and of their food also shared with the children, the latter not budging as long as there were eatables in sight, they allowed their glances to roam near and far, and their eyes rested on the town lying there spread out in its wreath of mountains, with its haze of shiny smoke. For the plentiful noonday meal which the Seldwylians prepared each and every day used to conjure up a silvery cloud of smoke surrounding the roofs and visible from afar, and this would float right along the sides of their mountains.

"These loafers at Seldwyla are again living on the fat of the land," said Manz, one of the two peasants, and Marti, the other, replied: "Yesterday a man called on me on account of these fallow fields." "From the district council? Yes, he saw me too," rejoined Manz. "Hm, and probably also said you might use the land and pay the rental to the council?" "Yes, until it should have been decided whom the land belongs to and what is to be done with it. But I wouldn't think of it, with the land in the condition it's in, and told him they might sell the land and keep the money till the owner had been found, which probably will never be done. For, as we know, whatever is once in the hands of the custodian at Seldwyla, does not easily leave it again. Besides, the whole matter is rather involved, I've heard. But these Seldwyla folks would like nothing better than to receive every little while some money that they could spend in their foolish way. Of course, that they could also do with the sum received from a sale. However, we here would not be so stupid as to bid very high for it, and then at least we should know whom the land belongs to." "Just what I think myself, and I said the same thing to the fellow."

They kept silent for a moment, and then Manz added: "A pity it is, all the same, that this fine soil is thus going

gute Boden so daliegen muß, es ist nicht zum Ansehen, das geht nun schon in die zwanzig Jahre so, und keine Seele fragt darnach; denn hier im Dorf ist niemand, der irgendeinen Anspruch auf den Acker hat, und niemand weiß auch, wo die Kinder des verdorbenen Trompeters hingekommen sind.«

»Hm!« sagte Marti, »das wäre so eine Sache! Wenn ich den schwarzen Geiger ansehe, der sich bald bei den Heimatlosen aufhält, bald in den Dörfern zum Tanz aufspielt, so möchte ich darauf schwören, daß er ein Enkel des Trompeters ist, der freilich nicht weiß, daß er noch einen Acker hat. Was täte er aber damit? Einen Monat lang sich, besaufen und dann nach, wie vor! Zudem, wer dürfte da einen Wink geben, da man es doch nicht sicher wissen kann!«

»Da könnte man eine schöne Geschichte anrichten!« antwortete Manz, »wir haben so genug zu tun, diesem Geiger das Heimatsrecht in unserer Gemeinde abzustreiten, da man uns den Fetzel fortwährend aufhalsen will. Haben sich seine Eltern einmal unter die Heimatlosen begeben, so mag er auch dableiben und dem Kesselvolk das Geigelein streichen. Wie in aller Welt können wir wissen, daß er des Trompeters Sohnessohn ist? Was mich betrifft, wenn ich den Alten auch, in dem dunklen Gesicht vollkommen zu erkennen glaube, so sage ich: irren ist menschlich, und das geringste Fetzchen Papier, ein Stücklein von einem Taufschein würde meinem Gewissen besser tun als zehn sündhafte Menschengesichter!«

»Eia, sicherlich!« sagte Marti, »er sagt zwar, er sei nicht schuld, daß man ihn nicht getauft habe! Aber sollen wir unsern Taufstein tragbar machen und in den Wäldern herumtragen? Nein, er steht fest in der Kirche, und dafür ist die Totenbahre tragbar, die draußen an der Mauer hängt. Wir sind schon übervölkert im Dorf und brauchen bald zwei Schulmeister!«

Hiemit war die Mahlzeit und das Zwiegespräch der Bauern geendet, und sie erhoben sich, den Rest ihrer heutigen Vormittagsarbeit zu vollbringen. Die beiden Kinder hingegen, welche schon den Plan entworfen hatten, mit den Vätern nach Hause zu ziehen, zogen ihr Fuhrwerk unter den Schutz der jungen Linden und begaben sich dann auf einen Streifzug in dem wilden Acker, da derselbe mit seinen Unkräutern, Stauden und Steinhaufen eine ungewohnte und merkwürdige Wildnis darstellte. Nachdem sie in der Mitte dieser grünen Wildnis einige Zeit hingewandert,

to waste every year. I can scarce bear to see it. This has now been going on for a score of years, and nobody cares a rap about it, it seems, for here in the village there is really nobody who has any claim to it, nor does anybody know what has become of the children of that hornblower, the one who went to the dogs."

"Hm," muttered Marti, "that is as may be. When I have a look at the black fiddler, the one who is a vagrant for a spell, and then at other times plays the fiddle at dances, I could almost swear that he is a grandson of that hornblower, and who, of course, does not know that he is entitled to these fields. And what in the world could he do with them? To go on a month's spree, and then to be as badly off as before. Besides, what can one say for sure? After all, there is nothing to prove it."

"Indeed, yes, one might do harm by interfering," rejoined Manz. "As it is we have to do with our own affairs, and it takes trouble enough now to keep this hobo from acquiring home rights in our commune. All the time they want to burden us with that expense. But if his folks once have joined the stray sheep, let him keep to them and play his fiddle for a living. How can we really know whether he is the hornblower's grandson or no? As far as I'm concerned, although I believe I can recognize the old fellow in his dark face, I say to myself: It is human to err, and the slightest scrap of a legal document, a bit of a baptismal record or something, would be to my mind better proof than ten sinful human faces."

"My opinion exactly," opined Marti, "although he says it is not his fault that he never was baptized. But are we to lug our baptismal fount around in the woods? No indeed. That stands immovable in the church, and on the other hand, to carry around the dead we have the stretcher which is always hanging from the wall. As it is, we are too many now in our village and shall soon need another schoolmaster."

With that the colloquy and the midday meal of the two peasants came to an end, and they now rose and prepared to finish the rest of their day's task. The two children, on the other hand, having vainly planned to drive home with their fathers, now pulled their little vehicle into the shade of the linden saplings close by, and next undertook a campaign of adventure and discovery into the vast wilderness of the waste fields. To them this wilderness was interminable, with its immense weeds, its overgrown flower stalks, and its huge piles of stone and rock. After wandering, hand in hand, for some time in the very center of this waste, and after having amused

Hand in Hand, und sich daran belustigt, die verschlungenen Hände über die hohen Distelstauden zu schwingen, ließen sie sich endlich im Schatten einer solchen nieder, und das Mädchen begann seine Puppe mit den langen Blättern des Wegekrautes zu bekleiden, so daß sie einen schönen grünen und ausgezackten Rock bekam; eine einsame rote Mohnblume, die da noch blühte, wurde ihr als Haube über den Kopf gezogen und mit einem Grase festgebunden, und nun sah die kleine Person aus wie eine Zauberfrau, besonders nachdem sie noch ein Halsband und einen Gürtel von kleinen roten Beerchen erhalten. Dann wurde sie hoch in die Stengel der Distel gesetzt und eine Weile mit vereinten Blicken angeschaut, bis der Knabe sie genugsam besehen und mit einem Steine herunterwarf. Dadurch geriet aber ihr Putz in Unordnung, und das Mädchen entkleidete sie schleunigst, um sie aufs neue zu schmücken; doch als die Puppe eben wieder nackt und bloß war und nur noch der roten Haube sich erfreuete, entriß der wilde Junge seiner Gefährtin das Spielzeug und warf es hoch in die Luft. Das Mädchen sprang klagend darnach, allein der Knabe fing die Puppe zuerst wieder auf, warf sie aufs neue empor, und indem das Mädchen sie vergeblich zu haschen sich bemühte, neckte er es auf diese Weise eine gute Zeit. Unter seinen Händen aber nahm die fliegende Puppe Schaden, und zwar am Knie ihres einzigen Beines, allwo ein kleines Loch einige Kleiekörner durchsickern ließ. Kaum bemerkte der Peiniger dies Loch, so verhielt er sich mäuschenstill und war mit offenem Munde eifrig beflissen, das Loch mit seinen Nägeln zu vergrößern und dem Ursprung der Kleie nachzuspüren. Seine Stille erschien dem armen Mädchen höchst verdächtig, und es drängte sich herzu und mußte mit Schrecken sein böses Beginnen gewahren. »Sieh mal!« rief er und schlenkerte ihr das Bein vor der Nase herum, daß ihr die Kleie ins Gesicht flog, und wie sie darnach langen wollte und schrie und flehte, sprang er wieder fort und ruhte nicht eher, bis das ganze Bein dürr und leer herabhing als eine traurige Hülse. Dann warf er das mißhandelte Spielzeug hin und stellte sich höchst frech und gleichgültig, als die Kleine sich weinend auf die Puppe warf und dieselbe in ihre Schürze hüllte. Sie nahm sie aber wieder hervor und betrachtete wehselig die Ärmste, und als sie das Bein sah, fing sie abermals an, laut zu weinen, denn dasselbe hing an dem Rumpfe nicht	themselves in swinging their joined hands over the top of the giant thistles, they at last sat down in the shade of a perfect forest of weeds, and the little girl began to clothe her doll with the long leaves of some of these plants, so that the doll soon wore a beautiful habit of green, with fringed borders, while a solitary poppy blossom she had found was drawn over dolly's head as a brilliant bonnet, and this she tied fast with a grass blade for ribbon. Now the little doll looked exactly like a good fairy, especially after being further ornamented with a necklace and a girdle of small scarlet berries. Then she sat it down high in the cup on the stalk of the thistle, and for a minute or so the two jointly admired the strangely beautified dolly. The boy tired first of this and brought dolly down with a well-aimed pebble. But in that way dolly's finery got disordered, and the little girl undressed it quickly and set to anew to decorate her pet. But just when the doll had been disrobed and only wore the poppy flower on her head, the boy grasped the doll, and threw it high into the air. The girl, though, with loud plaints jumped to catch it, and the boy again caught it first and tossed it again and again, the little girl all the while vainly attempting to recover it. Quite a while this wild game lasted, but in the violent hands of the boy the flying doll now came to grief, and sustained a small fracture near the knee of her sole remaining limb. And from a small aperture some sawdust and bran began to escape. Hardly had he perceived that when he became quiet as a mouse, with open lips endeavoring eagerly to enlarge the little hole with his nails, in order to investigate the inside and find out whence the scattered bran came. The poor little girl, rendered suspicious by the boy's sudden silence, now squeezed up and noticed with terror his efforts. "Just look!" shouted the boy and swung the doll's leg right before his playmate's nose, so that the bran spurted into her face. When she tried to recover her doll, and pleaded and shrieked, he sprang away with his prey, and did not desist before the whole leg had been emptied of its filling and hung, a mere hollow shell, from his hand. Then, to crown his misdeeds, he actually threw the remains of the doll away, and behaved in a rude and grossly indifferent manner when the little girl gathered up her treasure and put it weeping in her apron. But she took it out after a while and gazed with tears at what was left. When she fathomed the full extent of the damage, she resumed weeping, and it was particularly the ruined leg that grieved her; indeed it hung just as limp and thin as the tail of a salamander. When she wept aloud for sorrow the sinner evinced evidently some qualms of conscience, and he stood stock-still, his features suffused with anxiety and repentance. When she became aware of this state of the case, she stopped crying and

anders denn das Schwänzchen an einem Molche. Als sie gar so unbändig weinte, ward es dem Missetäter endlich etwas übel zu Mut, und er stand in Angst und Reue vor der Klagenden, und als sie dies merkte, hörte sie plötzlich auf und schlug ihn einigemal mit der Puppe, und er tat, als ob es ihm weh täte, und schrie »Au!«, so natürlich, daß sie zufrieden war und nun mit ihm gemeinschaftlich die Zerstörung und Zerlegung fortsetzte. Sie bohrten Loch auf Loch in den Marterleib und ließen aller Enden die Kleie entströmen, welche sie sorgfältig auf einem flachen Steine zu einem Häufchen sammelten, umrührten und aufmerksam betrachteten. Das einzige Feste, was noch an der Puppe bestand, war der Kopf und mußte jetzt vorzüglich die Aufmerksamkeit der Kinder erregen; sie trennten ihn sorgfältig los von dem ausgequetschten Leichnam und guckten erstaunt in sein hohles Innere. Als sie die bedenkliche Höhlung sahen und auch die Kleie sahen, war es der nächste und natürlichste Gedankensprung, den Kopf mit der Kleie auszufüllen, und so waren die Fingerchen der Kinder nun beschäftigt, um die Wette Kleie in den Kopf zu tun, so daß zum ersten Mal in seinem Leben etwas in ihm steckte. Der Knabe mochte es aber immer noch für ein totes Wissen halten, weil er plötzlich eine große blaue Fliege fing und, die Summende zwischen beiden hohlen Händen haltend, dem Mädchen gebot, den Kopf von der Kleie zu entleeren. Hierauf wurde die Fliege hineingesperrt und das Loch mit Gras verstopft. Die Kinder hielten den Kopf an die Ohren und setzten ihn dann feierlich auf einen Stein; da er noch mit der roten Mohnblume bedeckt war, so glich der Tönende jetzt einem weissagenden Haupte, und die Kinder lauschten in tiefer Stille seinen Kunden und Märchen, indessen sie sich umschlungen hielten. Aber jeder Prophet erweckt Schrecken und Undank; das wenige Leben in dem dürftig geformten Bilde erregte die menschliche Grausamkeit in den Kindern, und es wurde beschlossen, das Haupt zu begraben. So machten sie ein Grab und legten den Kopf, ohne die gefangene Fliege um ihre Meinung zu befragen, hinein und errichteten über dem Grabe ein ansehnliches Denkmal von Feldsteinen. Dann empfanden sie einiges Grauen, da sie etwas Geformtes und Belebtes begraben hatten, und entfernten sich ein gutes Stück von der unheimlichen Stätte. Auf einem ganz mit grünen Kräutern bedeckten Plätzchen legte sich das Dirnchen auf

struck him several times with her doll, and he pretended that she hurt him and exclaimed in a natural manner: "Outch!" So naturally indeed did he do so that she was satisfied and now engaged with him in the great sport of further and complete destruction. Together they bored hole upon hole into the martyred body, and let the bran out everywhere. This bran they collected with great pains, deposited it on a big flat stone, and stirred it over and over to ascertain its mysterious properties. The sole part of the doll still in its former state was the head, and thus of course it attracted the special attention of the two children. With great care they separated it from the trunk, and peered in amazement at its hollow interior. Seeing this great hollow the thought occurred to them to fill it up with the loose bran. With their tiny baby fingers they stuffed and stuffed by turns the bran into the empty space, and for the first time in its existence this head was filled with something. The boy, however, evidently deemed the task incomplete; probably it required some life, something moving, to satisfy him. So he caught a huge blue fly, and while he held it tight he instructed the little girl to let out the bran once more. Then he placed the fly into the hollow head, and stopped up the exit with a small bunch of grass. The two children held the head to their ears, and then put it solemnly upon a great rock. Since the head was still covered with the scarlet poppy, this receptacle of sound now closely resembled a soothsaying oracle, and the two listened with great respect to queer noises it emitted, in deep silence as if fairy tales were being told, holding each other close meanwhile. But every prophet awakens not only respect but also terror and ingratitude. The odd noises inside the hollow head aroused the human cruelty of the children, and jointly they resolved to bury it. They dug a shallow grave, and placed the head in it, without first obtaining the views of the imprisoned fly on it. Then they erected over the grave a monument of stone. But awe seized them at this instance, since they had buried something living and conscious, and they went away from the scene of this pagan sacrifice. In a spot wholly overgrown with green herbs the little girl lay down on her back, being tired, and began singing, over and over again, a few simple words in a monotonous voice, and the little boy sat near and joined singing, and he, too, was so tired as almost to fall asleep. The sun shone right into the open mouth of the singing girl, illuminating her white little teeth, and rendered her scarlet lips semitransparent. The boy saw these white teeth, and he held her head and curiously investigating them he said: "Guess how many teeth you have." The little girl reflected for a moment, and then she said at random: "A hundred!" "No," said the boy, "two and thirty." But he added: "Wait,

den Rücken, da es müde war, und begann in eintöniger Weise einige Worte zu singen, immer die nämlichen, und der Junge kauerte daneben und half, indem er nicht wußte, ob er auch vollends umfallen solle, so lässig und müßig war er. Die Sonne schien dem singenden Mädchen in den geöffneten Mund, beleuchtete dessen blendendweiße Zähnchen und durchschimmerte die runden Purpurlippen. Der Knabe sah die Zähne, und dem Mädchen den Kopf haltend und dessen Zähnchen neugierig untersuchend, rief er: »Rate, wie viele Zähne hat man?« Das Mädchen besann sich einen Augenblick, als ob es reiflich nachzählte, und sagte dann auf Geratewohl: »Hundert!« – »Nein, zweiunddreißig!« rief er, »wart, ich will einmal zählen!« Da zählte er die Zähne des Kindes, und weil er nicht zweiunddreißig herausbrachte, so fing er immer wieder von neuem an. Das Mädchen hielt lange still, als aber der eifrige Zähler nicht zu Ende kam, raffte es sich auf und rief: »Nun will ich deine zählen!« Nun legte sich der Bursche hin ins Kraut, das Mädchen über ihn, umschlang seinen Kopf, er sperrte das Maul auf, und es zählte Eins, zwei, sieben, fünf, zwei, eins; denn die kleine Schöne konnte noch nicht zählen. Der Junge verbesserte sie und gab ihr Anweisung, wie sie zählen solle, und so fing auch sie unzähligemal von neuem an, und das Spiel schien ihnen am besten zu gefallen von allem, was sie heut unternommen. Endlich aber sank das Mädchen ganz auf den kleinen Rechenmeister nieder, und die Kinder schliefen ein in der hellen Mittagssonne.

Inzwischen hatten die Väter ihre Äcker fertig gepflügt und in frischduftende braune Fläche umgewandelt. Als nun, mit der letzten Furche zu Ende gekommen, der Knecht des einen halten wollte, rief sein Meister: »Was hältst du? Kehr noch einmal um!« – »Wir sind ja fertig!« sagte der Knecht. »Halt's Maul und tu, wie ich dir sage!« der Meister. Und sie kehrten um und rissen eine tüchtige Furche in den mittlern herrenlosen Acker hinein, daß Kraut und Steine flogen. Der Bauer hielt sich aber nicht mit der Beseitigung derselben auf, er mochte denken, hiezu sei noch Zeit genug vorhanden, und er begnügte sich, für heute die Sache nur aus dem Gröbsten zu tun. So ging es rasch die Höhe empor in sanftem Bogen, und als man oben angelangt und das liebliche Windeswehen eben wieder den Kappenzipfel des Mannes zurückwarf, pflügte auf der anderen Seite der Nachbar vorüber, mit dem

I will count them!" And he started to count them, and counted over and over, and it was at no time thirty-two, and so he resumed his count. The girl kept patient for a long time, but at last she got up and said: "Now I will count yours." And the boy lay down amongst the herbs, the little one above him, and she embraced his head, he opened wide his mouth, and she began to count: One, two, seven, five, two, one; for the little thing knew not yet how to count. The boy corrected her and instructed her how to go about it, and thus she also started again and again, and curiously enough it was precisely this little game that pleased them best of all that day. But at last the little girl sank down on the soft couch of herbs, and the two children fell asleep in the full glare of the noon sun.

Meanwhile the fathers had finished their job of plowing and had changed the stubble field into a brown plain, strongly scenting the earth. When at the end of the last furrow the helper of one of the two wanted to stop, his master shouted: "Why do you stop? Turn up another furrow!" "But we're done," said the helper. "Shut your mouth, and do what I tell you," replied the other. And they did turn once more and tore a big furrow right into the middle, the ownerless, field, so that weeds and stones flew about. But the peasant took no time to remove these. Probably he considered that there was ample time for that some other day. He was satisfied to do the thing for the nonce only in its main feature. Thus he went up the height softly, and when up on top and the delicious play of the wind now turned once more the tip of his white cap backwards, on the other side of the fallow field the second peasant was just plowing a similar furrow, the wind having also reversed the tip of his cap, and cut also a goodly furrow off from the same fallow field. Each

Zipfel nach vorn, und schnitt ebenfalls eine ansehnliche Furche vom mittlern Acker, daß die Schollen nur so zur Seite flogen. Jeder sah wohl, was der andere tat, aber keiner schien es zu sehen, und sie entschwanden sich wieder, indem jedes Sternbild still am andern vorüberging und hinter diese runde Welt hinabtauchte. So gehen die Weberschiffchen des Geschickes aneinander vorbei, und »was er webt, das weiß kein Weber!«

Es kam eine Ernte um die andere, und jede sah die Kinder größer und schöner und den herrenlosen Acker schmäler zwischen seinen breitgewordenen Nachbaren. Mit jedem Pflügen verlor er hüben und drüben eine Furche, ohne daß ein Wort darüber gesprochen worden wäre und ohne daß ein Menschenauge den Frevel zu sehen schien. Die Steine wurden immer mehr zusammengedrängt und bildeten schon einen ordentlichen Grat auf der ganzen Länge des Ackers, und das wilde Gesträuch darauf war schon so hoch, daß die Kinder, obgleich sie gewachsen waren, sich, nicht mehr sehen konnten, wenn eines diesund das andere jenseits ging. Denn sie gingen nun nicht mehr gemeinschaftlich auf das Feld, da der zehnjährige Salomon oder Sali, wie er genannt wurde, sich schon wacker auf Seite der größeren Burschen und der Männer hielt; und das braune Vrenchen, obgleich es ein feuriges Dirnchen war, mußte bereits unter der Obhut seines Geschlechts gehen, sonst wäre es von den andern als ein Bubenmädchen ausgelacht worden. Dennoch nahmen sie während jeder Ernte, wenn alles auf den Äckern war, einmal Gelegenheit, den wilden Steinkamm, der sie trennte, zu besteigen und sich gegenseitig von demselben herunterzustoßen. Wenn sie auch sonst keinen Verkehr mehr miteinander hatten, so schien diese jährliche Zeremonie um so sorglicher gewahrt zu werden, als sonst nirgends die Felder ihrer Väter zusammenstießen.

Indessen sollte der Acker doch endlich verkauft und der Erlös einstweilen amtlich aufgehoben werden. Die Versteigerung fand an Ort und Stelle statt, wo sich aber nur einige Gaffer einfanden außer den Bauern Manz und Marti, da niemand Lust hatte, das seltsame Stückchen zu erstehen und zwischen den zwei Nachbaren zu bebauen. Denn obgleich diese zu den besten Bauern des Dorfes gehörten und nichts weiter getan hatten, als was zwei Drittel der übrigen unter diesen Umständen auch getan haben wür-

of them saw, of course, what the other did, but neither seemed to do so, and thus they once more strode away one from the other, each falling star finally disappearing below the curve of the ground. Thus the woof of Fate spins its net around us, "and what he weaves no weaver knows."

One harvest after another went by and the two children grew steadily taller and handsomer, and the ownerless fields as steadily smaller between the two neighbors. With every new plowing the section between lost hither and thither one furrow, without there being a word said about it, and without a human eye apparently noting the misdeed. The stones and rocks became more and more compact and formed already a perfect and continuous ridge the whole length of the field, and the shrubs and weeds on it had already attained such an altitude that the two children, although they, too, had grown, could no longer see each other across them. They no longer went to the field together, since ten-year-old Salomon, or Sali, as he was mostly called, now kept with the bigger boys or the men, and dusky Vreni, though a fiery little thing, had already to place herself under the supervision of those of her sex, for fear of being laughed at as a tomboy. In spite of all that they improved the occasion of the harvest, when everybody was out in the fields, to climb once on top of the huge stony ridge, or breastworks, which ordinarily divided them, and to wage a toy war, pushing each other down from it, as the culmination of the battle. Even though they had no longer anything more to do with each other, this annual ceremony was maintained by them all the more carefully since the land of their fathers did not meet anywhere else.

However, now the fallow field was to be sold, after all, and the sum realized provisionally kept by the authorities. The day came at last, and the public sale took place on the spot itself. But beside Manz and Marti there were present only a few curious ones, since nobody but they felt like buying the odd piece of ground and cultivating it between the property of the two peasants. For although these two belonged among the best farmers of the village, and had done nothing but what two-thirds of the others would also have done under like circumstances, still now they were looked at askance because of it, and nobody

den, so sah man sie doch jetzt stillschweigend darum an, und niemand wollte zwischen ihnen eingeklemmt sein mit dem geschmälerten Waisenfelde. Die meisten Menschen sind fähig oder bereit, ein in den Lüften umgehendes Unrecht zu verüben, wenn sie mit der Nase darauf stoßen; sowie es aber von einem begangen ist, sind die übrigen froh, daß sie es doch nicht gewesen sind, daß die Versuchung nicht sie betroffen hat, und sie machen nun den Auserwählten zu dem Schlechtigkeitsmesser ihrer Eigenschaften und behandeln ihn mit zarter Scheu als einen Ableiter des Übels, der von den Göttern gezeichnet ist, während ihnen zugleich noch der Mund wässert nach den Vorteilen, die er dabei genossen. Manz und Marti waren also die einzigen, welche ernstlich auf den Acker boten; nach einem ziemlich hartnäckigen Überbieten erstand ihn Manz, und er wurde ihm zugeschlagen. Die Beamten und die Gaffer verloren sich vom Felde; die beiden Bauern, welche sich auf ihren Äckern noch zu schaffen gemacht, trafen beim Weggehen wieder zusammen, und Marti sagte: »Du wirst nun dein Land, das alte und das neue, wohl zusammenschlagen und in zwei gleiche Stücke teilen? Ich hätte es wenigstens so gemacht, wenn ich das Ding bekommen hätte.« – »Ich werde es allerdings auch tun«, antwortete Manz, »denn als ein Acker würde mir das Stück zu groß sein. Doch was ich sagen wollte Ich habe bemerkt, daß du neulich noch am untern Ende dieses Ackers, der jetzt mir gehört, schräg hineingefahren bist und ein gutes Dreieck abgeschnitten hast. Du hast es vielleicht getan in der Meinung, du werdest das ganze Stück an dich bringen und es sei dann sowieso dein. Da es nun aber mir gehört, so wirst du wohl einsehen, daß ich eine solche ungehörige Einkrümmung nicht brauchen noch dulden kann, und wirst nichts dagegen haben, wenn ich den Strich wieder grad mache! Streit wird das nicht abgeben sollen!«

Marti erwiderte ebenso kaltblütig, als ihn Manz angeredet hatte: »Ich sehe auch nicht, wo Streit herkommen soll! Ich denke, du hast den Acker gekauft, wie er da ist, wir haben ihn alle gemeinschaftlich besehen, und er hat sich seit einer Stunde nicht um ein Haar verändert!«

»Larifari!« sagte Manz, »was früher geschehen, wollen wir nicht aufrühren! Was aber zuviel ist, ist zuviel, und alles muß zuletzt eine ordentliche grade Art haben; diese drei Acker sind von jeher so grade nebeneinander gelegen, wie nach dem

wanted to be squeezed in between them in the diminished and orphaned field. For most men are so made as to be quite ready to commit a wrong which is more or less in vogue, especially if the circumstances of the case facilitate the wrong. But as soon as the wrong has been perpetrated by some one else, they are glad that it was not they who had been exposed to the temptation, and then they regard the guilty one almost as a warning example in regard to their own failings, and treat him with a delicate aversion as a sort of lightning rod of evil itself, as one marked by the gods themselves, while all the while their mouths are watering for the advantages thus accrued to him by means of his sin. Manz and Marti were, therefore, the only ones who seriously bid on the ownerless land, and after a rather spirited contest, during which the price was driven up higher than had been supposed, it was Manz to whom it was awarded. The officials and the lookers-on soon drifted away, and the two neighbors who had been busy on their fields after the sale, met again, and Marti said: "I suppose you will now put your land, the old and the new, together, halve it, and work it in that way? That, at least, is what I should have done if I had got the land." "That indeed is what I mean to do," answered Manz, "for as one single field it would not be easy to manage. But there is another thing I want to say. I noticed the other day that you drove into the lower end of this field that has now become mine, and that you cut off quite a good-sized triangle. It may be you thought at the time that you yourself would soon own the whole of it and that then it would make no difference anyway. But since now it belongs to me, you will admit that I cannot and will not permit such a curtailment of my property rights, and you will not take it amiss if I again straighten out the right lines. Of course you will not. There need be no hard feelings on that score."

Marti, however, replied just as coolly: "Neither do I look for any trouble. For my opinion is you have purchased the field just as it is. We both examined it before the sale, and of course it has not changed within an hour or so."

"Nonsense," said Manz, "what was done formerly, under different conditions, we will not go into. But too much is too much, and everything has its limit, and must be adjusted according to reason in the end. These three fields have from of old been lying one next to the other

Richtscheit gezeichnet; es ist ein ganz absonderlicher Spaß von dir, wenn du nun einen solchen lächerlichen und unvernünftigen Schnörkel dazwischenbringen willst, und wir beide würden einen Übernamen bekommen, wenn wir den krummen Zipfel da bestehen ließen. Er muß durchaus weg!«

Marti lachte und sagte: »Du hast ja auf einmal eine merkwürdige Furcht vor dem Gespötte der Leute! Das läßt sich aber ja wohl machen; mich geniert das Krumme gar nicht; ärgert es dich, gut, so machen wir es grad, aber nicht auf meiner Seite, das geb ich dir schriftlich, wenn du willst!«

»Rede doch nicht so spaßhaft«, sagte Manz, »es wird wohl grad gemacht, und zwar auf deiner Seite, darauf kannst du Gift nehmen!«

»Das werden wir ja sehen und erleben!« sagte Marti, und beide Männer gingen auseinander, ohne sich weiter anzublicken; vielmehr starrten sie nach verschiedener Richtung ins Blaue hinaus, als ob sie da wunder was für Merkwürdigkeiten im Auge hätten, die sie betrachten müßten mit Aufbietung aller ihrer Geisteskräfte.

Schon am nächsten Tage schickte Manz einen Dienstbuben, ein Tagelöhnermädchen und sein eigenes Söhnchen Sali auf den Acker hinaus, um das wilde Unkraut und Gestrüpp auszureuten und auf Haufen zu bringen, damit nachher die Steine um so bequemer weggefahren werden könnten. Dies war eine Änderung in seinem Wesen, daß er den kaum eilfjährigen Jungen, der noch zu keiner Arbeit angehalten worden, nun mit hinaussandte, gegen die Einsprache der Mutter. Es schien, da er es mit ernsthaften und gesalbten Worten tat, als ob er mit dieser Arbeitsstrenge gegen sein eigenes Blut das Unrecht betäuben wollte, in dem er lebte und welches nun begann, seine Folgen ruhig zu entfalten. Das ausgesandte Völklein jätete inzwischen lustig an dem Unkraut und hackte mit Vergnügen an den wunderlichen Stauden und Pflanzen allerart, die da seit Jahren wucherten. Denn da es eine außerordentliche, gleichsam wilde Arbeit war, bei der keine Regel und keine Sorgfalt erheischt wurde, so galt sie als eine Lust. Das wilde Zeug, an der Sonne gedörrt, wurde aufgehäuft und mit großem Jubel verbrannt, daß der Qualm weithin sich verbreitete und die jungen Leutchen darin herumsprangen wie besessen. Dies war das letzte Freudenfest auf dem Unglücksfelde, und das junge Vrenchen, Martis Tochter, kam auch hinausgeschlichen und half tapfer mit. Das Unge-

just as though marked with the measuring tape. You may think it funny to put in such an unjustifiable objection or claim. We both of us would get a new nickname if I let you keep that crooked end of it without rhyme or reason. It must come back where it by right belongs."

But Marti only laughed and said: "All at once so afraid of what people may think? But then, it's easily arranged. I have no objection at all to such a crooked-shaped bit of land. If you don't like it, all right, we can straighten it out. But not on my side, I swear."

"Don't talk so strange," replied Manz with some heat. "Of course it will be straightened out, and that on your side. You can bet your bottom dollar on that."

"Well, we'll see about that," was Marti's parting remark, and the two men separated without even looking at each other. On the contrary, they gazed steadfastly in different directions, as if something of enormous interest were floating in the air which it was absolutely necessary to keep an eye on.

On the next day already Manz sent his hired boy, also a wench working for daily wage, and his own boy Sali out to the new field, to begin removing the weeds and wild growths, and to pile them up at certain places, so as to make the loading up and carting away of the crop of stones all the easier. This noted a change in his character, this sending the little boy, scarcely eleven, whom he had never before driven to hard work such as weeding, out to field labor, and this against the will of the mother. It seemed indeed, since he defended his order with solemn and high-sounding words, as if he wanted to daze his own better conscience. At any rate, the slight wrong thus done to his own flesh and blood in insisting on onerous and unfit labor, was but one of the consequences growing out of the original wrong done by him for years in regard to the field itself. One by one more wrong, more evil unfolded itself. The three meanwhile weeded away industriously on the long strip of ground, and hacked away at the queer plants that had been flourishing on the soil for so many years. And to the young people doing this hard work, albeit it taxed and tried their strength greatly, it really was something of an amusement, since it was no carefully graduated and scaled task, but rather a wild job of destruction. After piling all this vegetable refuse up in heaps and letting the sun dry it, it was set afire with great jubilation and noise, and when the murky flames shot up and broad swaths of smoke waved irregularly, the young people jumped and danced about like a band of wild Indians. But this was the last festival

wöhnliche dieser Begebenheit und die lustige Aufregung gaben einen guten Anlaß, sich seinem kleinen Jugendgespielen wieder einmal zu nähern, und die Kinderwaren recht glücklich und munter bei ihrem Feuer. Es kamen noch andere Kinder hinzu, und es sammelte sich eine ganze vergnügte Gesellschaft; doch immer, sobald sie getrennt wurden, suchte Sali alsobald wieder neben Vrenchen zu gelangen, und dieses wußte desgleichen immer vergnügt lächelnd zu ihm zu schlüpfen, und es war beiden Kreaturen, wie wenn dieser herrliche Tag nie enden müßte und könnte. Doch der alte Manz kam gegen Abend herbei, um zu sehen, was sie ausgerichtet, und obgleich sie fertig waren, so schalt er doch ob dieser Lustbarkeit und scheuchte die Gesellschaft auseinander. Zugleich zeigte sich Marti auf seinem Grund und Boden, und seine Tochter gewahrend, pfiff er derselben schrill und gebieterisch durch den Finger, daß sie erschrocken hineilte, und er gab ihr, ohne zu wissen warum, einige Ohrfeigen, also daß beide Kinder in großer Traurigkeit und weinend nach, Hause gingen, und sie wußten jetzt eigentlich sowenig, warum sie so traurig waren, als warum sie vorhin so vergnügt gewesen; denn die Rauheit der Väter, an sich ziemlich neu, war von den arglosen Geschöpfen noch nicht begriffen und konnte sie nicht tiefer bewegen.

Die nächsten Tage war es schon eine härtere Arbeit, zu welcher Mannsleute gehörten, als Manz die Steine aufnehmen und wegfahren ließ. Es wollte kein Ende nehmen, und alle Steine der Welt schienen da beisammen zu sein. Er ließ sie aber nicht ganz vom Felde wegbringen, sondern jede Fuhre auf jenem streitigen Dreiecke abwerfen, welches von Marti schon säuberlich umgepflügt war. Er hatte vorher einen graden Strich gezogen als Grenzscheide und belastete nun dies Fleckchen Erde mit allen Steinen, welche beide Männer seit unvordenklichen Zeiten herübergeworfen, so daß eine gewaltige Pyramide entstand, die wegzubringen sein Gegner bleibenlassen würde, dachte er. Marti hatte dies am wenigsten erwartet; er glaubte, der andere werde nach alter Weise mit dem Pfluge zu Werke gehen wollen, und hatte daher abgewartet, bis er ihn als Pflüger ausziehen sähe. Erst als die Sache schon beinahe fertig, hörte er von dem schönen Denkmal, welches Manz da errichtet, rannte voll Wut hinaus, sah die Bescherung, rannte zurück und holte den Gemeindeammann, um vorläufig gegen den

on the ominous new field, and little Vreni, Marti's young daughter, also crept out and joined the revels. The unusual occasion and the spirit of rampant gaiety easily brought it about that the two playmates of yore once more came in contact and were happy and jolly at their bonfire. Other children, too, gathered, until there was quite a crowd of youthful, excited merrymakers assembled. But always it happened that, as soon as the two became separated in the throng, Vreni would rejoin Sali, or Sali Vreni. When it was she it was a treat to watch her face when she slipped her little hand in that of the boy, her animated features and her glowing eyes fairly brimming with pleasure. To both of them it seemed as though this glorious day could never end. Old Manz, though, came out toward evening, to see what had been accomplished, and despite the fact that their labor had been done well and as directed, he scolded at the childish jollification and drove the young people off his ground. Almost at the same time Marti visited his own section adjoining, and noticing his little daughter from afar, he whistled to her shrill and peremptory, and when she obeyed the summons in frightened haste he struck her harshly in the face without giving any reason. So that both little ones went home weeping and sad; yet they were both still so much children that they scarcely knew at this time why they were so sad or knew before why they felt so happy. As for the rudeness of their fathers they did not understand the underlying motive of it, and it did not touch their hearts.

During the next days the labor became harder and more strenuous, and some men had to be hired for it. For the task was this time to load and clean off the huge crop of stones along the entire length of the field. There seemed to be no end to this work, and one would have said that all the stones in the world had been collected there. But Manz did not have the stones carted off entirely from the field, but every load was taken to the triangular piece of ground in dispute, where it was dumped. It was dumped on the neatly plowed soil that Marti had toiled over. Manz had previously drawn a straight line as boundary, and now he loaded this spot down with all these thousands upon thousands of pebbles, rocks and bowlders which he and Marti had for whole decades thrown upon ownerless soil. The heap grew, and grew for days and weeks, until there was a mighty pyramid of stone which, as Manz felt convinced, his adversary would surely be loath to trouble with. Marti, in fact, had expected nothing of the kind. He had rather thought that Manz would go to work with his plow, as he used to do, and had therefore waited to see him appear in that part. And Marti did not hear of the rocky monument until almost completed. When he ran out in the full blast of his anger,

Steinhaufen zu protestieren und den Fleck gerichtlich in Beschlag nehmen zu lassen, und von diesem Tage an lagen die zwei Bauern im Prozeß miteinander und ruhten nicht, ehe sie beide zugrunde gerichtet waren.

Die Gedanken der sonst so wohlweisen Männer waren nun so kurz geschnitten wie Häcksel; der beschränkteste Rechtssinn von der Welt erfüllte jeden von ihnen, indem keiner begreifen konnte noch wollte, wie der andere so offenbar unrechtmäßig und willkürlich den fraglichen unbedeutenden Ackerzipfel an sich reißen könne. Bei Manz kam noch ein wunderbarer Sinn für Symmetrie und parallele Linien hinzu, und er fühlte sich wahrhaft gekränkt durch den aberwitzigen Eigensinn, mit welchem Marti auf dem Dasein des unsinnigsten und mutwilligsten Schnörkels beharrte. Beide aber trafen zusammen in der Überzeugung, daß der andere, den andern so frech und plump übervorteilend, ihn notwendig für einen verächtlichen Dummkopf halten müsse, da man dergleichen etwa einem armen haltlosen Teufel, nicht aber einem aufrechten, klugen und wehrhaften Manne gegenüber sich erlauben könne, und jeder sah sich in seiner wunderlichen Ehre gekränkt und gab sich rückhaltlos der Leidenschaft des Streites und dem daraus erfolgenden Verfalle hin, und ihr Leben glich fortan der träumerischen Qual zweier Verdammten, welche, auf einem schmalen Brette einen dunklen Strom hinabtreibend, sich befehden, in die Luft hauen und sich selber anpacken und vernichten, in der Meinung, sie hätten ihr Unglück gefaßt. Da sie eine faule Sache hatten, so gerieten beide in die allerschlimmsten Hände von Tausendkünstlern, welche ihre verdorbene Phantasie auftrieben zu ungeheuren Blasen, die mit den nichtsnutzigsten Dingen angefüllt wurden. Vorzüglich waren es die Spekulanten aus der Stadt Seldwyla, welchen dieser Handel ein gefundenes Essen war, und bald hatte jeder der Streitenden einen Anhang von Unterhändlern, Zuträgern und Ratgebern hinter sich, die alles bare Geld auf hundert Wegen abzuziehen wußten. Denn das Fleckchen Erde mit dem Steinhaufen darüber, auf welchem bereits wieder ein Wald von Nesseln und Disteln blühte, war nur noch der erste Keim oder der Grundstein einer verworrenen Geschichte und Lebensweise, in welcher die zwei Fünfzigjährigen noch neue Gewohnhei-

and saw it all, he hastened home and fetched the village magistrate in order to protest against the accumulation of stones on "his" ground, and to have the small bit of ground officially declared as in litigation. From that sinister day on the two peasants sued and countersued each other in court, and neither desisted until both were completely ruined.

The thinking of these two ordinarily shrewd and fair men became fundamentally wrong and fallacious. They were unable to view anything henceforth as unrelated with their quarrel. Their arguments fell short of the mark in everything. The most narrow sense of legality, of what was permitted and what not, filled the head of each of them, and neither was able to understand how the other could seize so entirely without reason or right this bit of soil, in itself so insignificant. In the case of Manz there was added a wonderful sense for symmetry and parallel lines, and he felt really and truly shortened in his rights by Martins insistence on retaining hold of a fragment of property laid out on different geometrical lines. But both tallied in their conceptions in this that the other must think him a veritable fool to try and get the better of him in this particular manner, in this impudent and unparalleled manner, since to make such an attempt at all was perhaps thinkable in the case of a mere nobody, of a man without reputation and substance, but surely not in the case of an upstanding, energetic and able man, of one who was both willing and able to take care of his interests. And it was this consideration above all that rankled and festered in the heart of each of the two once so friendly neighbors. Each felt himself hurt in his quaint sense of honor, and let himself go headlong in the rush of passion and of combativeness, without even attempting at any time to stop the resultant moral and material decay and ruin. Their two lives henceforth resembled the torture of two lost souls who, upon a narrow board, carried along a dark and fearsome river, yet deal tremendous blows at the air, seize upon each other and destroy each other finally, all in the false belief of having seized and trying to destroy their evil fate itself. As their whole matter in dispute was in itself and on both sides not clean or lucid, they soon got into the hands of all sorts of swindlers and cutthroats, of pettifoggers and evil counselors, men who filled their imagination with glittering bubbles, containing no substance whatever. And especially it was the speculators and dishonest agents of Seldwyla who found this case one after their own heart, and soon each of the two litigants had a whole train of advisers, go-betweens and spies around him, fellows who in all sorts of crooked ways knew how to draw cash money out of them. For the quarrel for that tiny fragment of soil with the stone pyramid on top on which already

ten und Sitten, Grundsätze und Hoffnungen annahmen, als sie bisher geübt. Je mehr Geld sie verloren, desto sehnsüchtiger wünschten sie welches zu haben, und je weniger sie besaßen, desto hartnäckiger dachten sie reich zu werden und es dem andern zuvorzutun. Sie ließen sich zu jedem Schwindel verleiten und setzten auch jahraus, jahrein in alle fremden Lotterien, deren Lose massenhaft in Seldwyla zirkulierten. Aber nie bekamen sie einen Taler Gewinn zu Gesicht, sondern hörten nur immer vom Gewinnen anderer Leute und wie sie selbst beinahe gewonnen hätten, indessen diese Leidenschaft ein regelmäßiger Geldabfluß für sie war. Bisweilen machten sich die Seldwyler den Spaß, beide Bauern, ohne ihr Wissen, am gleichen Lose teilnehmen zu lassen, so daß beide die Hoffnung auf Unterdrückung und Vernichtung des andern auf ein und dasselbe Los setzten. Sie brachten die Hälfte ihrer Zeit in der Stadt zu, wo jeder in einer Spelunke sein Hauptquartier hatte, sich den Kopf heißmachen und zu den lächerlichsten Ausgaben und einem elenden und ungeschickten Schlemmen verleiten ließ, bei welchem ihm heimlich doch selber das Herz blutete, also daß beide, welche eigentlich nur in diesem Hader lebten, um für keine Dummköpfe zu gelten, nun solche von der besten Sorte darstellten und von jedermann dafür angesehen wurden. Die andere Hälfte der Zeit lagen sie verdrossen zu Hause oder gingen ihrer Arbeit nach, wobei sie dann durch ein tolles böses Überhasten und Antreiben das Versäumte einzuholen suchten und damit jeden ordentlichen und zuverlässigen Arbeiter verscheuchten. So ging es gewaltig rückwärts mit ihnen, und ehe zehn Jahre vorüber, steckten sie beide von Grund aus in Schulden und standen wie die Störche auf einem Beine auf der Schwelle ihrer Besitztümer, von der jeder Lufthauch sie herunterwehte. Aber wie es ihnen auch erging, der Haß zwischen ihnen wurde täglich größer, da jeder den andern als den Urheber seines Unsterns betrachtete, als seinen Erbfeind und ganz unvernünftigen Widersacher, den der Teufel absichtlich in die Welt gesetzt habe, um ihn zu verderben. Sie spien aus, wenn sie sich nur von weitem sahen; kein Glied ihres Hauses durfte mit Frau, Kind oder Gesinde des andern ein Wort sprechen, bei Vermeidung der gröbsten Mißhandlung. Ihre Weiber verhielten sich verschieden bei dieser Verarmung und Verschlechterung des ganzen Wesens. Die Frau des Marti, welche von

a perfect forest of weeds, thistles and nettles had grown anew, was only the first stage in a labyrinth of errors that little by little changed the whole character and method of living for the two. It was singular, too, how in the case of two men of about fifty there could shoot up and become fixed an entire crop of new habits and morals, principles and hopes, all of a kind which were foreign to their former natures, how men who all their lives had been noted for their hard common-sense could become day-dreamers and gullible oafs. And the more money they lost by all this the more they longed to acquire more, and the less they possessed the more persistently they endeavored to become rich and to shine before their fellows. Thus they easily allowed themselves to be hoodwinked by the clumsiest tricks, and year after year they would play in all the foreign lotteries of which Seldwyla agents were praising to them the splendid chances. But never so much as a dollar came their way in prizes. On the other hand, they forever heard of the big winnings in these lotteries made by others; they also were told that it had hung just by a hair that they would have done as well, and thus they were constantly bled by these leeches of their scantier and scantier means. Now and then the rascally Seldwylians played a trick on the two deadly enemies which for its peculiar raciness was specially relished by them, the people of Seldwyla, that is. They would sell the two peasants sections of the same lottery tickets, so that Manz as well as Marti would build their hopes of a rich strike on precisely the same fallacious foundation, and also in the end would feel the same despondency from the same source. Half their time the two now spent in town, and there each had his headquarters in a miserable tavern. There they would indulge in foolish bragging and bluster, would drink too much and play the Lord Bountiful to loafers that would flatter the simpletons to the top of their bent, and all the while the dark doubt would assail them that they who in order not to be reckoned dunces had gone to law about a trifling object, had now really become just that and furthermore, were so reckoned by general consent. The other half of the time they spent at home, morose and incapable of steady work or sober reflection. Habitually neglecting their farm labor, at times they tried to make up for that by undue haste, overworking their help and thus soon unable to retain any respectable men in their employ. Thus things went from bad to worse little by little, and within less than ten years both of them were overburdened with debts, and stood like storks with one leg upon their farms, so that the slightest change might blow them over. But no matter how else they fared, the hatred between them grew more intense every day, since each looked upon the other as the cause of his

guter Art war, hielt den Verfall nicht aus, härmte sich ab und starb, ehe ihre Tochter vierzehn Jahre alt war. Die Frau des Manz hingegen bequemte sich der veränderten Lebensweise an, und um sich als eine schlechte Genossin zu entfalten, hatte sie nichts zu tun, als einigen weiblichen Fehlern, die ihr von jeher angehaftet, den Zügel schießen zu lassen und dieselben zu Lastern auszubilden. Ihre Naschhaftigkeit wurde zu wilder Begehrlichkeit, ihre Zungenfertigkeit zu einem grundfalschen und verlogenen Schmeichel- und Verleumdungswesen, mit welchem sie jeden Augenblick das Gegenteil von dem sagte, was sie dachte, alles hintereinanderhetzte und ihrem eigenen Manne ein X für ein U vormachte; ihre ursprüngliche Offenheit, mit der sie sich der unschuldigeren Plauderei erfreut, ward nun zur abgehärteten Schamlosigkeit, mit der sie jenes falsche Wesen betrieb, und so, statt unter ihrem Manne zu leiden, drehte sie ihm eine Nase; wenn er es arg trieb, so machte sie es bunt, ließ sich nichts abgehen und gedieh zu der dicksten Blüte einer Vorsteherin des zerfallenden Hauses.

So war es nun schlimm bestellt um die armen Kinder, welche weder eine gute Hoffnung für ihre Zukunft fassen konnten noch sich auch nur einer lieblich frohen Jugend erfreuten, da überall nichts als Zank und Sorge war. Vrenchen hatte anscheinend einen schlimmern Stand als Sali, da seine Mutter tot und es einsam in einem wüsten Hause der Tyrannei eines verwilderten Vaters anheimgegeben war. Als es sechzehn Jahre zählte, war es schon ein schlankgewachsenes, ziervolles Mädchen; seine dunkelbraunen Haare ringelten sich unablässig fast bis über die blitzenden braunen Augen, dunkelrotes Blut durchschimmerte die Wangen des bräunlichen Gesichtes und glänzte als tiefer Purpur auf den frischen Lippen, wie man es selten sah und was dem dunklen Kinde ein eigentümliches Ansehen und Kennzeichen gab. Feurige Lebenslust und Fröhlichkeit zitterte in jeder Fiber dieses Wesens; es lachte

misfortune, as his archenemy, as his foe without rhyme or reason, as the one being in the world whom the devil purposely had invented to ruin him. They spat out before each other when they saw the adversary approaching from afar. Nobody belonging to them was permitted to speak to wife, child or servants of the other, on pain of instant brutal punishment. Their wives behaved differently under these circumstances. Marti's wife, who came of good family and was of a fine disposition, did not long survive the rapid downfall of her house and family, sorrowed silently and died before her little daughter was fourteen. The wife of Manz, on the other hand, altered her whole character. Only for the worse, of course. And to do that all she needed to do was to aggravate some of her natural defects, let them go on, so to speak, without bridling them at all. Her passion for tidbits and sweets became boundless; her love of gossip deteriorated into a veritable craze, and she soon became unable to tell the truth about anything or anybody. She habitually spoke the very contrary of what was in her thoughts, cheated and deceived her own husband, and found keen pleasure in getting everybody by the ears. Her original frankness and her harmless delight in satisfying her feminine curiosity turned into evil intrigue and the inclination to make mischief between neighbors and friends. Instead of suffering patiently under the rudeness and changed habits of her husband, she fooled him and laughed behind his back in doing so. No matter if he now and then behaved with cruelty to her and his household, she did not care. She denied herself nothing, became more luxurious in her tastes as his money affairs grew steadily more involved, and fattened on the very misfortunes that were rapidly leading to complete ruin.

That with all that the two children fared any better was scarcely to be expected. While still mere human buds and incapable of meeting the harsh fate slowly preparing for them, they were done out of their youth and out of the hopes and advantages incident to their tender years. Vreni indeed was worse off in this respect than Sali, the boy, since her mother was dead and she was exposed in a wasted home to the tyranny of a father whose violent instincts found no check whatever. When sixteen Vreni had developed into a slender and charming young girl. Her hair of dark-brown naturally curled down to her flashing eyes; her swiftly coursing blood seemed to shimmer through the delicate oval of her dusky cheeks, and the scarlet of her dainty lips made a strikingly vivid contrast, so that everybody looked twice when she passed. And despite her sad bringing-up, an ardent love of life and an inextinguishable cheerfulness were trembling in every fibre of Vreni's being. Laughing and smiling at the least encouragement she forgot her troubles easily, and

und war aufgelegt zu Scherz und Spiel, wenn das Wetter nur im mindesten lieblich war, d.h. wenn es nicht zu sehr gequält wurde und nicht zu viel Sorgen ausstand. Diese plagten es aber häufig genug; denn nicht nur hatte es den Kummer und das wachsende Elend des Hauses mitzutragen, sondern es mußte noch sich selber in acht nehmen und mochte sich gern halbwegs ordentlich und reinlich kleiden, ohne daß der Vater ihm die geringsten Mittel dazu geben wollte. So hatte Vrenchen die größte Not, ihre anmutige Person einigermaßen auszustaffieren, sich ein allerbescheidenstes Sonntagskleid zu erobern und einige bunte, fast wertlose Halstüchelchen zusammenzuhalten. Darum war das schöne wohlgemute junge Blut in jeder Weise gedemütigt und gehemmt und konnte am wenigsten der Hoffart anheimfallen. Überdies hatte es bei schon erwachendem Verstande das Leiden und den Tod seiner Mutter gesehen, und dies Andenken war ein weiterer Zügel, der seinem lustigen und feurigen Wesen angelegt war, so daß es nun höchst lieblich, unbedenklich und rührend sich ansah, wenn trotz alledem das gute Kind bei jedem Sonnenblick sich ermunterte und zum Lächeln bereit war.

Sali erging es nicht so hart auf den ersten Anschein; denn er war nun ein hübscher und kräftiger junger Bursche, der sich zu wehren wußte und dessen äußere Haltung wenigstens eine schlechte Behandlung von selbst unzulässig machte. Er sah wohl die üble Wirtschaft seiner Eltern und glaubte sich erinnern zu können, daß es einst nicht so gewesen; ja er bewahrte noch das frühere Bild seines Vaters wohl in seinem Gedächtnisse als eines festen, klugen und ruhigen Bauers, desselben Mannes, den er jetzt als einen grauen Narren, Händelführer und Müßiggänger vor sich sah, der mit Toben und Prahlen auf hundert törichten und verfänglichen Wegen wandelte und mit jeder Stunde rückwärts ruderte wie ein Krebs. Wenn ihm nun dies mißfiel und ihn oft mit Scham und Kummer erfüllte, während es seiner Unerfahrenheit nicht klar war, wie die Dinge so gekommen, so wurden seine Sorgen wieder betäubt durch die Schmeichelei, mit der ihn die Mutter behandelte. Denn um in ihrem

was always ready for a frolic and a romp if domestic weather permitted at all, that is, if her father did not hinder and torture her too cruelly. However, with all her lightheartedness and her buoyant temperament, the deepening shadows over the house inevitably enshrouded her all too often. She had to bear the brunt of her father's soured disposition, and she had hardly any help in trying to keep house for him after a fashion. On her young shoulders mainly rested the embarrassments of a home constantly threatened by importunate creditors and wild boon companions of her dissolute father. And not alone that. With the natural taste of her sex for a neat and clean appearance her father refused her nearly every means to gratify it. Thus she had great trouble to ornament her pretty person the way it deserved. But somehow she managed to do it, to possess always a becoming holiday attire, including even a couple of vividly colored kerchiefs that set off marvelously her darksome beauty. Full of youthful animation and gaiety she found it hard to mostly have to renounce all the social pleasures of her years; but at least this prevented her from falling into the opposite extreme. Besides, young as she was, she had witnessed the declining days and the death of her mother, and had been deeply impressed by it, so that this had acted as another restraint on her joyous disposition. It was almost a pathetic sight to observe how notwithstanding all these serious obstacles pretty Vreni instantly would respond to the calls of joy if the occasion was at all favorable, as a flower after drooping in a heavy rainstorm will raise its head at the first rays of the reappearing sun.

Sali was not faring quite so ill. He was a good-looking and vigorous young fellow who knew how to take care of himself and whose size and physical strength alone would have forbidden harsh bodily mistreatment. He saw, of course, how his parents were sliding down-hill more and more, and he seemed to remember a time when things had been otherwise. He even carried in his memory the picture of his father as that of an upstanding, determined, serious and energetic peasant, while now he saw before him all the while a man who was a gray-headed dolt, a quarrelsome fool, who with all his fits of impotent rage and all his brag and bluster was every hour more and more crawling backwards like a crawfish. But when these things displeased him and filled him with shame and sorrow, although he could not very well understand how it all had come about, the influence of his mother came to deaden this feeling and to fill him with an unjustified hope of improvement. She would flatter her son in the same extravagant and wholly unreasonable manner which had become her second nature in dealing with the new troubles that were gradually overcoming

Unwesen ungestörter zu sein und einen guten Parteigänger zu haben, auch um ihrer Großtuerei zu genügen, ließ sie ihm zukommen, was er wünschte, kleidete ihn sauber und prahlerisch und unterstützte ihn in allem, was er zu seinem Vergnügen vornahm. Er ließ sich dies gefallen ohne viel Dankbarkeit, da ihm die Mutter viel zuviel dazu schwatzte und log; und indem er so wenig Freude daran empfand, tat er lässig und gedankenlos, was ihm gefiel, ohne daß dies jedoch etwas Übles war, weil er für jetzt noch unbeschädigt war von dem Beispiele der Alten und das jugendliche Bedürfnis fühlte, im ganzen einfach, ruhig und leidlich tüchtig zu sein. Er war ziemlich genau so, wie sein Vater in diesem Alter gewesen war, und dieses flößte demselben eine unwillkürliche Achtung vor dem Sohne ein, in welchem er mit verwirrtem Gewissen und gepeinigter Erinnerung seine eigene Jugend achtete. Trotz dieser Freiheit, welche Sali genoß, ward er seines Lebens doch nicht froh und fühlte wohl, wie er nichts Rechtes vor sich hatte und ebensowenig etwas Rechtes lernte, da von einem zusammenhängenden und vernunftgemäßen Arbeiten in Manzens Hause längst nicht mehr die Rede war. Sein bester Trost war daher, stolz auf seine Unabhängigkeit und einstweilige Unbescholtenheit zu sein, und in diesem Stolze ließ er die Tage trotzig verstreichen und wandte die Augen von der Zukunft ab.

Der einzige Zwang, dem er unterworfen, war die Feindschaft seines Vaters gegen alles, was Marti hieß und an diesen erinnerte. Doch wußte er nichts anderes, als daß Marti seinem Vater Schaden zugefügt und daß man in dessen Hause ebenso feindlich gesinnt sei, und es fiel ihm daher nicht schwer, weder den Marti noch seine Tochter anzusehen und seinerseits auch einen angehenden, doch ziemlich zahmen Feind vorzustellen. Vrenchen hingegen, welches mehr erdulden mußte als Sali und in seinem Hause viel

the whole family. For in order to lead her life of self-indulgence the more easily and to have one critical observer the less, and to make her son her partisan, but also as a vent for her love of display, she contrived to let her son have everything he had a desire for. She saw to it that he was always dressed with care, and entirely too expensively for the means of the family, and indulged him in his pleasures. He on his part accepted all that without much thought or gratitude, since he noticed at the same time how his mother was juggling with and tricking his father, and how she was continually telling untruths and vainly boasting. And while thus allowing his mother to spoil him without paying much attention to the process itself, no great harm was yet done in his case, since he had so far not been much tainted by the vices and sins of mother or father. Indeed, in his youthful pride he had the strong wish to become, if possible, a man such as he recalled his own father once to have been, a man of substance and of rational and successful conduct of his life. Sali was really very much as his father knew himself to have been at his own age, and a queer remnant of respectability urged the father to treat his son well. In honoring him he seemed to honor his old self. Confused reminiscences at such times drifted through his beclouded soul, and they afforded him a species of subconscious delight. But although in this manner Sali escaped some of the natural consequences of the process of domestic decay which was going on around him, he was not able to genuinely enjoy his life and to make rational plans for an assured future. He felt well enough that he was resting on quicksand, that he was neither doing anything much to bring himself into a position of independence nor to look for any secured future; nor was he learning much towards that end in the broken-down household and on the neglected farm of his father. The work done there was done haphazard style, and no systematic and orderly effort was made to get things done in season. His best consolation, therefore, was to preserve his good reputation, to work with a will on the farm when he could, and to turn his eyes away from a threatening future.

The sole orders laid upon him by his father were to avoid any sort of intercourse with all that bore the name of Marti. All he knew about the matter personally was that Marti had done wrong to his father, and that in Marti's house precisely the same bitter enmity was felt towards the Manz family. Of the details involved in this state of affairs, of the manner in which the old-time good-neighborliness and friendship existing for so many years between the two families had been turned into hatred and scorn Sali knew nothing, these things having shaped themselves at a period of his life when his boyish

verlassener war, fühlte sich weniger zu einer förmlichen Feindschaft aufgelegt und glaubte sich nur verachtet von dem wohlgekleideten und scheinbar glücklicheren Sali; deshalb verbarg sie sich vor ihm, und wenn er irgendwo nur in der Nähe war, so entfernte sie sich eilig, ohne daß er sich die Mühe gab, ihr nachzublicken. So kam es, daß er das Mädchen schon seit ein paar Jahren nicht mehr in der Nähe gesehen und gar nicht wußte, wie es aussah, seit es herangewachsen. Und doch wunderte es ihn zuweilen ganz gewaltig, und wenn überhaupt von den Martis gesprochen wurde, so dachte er unwillkürlich nur an die Tochter, deren jetziges Aussehen ihm nicht deutlich und deren Andenken ihm gar nicht verhaßt war.

Doch war sein Vater Manz nun der erste von den beiden Feinden, der sich nicht mehr halten konnte und von Haus und Hof springen mußte. Dieser Vortritt rührte daher, daß er eine Frau besaß, die ihm geholfen, und einen Sohn, der doch auch einiges mit brauchte, während Marti der einzige Verzehrer war in seinem wackeligen Königreich, und seine Tochter durfte wohl arbeiten wie ein Haustierchen, aber nichts gebrauchen. Manz aber wußte nichts anderes anzufangen, als auf den Rat seiner Seldwyler Gönner in die Stadt zu ziehen und da sich als Wirt aufzutun. Es ist immer betrüblich anzusehen, wenn ein ehemaliger Landmann, der auf dem Felde alt geworden ist, mit den Trümmern seiner Habe in eine Stadt zieht und da eine Schenke oder Kneipe auftut, um als letzten Rettungsanker den freundlichen und gewandten Wirt zu machen, während es ihm nichts weniger als freundlich zu Mut ist. Als die Manzen vom Hofe zogen, sah man erst, wie arm sie bereits waren; denn sie luden lauter alten und

brain had been unable to grasp their true meaning. He had perforce been content with the verdict of his father, obeying the latter's prohibition to further consort with the Marti people without attempting to ascertain the underlying causes of the quarrel. So far he had not found it difficult to do as his father told him, and he did not meddle in the least with the whole business. He made no effort to either see or avoid Marti and his daughter Vreni, and while he assumed that his father must be in the right of it, he was no active enemy of the Martis. Vreni, on her part, was differently constituted from the lad. Having to suffer much more than Sali at home and feeling more deeply than he, woman-fashion, her almost total isolation, she was not so ready to let a sentiment of declared enmity enter her young and untried heart. In fact, she rather believed herself scorned and despised by the much better clad and apparently also much more fortunate former playmate. It was, therefore, only from a feeling of embarrassment that she hid from him, and whenever he came near enough to perceive her, she fled from him. He indeed never troubled to glance at her. So it happened that Sali had not seen the girl near enough for a couple of years to know what she was like. He had no notion that she was now almost grown-up, and that she was distinctly beautiful. And yet, once in a while he would remember her as his little playmate, as the merry companion of his carefree boyhood, and when at his home the Martis were mentioned he instinctively wondered what had become of her and how she would look now. He certainly did not hate her. In his memory she lived in a shadowy sort of way as a rather attractive girl.

It was his father, Manz, now who first had to go under. He was no longer able to stave off his creditors and had to leave farm and house behind. That he, though somewhat of better means originally than his neighbor and foe, was first to collapse was owing to his wife, who had lived in quite an extravagant style, and then he, too, had a son who, after all, cost him something. Marti, as we know, had but a little daughter who was scarcely any expense to him. Manz did not know what else to do but to follow the advice of some Seldwyla patrons and move to town, there to turn mine host of an inn or low tavern. It is always a sad sight to see a former peasant of some substance, a man who has been leading for many years a life of unremitting toil, it is true, but also one of independence and usefulness, after growing old among his acres, seek refuge from ill-fortune in town, taking the small remnants of his belongings with him and open a poor, shabby resort, in order to play, as the last safety anchor, the amiable and seductive host, all the while feeling by no means in a holiday mood himself. When the Manz family then left their farm to take this desperate

zerfallenden Hausrat auf, dem man es ansah, daß seit vielen Jahren nichts erneuert und angeschafft worden war. Die Frau legte aber nichtsdestominder ihren besten Staat an, als sie sich oben auf die Gerümpelfuhre setzte, und machte ein Gesicht voller Hoffnungen, als künftige Stadtfrau schon mit Verachtung auf die Dorfgenossen herabsehend, welche voll Mitleid hinter den Hecken hervor dem bedenklichen Zuge zuschauten. Denn sie nahm sich vor, mit ihrer Liebenswürdigkeit und Klugheit die ganze Stadt zu bezaubern, und was ihr versimpelter Mann nicht machen könne, das wolle sie schon ausrichten, wenn sie nur erst einmal als Frau Wirtin in einem stattlichen Gasthofe säße. Dieser Gasthof bestand aber in einer trübseligen Winkelschenke in einem abgelegenen schmalen Gäßchen, auf der eben ein anderer zugrunde gegangen war und welche die Seldwyler dem Manz verpachteten, da er noch einige hundert Taler einzuziehen hatte. Sie verkauften ihm auch ein paar Fäßchen angemachten Weines und das Wirtschaftsmobiliar, das aus einem Dutzend weißen geringen Flaschen, ebensoviel Gläsern und einigen tannenen Tischen und Bänken bestand, welche einst blutrot angestrichen gewesen und jetzt vielfältig abgescheuert waren. Vor dem Fenster knarrte ein eiserner Reifen in einem Haken, und in dem Reifen schenkte eine blecherne Hand Rotwein aus einem Schöppchen in ein Glas. Überdies hing ein verdorrter Busch von Stechpalme über der Haustüre, was Manz alles mit in die Pacht bekam. Um deswillen war er nicht so wohlgemut wie seine Frau, sondern trieb mit schlimmer Ahnung und voll Ingrimm die mageren Pferde an, welche er vom neuen Bauern geliehen. Das letzte schäbige Knechtchen, das er gehabt, hatte ihn schon seit einigen Wochen verlassen. Als er solcherweise abfuhr, sah er wohl, wie Marti voll Hohn und Schadenfreude sich unfern der Straße zu schaffen machte, fluchte ihm und hielt denselben für den alleinigen Urheber seines Unglückes. Sali aber, sobald das Fuhrwerk im Gange war, beschleunigte seine Schritte, eilte voraus und ging allein auf Seitenwegen nach der Stadt.

step, it was first apparent how poor they had already grown. For all the household goods that were loaded on a cart were in a deplorable state, defective and not repaired for many years. Nevertheless the wife put on her best finery, when seating herself on top of the crazy old vehicle, and made a face of such pride as though she already looked down upon her neighbors as would a city lady of taste and refinement, while all the while the villagers peeped from behind their hedges full of pity at the sorry show made by the exodus. For Mother Manz had settled it in her foolish noddle to turn the heads of all Seldwyla by her fine manners and her wheedling tongue, thinking that if her boorish husband did not understand how to handle and cajole the town folks, it was vastly different with herself who would soon show these Seldwyla people what an alluring hostess she would make at the head of a tavern or inn doing a rushing business. Great was her disenchantment, however, when she actually set eyes on this inn vaunted so much in advance by her addled spirits. For it was located in a small side-street of a rather disreputable quarter of Seldwyla, and the inn itself was one in which the predecessor, one of several that had gone the same way, had just been forcibly ousted because of being unable to pay his debts. His Seldwyla patrons had, in fact, rented this mean public house for a few hundred dollars a year to Manz in consideration of the fact that the latter still had some small sums outstanding in town, and because they could find nobody else to take the place at a venture. They also sold him a few barrels of inferior wine as well as the fixtures which consisted in the main of a couple of dozen glasses and bottles, and of some rude and hacked pine tables and benches that had once been painted a hue of deadly scarlet and were now reduced to a dingy brownish tint. Before the entrance door an iron hoop was clattering in the wind, and inside the hoop a tin hand was pouring out forever claret into a small shoppen vessel. Besides all these luxuries there was a sun-dried bunch of datura fastened above the door, all of which Manz had noted down in his lease. Knowing all this Manz was by no means so full of hopes and smiling humor as his spouse, but on the contrary whipped up his bony old horses, lent him by the new owner of his farm, with considerable foreboding. The last shabby helper he had had on his farm had left him several weeks before, and when he left the village on this his present errand he had not failed to note Marti who, full of grim joy and scorn, had busied himself with some trifling task along the road where his fallen foe had to pass. Manz saw it, cursed Marti, and held him to be the sole cause of his downfall. But Sali, as soon as the cart was fairly on the way, got down, speeded up his steps and reached the town along by-paths.

»Da wären wir!« sagte Manz, als die Fuhre vor dem Spelunkelein anhielt. Die Frau erschrak darüber, denn das war in der Tat ein trauriger Gasthof. Die Leute traten eilfertig unter die Fenster und vor die Häuser, um sich den neuen Bauernwirt anzusehen, und machten mit ihrer Seldwyler Überlegenheit mit leidig spöttische Gesichter. Zornig und mit nassen Augen kletterte die Manzin vom Wagen herunter und lief, ihre Zunge vorläufig wetzend, in das Haus, um sich heute vornehm nicht wieder blicken zu lassen; denn sie schämte sich des schlechten Gerätes und der verdorbenen Betten, welche nun abgeladen wurden. Sali schämte sich auch, aber er mußte helfen und machte mit seinem Vater einen seltsamen Verlag in dem Gäßchen, auf welchem alsbald die Kinder der Falliten herumsprangen und sich über das verlumpte Bauernpack lustig machten. Im Hause aber sah es noch trübseliger aus, und es glich einer vollkommenen Räuberhöhle. Die Wände waren schlecht geweißtes feuchtes Mauerwerk, außer der dunklen unfreundlichen Gaststube mit ihren ehemals blutroten Tischen waren nur noch ein paar schlechte Kämmerchen da, und überall hatte der ausgezogene Vorgänger den trostlosesten Schmutz und Kehricht zurückgelassen.

So war der Anfang, und so ging es auch fort. Während der ersten Woche kamen, besonders am Abend, wohl hin und wieder ein Tisch voll Leute aus Neugierde, den Bauernwirt zu sehen und ob es da vielleicht einigen Spaß absetzte. Am Wirt hatten sie nicht viel zu betrachten, denn Manz war ungelenk, starr, unfreundlich und melancholisch, und wußte sich gar nicht zu benehmen, wollte es auch nicht wissen. Er füllte langsam und ungeschickt die Schöppchen, stellte sie mürrisch vor die Gäste und versuchte etwas zu sagen, brachte aber nichts heraus. Desto eifriger warf sich nun seine Frau ins Geschirr und hielt die Leute wirklich einige Tage zusammen, aber in einem ganz andern Sinne, als sie meinte. Die ziemlich dicke Frau hatte sich eine eigene Haustracht zusammengesetzt, in der sie unwiderstehlich zu sein glaubte. Zu einem leinenen ungefärbten Landrock trug sie einen alten grünseidenen Spenzer, eine baumwollene Schürze und einen schlimmen weißen Halskragen. Von ihrem nicht mehr dichten Haar hatte sie an den Schlä-

"Well, here we are," said Manz, when the cart had reached its destination. His wife was crestfallen when she noticed the dreary and unpropitious aspect of the place. The people of the neighborhood stepped in front of their housedoors to have a look at the new innkeeper, and when they saw the rustic appearance of the outfit and the miserable trappings, they put on their Seldwyla smile of superiority. Wrathfully Mother Manz climbed down from her high seat, and tears of anger were in her eyes as she quickly fled into the house, her limber tongue for once forsaking her. On that day at least she was no more seen below. For she herself was well aware of the sorry show made by her, and all the more as the tattered condition of her furniture could not be concealed from prying eyes when the various articles were now being unloaded. Her musty and torn beds, particularly, she felt ashamed of. Sali, too, shared her feelings, but he was obliged to help his father in unloading, and the two made quite a stir in the neighborhood with their rustic manners and speech, furnishing the curious children with food for laughter. These little folks, indeed, amused themselves abundantly that day at the expense of the "ragged peasant bankrupts." Inside the house, though, things looked still more desolate; the place, in fact, had more the looks of a robbers' roost than of an inn. The walls were of badly calsomined brick, damp with moisture, and beside the dark and poorly furnished guest room downstairs there were but a couple of bare and uninviting bedrooms, and everywhere their predecessor had left behind nothing but spider's webs, filth and dust.

That was the beginning of it, and thus it continued to the end. During the first few weeks indeed there came, especially in the evenings, a number of people anxious to see, out of sheer curiosity, "the peasant landlord," hoping there would be "some fun." But out of the landlord himself they could not get much of that, for Manz was stiff, unfriendly, and melancholy, and did not in the least know how to treat his guests, nor did he want to know. Slowly and awkwardly he would pour out the wine demanded, put it before the customer with a morose air, and then make an unsuccessful attempt to enter into some sort of conversation, but brought forth only some stammered commonplaces, whereupon he gave it up. All the more desperately did his wife endeavor to entertain her guests, and by her ludicrous and absurd behavior really managed, for a few days at least, to amuse people. But she did this in quite a different way from that intended by her. Mother Manz was rather corpulent, and she had from her own inventive brain composed a costume in which to wait on her guests and in which she believed herself to be simply irresistible. With a stout linen skirt she wore an old waist of green silk, a long cotton apron

fen possierliche Schnecken gewickelt und in das Zöpfchen hinten einen hohen Kamm gesteckt. So schwänzelte und tänzelte sie mit angestrengter Anmut herum, spitzte lächerlich das Mann, daß es süß aussehen sollte, hüpfte elastisch an die Tische hin, und das Glas oder den Teller mit gesalzenem Käse hinsetzend, sagte sie lächelnd: »So so? so soli! herrlich herrlich, ihr Herren!« und solches dummes Zeug mehr; denn obwohl sie sonst eine geschliffene Zunge hatte, so wußte sie jetzt doch nichts Gescheites vorzubringen, da sie fremd war und die Leute nicht kannte. Die Seldwyler von der schlechtesten Sorte, die da hockten, hielten die Hand vor den Mund, wollten vor Lachen ersticken, stießen sich unter dem Tisch mit den Füßen und sagten »Potztausig! das ist ja eine Herrliche!« – »Eine Himmlische!« sagte ein anderer, »beim ewigen Hagel! es ist der Mühe wert, hierherzukommen, so eine haben wir lang nicht gesehen!« Ihr Mann bemerkte das wohl mit finsterm Blicke; er gab ihr einen Stoß in die Rippen und flüsterte: »Du alte Kuh! Was machst du denn?« – »Störe mich nicht«, sagte sie unwillig, »du alter Tolpatsch! siehst du nicht, wie ich mir Mühe gebe und mit den Leuten umzugehen weiß? Das sind aber nur Lumpen von deinem Anhang! Laß mich nur machen, ich will bald fürnehmere Kundschaft hier haben!« Dies alles war beleuchtet von einem oder zwei dünnen Talglichten; Sali, der Sohn, aber ging hinaus in die dunkle Küche, setzte sich auf den Herd und weinte über Vater und Mutter.

Die Gäste hatten aber das Schauspiel bald satt, welches ihnen die gute Frau Manz gewährte, und blieben wieder, wo es ihnen wohler war und sie über die wunderliche Wirtschaft lachen konnten; nur dann und wann erschien ein einzelner, der ein Glas trank und die Wände angähnte, oder es kam ausnahmsweise eine ganze Bande, die armen Leute mit einem vorübergehenden Trubel und Lärm zu täuschen. Es ward ihnen angst und bange in dem engen Mauerwinkel, wo sie kaum die Sonne sahen, und Manz, welcher sonst gewohnt war, tagelang in der Stadt zu liegen, fand es jetzt unerträglich zwischen diesen Mauern. Wenn er an die freie Weite der Felder dachte,

and a ridiculous broad collar around the neck. Out of her hair, no longer abundant, she had twisted corkscrew curls ornamenting her forehead, and in the back she had stuck a tall comb into her thin braids. Thus made up she mincingly danced on the tips of her toes before the particular guest to be entranced, pointed her mouth in a laughable manner, which she thought was "sweet," hopped about the table with forced elasticity, and serving the wine or the salted cheese she would exclaim smilingly: "Well, well, so alone? Lively, lively, you gentlemen!" And some more of such nonsense she would whisper in a stilted way, for the trouble was that although usually she could talk glibly about almost anything with her cronies from the village, she felt somewhat embarrassed with these city people, not being acquainted with the subjects of conversation they liked to touch on. The Seldwyla people of the roughest type who had dropped in for something to laugh at, put their hands before their mouths to prevent bursting out in her face, nearly suffocated with suppressed merriment, trod upon each other's feet under the table, and afterwards, in relating the matter, would say: "Zounds, that is a woman among a thousand, a paragon!" Another one said: "A heavenly creature, by the gods. It is worth while coming here just to watch her antics. Such a funny one we haven't had here for a long while." Her husband noticed these goings on, with a mien of thunder, and he would perhaps punch her in the ribs and say: "You old cow, what is the matter with you?" But then she gave him a superior glance, and would murmur: "Don't disturb me! You stupid old fool, don't you see how hard I am trying to please people? Those over there, of course, are only low fellows from among your own acquaintance, but if you don't interfere with me I shall soon have much more fashionable guests here, as you'll see." These illusions of hers were illuminated in a room with but two tallow dips, but Sali, her son, went out into the dark kitchen, sat down at the hearth and wept about father and mother.

However, these first guests had soon their fill of this kind of sport, and began to stay away, and then went back to their old haunts where they got better drink and more rational conversation, and there they would laughingly comment on the queer peasant innkeepers. Only once in a while now a single guest of this type would drop in, usually to verify previous reports heard by him, and such a one found as a rule nothing more exciting to do than to yawn and gaze at the wall. Or perhaps a band of roystering blades, having heard the place spoken of by others, would wind up a jolly evening by a brief visit, and then there would be noise enough, but not much else, and the old couple could often not even thus be roused from their melancholy. For by that time both

so stierte er finster brütend an die Decke oder auf den Boden, lief unter die enge Haustüre und wieder zurück, da die Nachbaren den bösen Wirt, wie sie ihn schon nannten, angafften. Nun dauerte es aber nicht mehr lange, und sie verarmten gänzlich und hatten gar nichts mehr in der Hand; sie mußten, um etwas zu essen, warten, bis einer kam und für wenig Geld etwas von dem noch vorhandenen Wein verzehrte, und wenn er eine Wurst oder dergleichen begehrte, so hatten sie oft die größte Angst und Sorge, dieselbe beizutreiben. Bald hatten sie auch den Wein nur noch in einer großen Flasche verborgen, die sie heimlich in einer anderen Kneipe füllen ließen, und so sollten sie nun die Wirte machen ohne Wein und Brot und freundlich sein, ohne ordentlich gegessen zu haben. Sie waren beinahe froh, wenn nur niemand kam, und hockten so in ihrem Kneipchen, ohne leben noch sterben zu können. Als die Frau diese traurigen Erfahrungen machte, zog sie den grünen Spenzer wieder aus und nahm abermals eine Veränderung vor, indem sie nun, wie früher die Fehler, so nun einige weibliche Tugenden aufkommen ließ und mehr ausbildete, da Not an den Mann ging. Sie übte Geduld und suchte den Alten aufrechtzuhalten und den Jungen zum Guten anzuweisen; sie opferte sich vielfältig in allerlei Dingen, kurz, sie übte in ihrer Weise eine Art von wohltätigem Einfluß, der zwar nicht weit reichte und nicht viel besserte, aber immerhin besser war als gar nichts oder als das Gegenteil und die Zeit wenigstens verbringen half, welche sonst viel früher hätte brechen müssen für diese Leute. Sie wußte manchen Rat zu geben nunmehr in erbärmlichen Dingen, nach ihrem Verstande, und wenn der Rat nichts zu taugen schien und fehlschlug, so ertrug sie willig den Grimm der Männer, kurzum, sie tat jetzt alles, da sie alt war, was besser gedient hätte, wenn sie es früher geübt.

wife and husband had grown heartily sick of their bargain. The new style of living felt to him almost as lonesome and cold as the grave. For he who as a lifelong farmer had been used to see the sun rise, to hear and feel the wind blow, to breathe the pure air of the country from morning till night, and to have the sunshine come and go, was now cooped up within these dingy, hopeless walls, had to draw in his lungs with every breath the contaminated atmosphere of this miserable neighborhood, and when he thus dreamed day-dreams of the wide expanse of the fields he once owned and tilled, a dull sort of despair settled down on him like a pall. For hours and hours every day he would stare in a dark humor at the smoke-begrimed ceiling of his inn, having mostly little else to do, and dull visions of a future unrelieved by a single ray of hope would float across his saturnine mind. Insupportable his present life seemed to him then. Then a purposeless restlessness would come over him, when he would get up from his seat a dozen times an hour, run to the housedoor and peer out, then run back and resume his watch. The neighbors had already given him a nickname. The "wicked landlord," they dubbed him, because his glance was troubled and fierce. Not long and they were totally impoverished, had not even enough ready money left to put in the little in drink and provisions needed for chance customers, so that the sausages and bread, the wine and liquor that were ordered by guests had to be got on trust. Often they even lacked the wherewithal to make a meal of, and had to go hungry for a while. It was a curious tavern they were keeping. When somebody strolled in by accident and demanded refreshment they were forced to send to the nearest competitor, around the corner, and obtain a measure of wine and some food, paying for it an hour or so later when they themselves had been paid. And with all that, they were expected to play the cheerful host and to talk pleasantly when their own stomachs were empty. They were almost glad when nobody came; then each of them would cower in a dark corner by the chimney, too lethargic to stir. When Mother Manz underwent these sad experiences she once more took off her green silk waist, and another metamorphosis was noticed. As formerly she had shown a number of feminine vices, so now she exhibited some feminine virtues, and these grew with the evil times. She began to practice patience and sought to cheer up her morose husband and to encourage her young son in trying for remunerative work. She sacrificed her own comfort and convenience even, went about like a happy busybody, and chattered incessantly merrily, all in an attempt to put some heart into the two men. In short, she exerted in her own queer way an undoubted beneficial influence on them, and while this did not lead

Um wenigstens etwas Beißbares zu erwerben und die Zeit zu verbringen, verlegten sich Vater und Sohn auf die Fischerei, das heißt mit der Angelrute, soweit es für jeden erlaubt war, sie in den Fluß zu hängen. Dies war auch eine Hauptbeschäftigung der Seldwyler, nachdem sie falliert hatten. Bei günstigem Wetter, wenn die Fische gern anbissen, sah man sie dutzendweise hinauswandern mit Rute und Eimer, und wenn man an den Ufern des Flusses wandelte, horchte alle Spanne lang einer, der angelte, der eine in einem langen braunen Bürgerrock, die bloßen Füße im Wasser, der andere in einem spitzen blauen Frack auf einer alten Weide stehend, den alten Filz schlief auf dem Ohre; weiterhin angelte gar einer im zerrissenen großblumigen Schlafrock, da er keinen andern mehr besaß, die lange Pfeife in der einen, die Rute in der anderen Hand, und wenn man um eine Krümmung des Flusses bog, stand ein alter kahlköpfiger Dickbauch faselnackt auf einem Stein und angelte; dieser hatte, trotz des Aufenthaltes am Wasser, so schwarze Füße, daß man glaubte, er habe die Stiefel anbehalten. Jeder hatte ein Töpfchen oder ein Schächtelchen neben sich, in welchem Regenwürmer wimmelten, nach denen sie zu andern Stunden zu graben pflegten. Wenn der Himmel mit Wolken bezogen und es ein schwüles dämmeriges Wetter war, welches Regen verkündete, so standen diese Gestalten am zahlreichsten an dem ziehenden Strome, regungslos gleich einer Galerie von Heiligen- oder Prophetenbildern. Achtlos zogen die Landleute mit Vieh und Wagen an ihnen vorüber, und die Schiffer auf dem Flusse sahen sie nicht an, während sie leise murrten über die störenden Schiffe.

to anything tangible it helped at least to make things bearable for the time being and was far better than the reverse would have been. She would rack her poor brains, and give this advice or that how to mend things, and if it miscarried she would have something fresh to propose. Mostly she proved in the wrong with her counsel, but now and then, in one of the many trivial ways that her petty mind was dwelling on she was successful. When the contrary resulted, she gaily took the blame, remained cheerful under discouragement, and, in short, did everything which, if she had only done it before things were past repair, might have really cured the desperate situation.

In order to have at least some food in the house and to pass the dull time, father and son now began to devote their leisure time to the sport of fishing, that is, with the angle, as far as it is permissible to everybody in Switzerland. This, be it said, was also one of the favorite pastimes of those decrepit Seldwylians who had come to grief in the world, most of them having failed in business. When the weather was favorable, namely, and when the fish took the bait most readily, one might see dozens of these gentry wander off provided with rod and pail, and on a walk along the shores of the river you might see one of them, every little distance, angling, the one in a long brown coat once of fashionable make, but with his bare feet in the water, the next attired in a tattered blue frock, astride an old willow tree, his ragged felt hat shoved over his left ear. Farther down even you might perceive a third whose meagre limbs were wrapped in a shabby old dressing gown, since that was the only article of clothing he had left, his long tobacco pipe in one hand, and an equally long fishing rod in the other. And in turning a bend of the river one was apt to encounter another queer customer who stood, quite nude, with his bald head and his fat paunch, on top of a flat rock in the river. This one had, though almost living in the water during the warm season, feet black as coal, so that it looked from a distance as if he had kept his boots on. Each of these worthies had a pot or a small box at his side, in which were swarming angle worms, and to obtain these they were industriously digging at all hours of the day not actually employed in fishing. Whenever the sky began to cloud up and the air became close and sultry, threatening rain, these quaint figures could be seen most numerously along the softly rolling stream, immovable like a congregation of ancient saints on their pillars. Without ever deigning to cast a glance in their direction, rustics from farm and forest used to pass them by, and the boatmen on the river did not even look their way, whereas these lone fishermen themselves used to curse in a forlorn way at these disturbers of their prey.

Wenn man Manz vor zwölf Jahren, als er mit einem schönen Gespann pflügte auf dem Hügel über dem Ufer, geweissagt hätte, er würde sich einst zu diesen wunderlichen Heiligen gesellen und gleich ihnen Fische fangen, so wäre er nicht übel aufgefahren. Auch eilte er jetzt hastig an ihnen vorüber hinter ihren Rücken und eilte stromaufwärts gleich einem eigensinnigen Schatten der Unterwelt, der sich zu seiner Verdammnis ein bequemes einsames Plätzchen sucht an den dunklen Wässern. Mit der Angelrute zu stehen, hatten er und sein Sohn indessen keine Geduld, und sie erinnerten sich der Art, wie die Bauern auf manche andere Weise etwa Fische fangen, wenn sie übermütig sind, besonders mit den Fländen in den Bächen; daher nahmen sie die Ruten nur zum Schein mit und gingen an den Borden der Bäche hinauf, wo sie wußten, daß es teure und gute Forellen gab.

Dem auf dem Lande zurückgebliebenen Marti ging es inzwischen auch immer schlimmer, und es war ihm höchst langweilig dabei, so daß er, anstatt auf seinem vernachlässigten Felde zu arbeiten, ebenfalls auf das Fischen verfiel und tagelang im Wasser herumplätscherte. Vrenchen durfte nicht von seiner Seite und mußte ihm Eimer und Gerät nachtragen durch nasse Wiesengründe, durch Bäche und Wassertümpel allerart, bei Regen und Sonnenschein, indessen sie das Notwendigste zu Hause liegenlassen mußte. Denn es war sonst keine Seele mehr da und wurde auch keine gebraucht, da Marti das meiste Land schon verloren hatte und nur noch wenige Äcker besaß, die er mit seiner Tochter liederlich genug oder gar nicht bebaute.

So kam es, daß, als er eines Abends einen ziemlich tiefen und reißenden Bach entlangging, in welchem die Forellen fleißig sprangen, da der Himmel voll Gewitterwolken hing, er unverhofft auf seinen Feind Manz traf, der an dem andern Ufer daherkam. Sobald er ihn sah, stieg ein schrecklicher Groll und Hohn in ihm auf; sie waren sich seit Jahren nicht so nahe gewesen, ausgenommen vor den Gerichtsschranken, wo sie nicht schelten durften, und Marti rief jetzt voll Grimm: »Was tust du hier, du Hund? Kannst du nicht in deinem Lotterneste bleiben, du Seldwyler Lumpenhund?«

»Wirst nächstens wohl auch ankommen, du Schelm!« rief Manz. »Fische fängst du ja auch schon und wirst deshalb nicht viel mehr zu versäumen haben!«

If Manz had been told twelve years before when he was still plowing with a fine team of horses across the hillock above the shore, that he, too, one day would join this strange brotherhood of the rod, he would probably have treated such a prophet rather roughly. But even today Manz hastened past those fishermen that were rather crowding one another, until he stood, upstream and alone, like a wrathful shadow of Hades, by himself, just as if he preferred even in the abode of the damned a spot of his own choosing. But to stand thus with a rod, for hours and hours, neither he nor his son Sali had the patience, and they remembered the manner in which peasants in their own neighborhood used to catch fish, especially to grasp them with their hands in the purling brooks. Therefore, they had their rods with them only as a ruse, and they walked upstream further and further, following the tortuous windings of the water, where they knew from of old that trout, dainty and expensive trout, were to be had.

Meanwhile Marti, though he had still nominal possession of his farm, had likewise been drifting from bad to worse, without any gleam of hope. And since all toil on his land could no more avert the final catastrophe, and time hung heavy on his hands, he also had taken to this sport of fishing. Instead of laboring in his neglected fields he often would fish for days and days at a time. Vreni at such times was not permitted to leave him, but had to follow him with pail and nets, through wet meadows and along brooks and waterholes, whether there was rain or shine, while neglecting her household labors at home. For at home not a soul had remained, neither was there any need, since Marti little by little had already lost nearly all his land, and now owned but a few more acres of it, and these he tilled either not at all or else, together with his daughter, in the slovenliest way.

Thus it came to pass that he, too, one early evening was walking along the borders of a rapid and deep brook, one in which trout were leaping plentifully, since the sky was overhung with dark and threatening clouds, when without any warning he encountered his enemy, Manz, who was coming along on the other side of it. As soon as he made him out a fearful anger began to gnaw at his very vitals. They had not been so near each other for years, except when in court facing the judge, and then they had not been permitted to vent their hatred and spite, and now Marti shouted full of venom: "What are you doing here, you dog? Can't you stay in your den in town? Oh, you Seldwylian loafer!"

"Don't talk as if you were something better, you scoundrel," growled Manz, "for I see you also catching fish, and thus it proves you have nothing better to do yourself!"

»Schweig, du Galgenhund!« schrie Marti, da hier die Wellen des Baches stärker rauschten, »du hast mich ins Unglück gebracht!« Und da jetzt auch die Weiden am Bache gewaltig zu rauschen anfingen im aufgehenden Wetterwind, so mußte Manz noch lauter schreien: »Wenn dem nur so wäre, so wollte ich mich freuen, du elender Tropf!« – »O du Hund!« schrie Marti herüber und Manz hinüber: »O du Kalb, wie dumm tust du!« Und jener sprang wie ein Tiger den Bach entlang und suchte herüberzukommen. Der Grund, warum er der Wütendere war, lag in seiner Meinung, daß Manz als Wirt wenigstens genug zu essen und zu trinken hätte und gewissermaßen ein kurzweiliges Leben führe, während es ungerechterweise ihm so langweilig wäre auf seinem zertrümmerten Hofe. Manz schritt indessen auch grimmig genug an der anderen Seite hin; hinter ihm sein Sohn, welcher, statt auf den bösen Streit zu hören, neugierig und verwundert nach Vrenchen hinübersah, welche hinter ihrem Vater ging, vor Scham in die Erde sehend, daß ihr die braunen krausen Haare ins Gesicht fielen. Sie trug einen hölzernen Fischeimer in der einen Hand, in der anderen hatte sie Schuh und Strümpfe getragen und ihr Kleid der Nässe wegen aufgeschürzt. Seit aber Sali auf der anderen Seite ging, hatte sie es schamhaft sinken lassen und war nun dreifach belästigt und gequält, da sie alle das Zeug tragen, den Rock zusammenhalten und des Streites wegen sich grämen mußte. Hätte sie aufgesehen und nach Sali geblickt, so würde sie entdeckt haben, daß er weder vornehm noch sehr stolz mehr aussah und selbst bekümmert genug war. Während Vrenchen so ganz beschämt und verwirrt auf die Erde sah und Sali nur diese in allem Elende schlanke und anmutige Gestalt im Auge hatte, die so verlegen und demütig dahinschritt, beachteten sie dabei nicht, wie ihre Väter still geworden, aber mit verstärkter Wut einem hölzernen Stege zueilten, der in kleiner Entfernung über den Bach führte und eben sichtbar wurde. Es fing an zu blitzen und erleuchtete seltsam die dunkle melancholische Wassergegend; es donnerte auch in den grauschwarzen Wolken mit dumpfem Grolle, und schwere Regentropfen fielen, als die verwilderten Männer gleichzeitig auf die schmale, unter ihren Tritten schwankende Brücke stürzten, sich gegenseitig packten und die Fäuste in die vor Zorn und ausbrechendem Kummer bleichen zitternden Gesichter schlugen. Es ist nichts Anmutiges und

"Shut your evil mouth, you fiend," shrieked Marti, since to make himself heard above the rush of waters he had to strain his voice. "You it is who have driven me into misery and poverty." And since the willows lining the brook now also were shaken by the gathering storm, Manz was forced to shout even louder: "If that is true, then I should feel glad, you woodenhead!" And thus, a duel of the most cruel taunts went on from both borders of the brook, and finally, driven beyond endurance, each of the two half-crazed men ran along the steep path, trying to find a way across the deep water. Of the two Marti was the most envenomed because he believed that his foe, being a landlord and managing an inn, must at least have food enough to eat and liquor to drink, besides leading a jolly sort of life, while he was barely able to eke out a meal or two on the coarsest fare. Besides, the memory of his wasted farm stung him to violence. But Manz, too, now stepped along lively enough on his side of the water, and behind him his son, who, instead of sharing his father's grim interest in the quarrel, peeped curiously and amazedly at Vreni. She, the girl, followed closely behind her father, deeply ashamed at what she heard and looking at the ground, so that her curly brown hair fell over her flushed face. She carried in her hand a wooden fishpail, and in the other her shoes and stockings, and had shortened her skirt to avoid its dragging in the wet. But since Sali was walking on the other side and seemed to watch her, she had allowed her skirt to drop, out of modesty, and was now thrice embarrassed and annoyed, since she had not alone to carry all, pail, nets, shoes and stockings, but also to hold up her skirt and to feel humiliated because of this bitter and vulgar quarrel. If she had lifted her eyes and read Sali's face, she would have seen that he no longer looked either proud or elegant as hitherto his image had dwelt in her mind, but that, on the contrary, the young man also wore a distressed and humbled mien. But while Vreni so entirely ashamed and disconcerted kept her eyes on the ground, and Sali stared in amazement at this dainty and graceful being that had so suddenly crossed his path, and who seemed so weighed down by the whole occurrence, they did not properly observe that their fathers by now had become silent but were both of them striving in increased rage to reach the small wooden bridge a short distance off and which led across to the other shore. Just then the first forks of lightning were weirdly illuminating the scene. The thunder was rolling in the dun clouds, and heavy drops of rain were already falling singly, when these two men, almost driven out of their senses, simultaneously reached the tiny bridge with their hurried and determined tread, and as soon as near enough seized each other with the iron grip of the rustic, striking with

nichts weniger als artig, wenn sonst gesetzte Menschen noch in den Fall kommen, aus Übermut, Unbedacht oder Notwehr unter allerhand Volk, das sie nicht näher berührt, Schläge auszuteilen oder welche zu bekommen; allein dies ist eine harmlose Spielerei gegen das tiefe Elend, das zwei alte Menschen überwältigt, die sich wohl kennen und seit lange kennen, wenn diese aus innerster Feindschaft und aus dem Gange einer ganzen Lebensgeschichte heraus sich mit nackten Händen anfassen und mit Fäusten schlagen. So taten jetzt diese beide ergrauten Männer; vor fünfzig Jahren vielleicht hatten sie sich als Buben zum letzten Mal gerauft, dann aber fünfzig lange Jahre mit keiner Hand mehr berührt, ausgenommen in ihrer guten Zeit, wo sie sich etwa zum Gruße die Hände geschüttelt, und auch dies nur selten bei ihrem trockenen und sichern Wesen. Nachdem sie ein oder zweimal geschlagen, hielten sie inne und rangen still zitternd miteinander, nur zuweilen aufstöhnend und elendiglich knirschend, und einer suchte den andern über das knackende Geländer ins Wasser zu werfen. Jetzt waren aber auch ihre Kinder nachgekommen und sahen den erbärmlichen Auftritt. Sali sprang eines Satzes heran, um seinem Vater beizustehen und ihm zu helfen, dem gehaßten Feinde den Garaus zu machen, der ohnehin der schwächere schien und eben zu unterliegen drohte. Aber auch Vrenchen sprang, alles wegwerfend, mit einem langen Aufschrei herzu und umklammerte ihren Vater, um ihn zu schützen, während sie ihn dadurch nur hinderte und beschwerte. Tränen strömten aus ihren Augen, und sie sah flehend den Sali an, der im Begriff war, ihren Vater ebenfalls zu fassen und vollends zu überwältigen. Unwillkürlich legte er aber seine Hand an seinen eigenen Vater und suchte denselben mit festem Arm von dem Gegner loszubringen und zu beruhigen, so daß der Kampf eine kleine Weile ruhte oder vielmehr die ganze Gruppe unruhig hin und her drängte, ohne auseinander zu kommen. Darüber waren die jungen Leute, sich mehr zwischen die Alten schiebend, in dichte Berührung gekommen, und in diesem Augenblicke erhellte ein Wolkenriß, der den grellen Abendschein durchließ, das nahe Gesicht des Mädchens, und Sali sah in dies ihm so wohlbekannte und doch soviel anders und schöner gewordene Gesicht. Vrenchen sah in diesem Augenblicke auch sein Erstaunen, und es lächelte ganz kurz und geschwind mitten in seinem Schrecken und in sei-

all the power they could summon with clenched fists into the hateful face of the adversary. Blows rained fast and furious, and each of the combatants gnashed his teeth with rage. It is not a becoming nor a handsome sight to see elderly men usually soberminded and slow to act in a personal encounter, no matter whether occasioned by anger, provocation or self-defense, but such a spectacle is harmless in comparison with that of two aged men who attack each other with uncontrolled fury because while knowing the other deeply and well, now out of the depths of that very knowledge and out of a fixed belief that the other has destroyed his very life, seize each other with their naked fists and try to commit murder from unrequited revenge. But thus these two men now did, both with hair gray to the roots. More than fifty years ago they had last fought with each other as lads, merely out of a youthful spirit of rivalry, but during the half century succeeding they had never laid hands on each other, except when, as good neighbors and fellow-peasants, they had grasped each other's hand in peace and concord, but even that, with their rather dry and undemonstrative ways, but rarely. After the first two or three frenzied blows, they both became silent, and now they struggled and wrestled in all the agony of senile impotence, their stiffened muscles and tendons stretched with the tension, murder in their glaring eyes, each groaning with the supreme effort to master the other. They now attempted, both of them, to end the fearsome fight by pushing the other over into the rushing flood below, the slender supports of the rails creaking under the pressure. But now at last their children had reached the spot, and Sali, with a bound, came to his father's help, to enable the latter to make an end of the hated foe, Marti being just about spent and exhausted. But Vreni also sprang, dropping all her burdens, to the rescue, and after the manner of women in such cases, embracing her father tightly and really thus rendering him unable to move and defend himself. Tears streamed from her eyes, and she looked with silent appeal at Sali, just at the moment when he was about also to grasp old Marti by the throat. Involuntarily he laid his hand upon the arm of his father, thus restraining him, and next attempted to wrest his father loose. The combat thus grew into a mutual swaying back and forth, and the whole group was impotently straining and pushing, without either party coming to a rest. But during this confused jumbling the two young people had, interfering between their elders, more and more approached each other, and just at this juncture a break in the dark bank of clouds overhead let the piercing rays of the setting sun reach the scene and illuminate it with a blinding flash, and then it was that Sali looked full into the countenance of the girl, rosy and

nen Tränen ihn an. Doch ermannte sich Sali, geweckt durch die Anstrengungen seines Vaters, ihn abzuschütteln, und brachte ihn mit eindringlich bittenden Worten und fester Haltung endlich ganz von seinem Feinde weg. Beide alte Gesellen atmeten hoch auf und begannen jetzt wieder zu schelten und zu schreien, sich voneinander abwendend; ihre Kinder aber atmeten kaum und waren still wie der Tod, gaben sich aber im Wegwenden und Trennen, ungesehen von den Alten, schnell die Hände, welche vom Wasser und von den Fischen feucht und kühl waren.

Als die grollenden Parteien ihrer Wege gingen, hatten die Wolken sich wieder geschlossen, es dunkelte mehr und mehr, und der Regen goß nun in Bächen durch die Luft. Manz schlenderte voraus auf den dunklen nassen Wegen, er duckte sich, beide Hände in den Taschen, unter den Regengüssen, zitterte noch in seinen Gesichtszügen und mit den Zähnen, und ungesehene Tränen rieselten ihm in den Stoppelbart, die er fließen ließ, um sie durch das Wegwischen nicht zu verraten. Sein Sohn hatte aber nichts gesehen, weil er in glückseligen Bildern verloren dicherging. Er merkte weder Regen noch Sturm, weder Dunkelheit noch Elend; sondern leicht, hell und warm war es ihm innen und außen, und er fühlte sich so reich und wohlgeboren wie ein Königssohn. Er sah fortwährend das sekundenlange Lächeln des nahen schönen Gesichtes und erwiderte dasselbe erst jetzt, eine gute halbe Stunde nachher, indem er voll Liebe in Nacht und Wetter hinein und das liebe Gesicht anlachte, das ihm allerwegen aus dem Dunkel entgegentrat, so daß er glaubte, Vrenchen müsse auf seinen Wegen dies Lachen notwendig sehen und seiner innewerden.

Sein Vater war des andern Tags wie zerschlagen und wollte nicht aus dem Hause. Der ganze Handel und das vieljährige Elend nahm heute eine neue, deutlichere Gestalt an und breitete sich dunkel aus in der drückenden Luft der Spelunke, also daß Mann und Frau matt und scheu um das Gespenst herumschlichen, aus der Stube

embellished by the excitement. It was to Sali like a glimpse of another, a brighter and more heavenly world. And Vreni at the same instant, too, quickly observed the impression she had made on her onetime playmate, and she smiled for the fraction of a second at him, right in the midst of her tears and her fright. Sali, however, recovered himself instantly, warned by the energetic struggles of his father to shake off the restraining arm of his son. By holding him firmly and by speaking with authority to his father, he managed to calm him down at last and to push him out of the reach of the other. Both old fellows breathed hard at this outcome of their desperate fight, and began again to heap insults on one another, finally turning away, however. Their children, though, were now silent in the midst of their relief. But in turning away and separating they for a moment glanced once more at each other, and their two hands, cool and moist from the water and the rain, met and each noticed a slight pressure.

When the two old men turned from the scene, the clouds once more closed, darkness fell, and the rain now poured down in torrents. Manz preceded his son upon the obscured wet paths, bent to the cold rain, and the terrific excitement still trembled in his features. His teeth were chattering, and unseen tears of defeated hatred ran into his stubbly beard. He let them run, and did not even wipe them away, because he was ashamed of them, and had no wish for his son to see them. But his son had seen nothing. He went through rain and storm in an ecstasy of happiness. He had forgotten all, his misery and the awful scene just witnessed, his poverty and the darkness around him. In his heart there was a happy song. Light and warm and full of joy everything within him was. He felt as rich and powerful as a king's son. He saw nothing but the smile of a second. He saw the beautiful face lit up by the miracle of love. And he returned that smile only now, a half hour later, and he laughed at the beautiful face and returned its gaze, looking into the night and storm as into a paradise, the face shining through the murk of rain like a guiding star. Indeed, he believed Vreni could not help noticing his answering smile miles away, and was smiling back at him.

Next day his father was stiff and sore and would not leave the house, and to him the whole wretched meeting with his foe and the whole development of the enmity between them, and the long years of misery that had grown out of it suddenly seemed to take on a new form and to become much plainer, while its influence spread around even in his dusky tavern. So much so that both

in die dunklen Kämmerchen, von da in die Küche und aus dieser wieder sich in die Stube schleppten, in welcher kein Gast sich sehen ließ. Zuletzt hockte jedes in einem Winkel und begann den Tag über ein müdes, halbtotes Zanken und Vorhalten mit dem andern, wobei sie zeitweise einschliefen, von unruhigen Tagträumen geplagt, welche aus dem Gewissen kamen und sie wieder weckten. Nur Sali sah und hörte nichts davon, denn er dachte nur an Vrenchen. Es war ihm immer noch zu Mut, nicht nur als ob er unsäglich reich wäre, sondern auch was Rechts gelernt hätte und unendlich viel Schönes und Gutes wüßte, da er nun so deutlich und bestimmt um das wußte, was er gestern gesehen. Diese Wissenschaft war ihm wie vom Himmel gefallen, und er war in einer unaufhörlichen glücklichen Verwunderung darüber; und doch war es ihm, als ob er es eigentlich von jeher gewußt und gekannt hätte, was ihn jetzt mit so wundersamer Süßigkeit erfüllte. Denn nichts gleicht dem Reichtum und der Unergründlichkeit eines Glückes, das an den Menschen herantritt in einer so klaren und deutlichen Gestalt, vom Pfäfflein getauft und wohlversehen mit einem eigenen Namen, der nicht tönt wie andere Namen.

Sali fühlte sich an diesem Tage weder müßig noch unglücklich, weder arm noch hoffnungslos; vielmehr war er vollauf beschäftigt, sich Vrenchens Gesicht und Gestalt vorzustellen, unaufhörlich, eine Stunde wie die andere; über dieser aufgeregten Tätigkeit aber verschwand ihm der Gegenstand derselben fast vollständig, das heißt, er bildete sich endlich ein, nun doch nicht zu wissen, wie Vrenchen recht genau aussehe, er habe wohl ein allgemeines Bild von ihr im Gedächtnis, aber wenn er sie beschreiben sollte, so könnte er das nicht. Er sah fortwährend dies Bild, als ob es vor ihm stände, und fühlte seinen angenehmen Eindruck, und doch sah er es nur wie etwas, das man eben nur einmal gesehen, in dessen Gewalt man liegt und das man doch noch nicht kennt. Er erinnerte sich genau der Gesichtszüge, welche das kleine Dirnchen einst gehabt,

Manz and his wife were moving about like ghosts, out of one room into another, into the cheerless kitchen and the bedchambers, and thence back again into the equally bare and dark guest room, where not a person was to be seen all day. At last they both began to grumble, one blaming the other for things that had gone wrong, dropping into an uneasy slumber from time to time from which a nightmare would waken them with a start, and in which their unquiet consciences upbraided them for past misdeeds. Only Sali heard and saw nothing of all this, for his mind was entirely engrossed with Vreni. Still the illusion was strong with him of being immeasurably wealthy, but beside that he had a hallucination that he was powerful and had learned how to conduct the most complicated and important affairs in the world. He felt as if he knew all the wisdom on earth, everything great and beautiful. And forever there stood before his dreamy soul, clear and distinct, that great happening of the night before, that wonderful creature with her enticing smile, that smile which had shed a blinding flash of happiness on his path. The consciousness of this great adventure dwelt with him like an unspeakable secret, of which he was the sole possessor and which had fallen to his share direct from heaven. It afforded him constant food for thought and wonderment. And yet with all that it seemed also to him that he had always known this would happen to him, and as if what now filled him with such marvelous sweetness had always dwelt in his heart. For nothing is just like this happiness of love, this sharing of a mystery between two persons, which approaches human beings in the form of unspeakable bliss, yet in a form so clear and precise, sanctioned and sanctified by the priest, and endowed with a name so mellifluously fine that no other word sounds half so sweet as Love.

On that day Sali felt neither lonesome nor unhappy; where he went and stood Vreni's image followed him and glowed in his inner self; and this without a moment's respite, one hour after another. But while his whole being was engrossed with the lovely image of the girl at the same time its outlines constantly became blurred, so that, after all, he lost the faculty of reproducing it clearly. If he had been asked to describe her in detail he would have been unable to do it. Always he saw her standing near him, with that wizard smile; he felt her warm breath and the whole indefinable charm of her presence, but it was for all that like something which is seen but once and then vanishes forever. Like something the potency of which one cannot escape and yet which one never can know. In dreaming thus he was able to recall fully the features of her when still a tiny maiden, and to experience a most pronounced pleasure in doing so, but the one Vreni of yesterday he could not recall as plainly. If

mit großem Wohlgefallen, aber nicht eigentlich derjenigen, welche er gestern gesehen. Hätte er Vrenchen nie wieder zu sehen bekommen, so hätten sich seine Erinnerungskräfte schon behelfen müssen und das liebe Gesicht säuberlich wieder zusammengetragen, daß nicht ein Zug daran fehlte. Jetzt aber versagten sie schlau und hartnäckig ihren Dienst, weil die Augen nach ihrem Recht und ihrer Lust verlangten, und als am Nachmittage die Sonne warm und hell die oberen Stockwerke der schwarzen Häuser beschien, strich Sali aus dem Tore und seiner alten Heimat zu, welche ihm jetzt erst ein himmlisches Jerusalem zu sein schien mit zwölf glänzenden Pforten und die sein Herz klopfen machte, als er sich ihr näherte.

Er stieß auf dem Wege auf Vrenchens Vater, welcher nach der Stadt zu gehen schien. Der sah sehr wild und liederlich aus, sein grau gewordener Bart war seit Wochen nicht geschoren, und er sah aus wie ein recht böser verlorener Bauersmann, der sein Feld verscherzt hat und nun geht, um andern Übles zuzufügen. Dennoch sah ihn Sali, als sie sich vorübergingen, nicht mehr mit Haß, sondern voll Furcht und Scheu an, als ob sein Leben in dessen Hand stände und er es lieber von ihm erflehen als ertrotzen möchte. Marti aber maß ihn mit einem bösen Blicke von oben bis unten und ging seines Weges. Das war indessen dem Sali recht, welchem es nun, da er den Alten das Dorf verlassen sah, deutlicher wurde, was er eigentlich da wolle, und er schlich sich auf altbekannten Pfaden so lange um das Dorf herum und durch dessen verdeckte Gäßchen, bis er sich Martis Haus und Hof gegenüber befand. Seit mehreren Jahren hatte er diese Stätte nicht mehr so nah gesehen; denn auch als sie noch hier wohnten, hüteten sich die verfeindeten Leute gegenseitig, sich ins Gehege zu kommen. Deshalb war er nun erstaunt über das, was er doch an seinem eigenen Vaterhause erlebt, und starrte voll Verwunderung in die Wüstenei, die er vor sich sah. Dem Marti war ein Stück Ackerland um das andere abgepfändet worden, er besaß nichts mehr als das Haus und den Platz davor nebst etwas Garten und dem Acker auf der Höhe am Flusse, von welchem er hartnäckig am längsten nicht lassen wollte.

indeed he had never seen Vreni again it might be that his memory would have pieced her personality together, little by little, until not the slightest bit had been wanting. But now all the strength of his mind did not suffice to render him this service, and this was because his senses, his eyes, imperatively demanded their rights and their solace, and when in the afternoon the sun was shining brilliantly and warm, gilding the roofs of all these blackened housetops, Sali almost unconsciously found himself on the way towards his old home in the country, which now seemed to him a heavenly Jerusalem with twelve shining portals, and which set his heart to beating feverishly as he approached it.

While on his way, though, he met Vreni's father, who with hurried and disordered steps was going in the direction of the town. Marti looked wild and unkempt, his gray beard had not been shorn for many weeks, and altogether he presented indeed the picture of what he was: a wicked and lost peasant who had got rid of his land and who now was intent on doing evil to others. Nevertheless, Sali under these radically different circumstances did not regard the crazed old man with hatred but rather with fear and awe, as though his own life was in the hands of this man and as though it were better to obtain it by favor than by force. Marti, however, measured the young man with a black look, glancing at him from his feet upwards, and then he went his way silently. But this encounter came most opportunely to Sali. For seeing the old man leaving the village on an errand it for the first time became quite clear to him what his own object had been in coming. Thus he proceeded stealthily on by-paths towards the village, and when reaching it cautiously felt his way through the small lanes until he had Marti's house and outbuildings right in front of him. For several years past he had not seen this spot so closely. For even while he still dwelt in the village itself he had been forbidden to approach the Marti farm, avoiding meeting the family with whom his father lived on terms of enmity. Therefore he was now full of wonder at what, just the same, he had had ample opportunity to observe in the case of his own father's property. Amazedly he stared at this once prosperous and well-cultivated farm now turned into a waste. For Marti had had one section after another of his property sequestrated by orders of the court, and now all that was left was the dwelling house itself and the space around it, with a bit of vegetable garden and a small field up above the river, which latter Marti had for some time been defending in a last desperate struggle with the judicial power.

Es war aber keine Rede mehr von einer ordentlichen Bebauung, und auf dem Acker, der einst so schön im gleichmäßigen Korne gewogt, wenn die Ernte kam, waren jetzt allerhand abfällige Samenreste gesäet und aufgegangen, aus alten Schachteln und zerrissenen Düten zusammengekehrt, Rüben, Kraut und dergleichen und etwas Kartoffeln, so daß der Acker aussah wie ein recht übel gepflegter Gemüseplatz und eine wunderliche Musterkarte war, dazu angelegt, um von der Hand in den Mund zu leben, hier eine Handvoll Rüben auszureißen, wenn man Hunger hatte und nichts Besseres wußte, dort eine Tracht Kartoffeln oder Kraut, und das übrige fortwuchern oder verfaulen zu lassen, wie es mochte. Auch lief jedermann darin herum, wie es ihm gefiel, und das schöne breite Stück Feld sah beinahe so aus wie einst der herrenlose Acker, von dem alles Unheil herkam. Deshalb war um das Haus nicht eine Spur von Ackerwirtschaft zu sehen. Der Stall war leer, die Türe hing nur in einer Angel, und unzählige Kreuzspinnen, den Sommer hindurch halb grün geworden, ließen ihre Fäden in der Sonne glänzen vor dem dunklen Eingang. An dem offenstehenden Scheunentor, wo einst die Früchte des festen Landes eingefahren, hing schlechtes Fischergeräte, zum Zeugnis der verkehrten Wasserpfuscherei; auf dem Hofe war nicht ein Huhn und nicht eine Taube, weder Katze noch Hund zu sehen; nur der Brunnen war noch als etwas Lebendiges da, aber er floß nicht mehr durch die Röhre, sondern sprang durch einen Riß nahe am Boden über diesen hin und setzte überall kleine Tümpel an, so daß er das beste Sinnbild der Faulheit abgab. Denn während mit wenig Mühe des Vaters das Loch zu verstopfen und die Röhre herzustellen gewesen wäre, mußte sich Vrenchen nun abquälen, selbst das lautere Wasser dieser Verkommenheit abzugewinnen und seine Wäscherei in den seichten Sammlungen am Boden vorzunehmen statt in dem vertrockneten und zerspellten Troge. Das Haus selbst war ebenso kläglich anzusehen; die Fenster waren vielfältig zerbrochen und mit Papier verklebt, aber doch waren sie das Freundlichste an dem Verfall; denn sie waren, selbst die zerbrochenen Scheiben, klar und sauber gewaschen, ja förmlich poliert, und glänzten so hell wie Vrenchens Augen, welche ihm in seiner Armut ja auch allen übrigen Staat ersetzen mußten. Und wie die krausen Haare und die rotgelben Kattunhalstücher zu Vrenchens Augen, stand zu

There was, it is true, no longer any question of a rational cultivation of the soil which once had borne so plentifully and where the wheat had waved like a golden sea toward harvest time. Instead of that now there was a mixed crop sprouting: rye, turnips, wheat and potatoes, with some other "garden truck" intermingling, all from seed that had come from paper packages left over or purchased in small quantities at random, so that the whole cultivated space looked like a negligently tended vegetable bed, in which cabbage, parsley and turnips predominated. It was plainly to be seen that the owner of it, too lazy or indifferent to do his farmer's work properly, had mainly had in mind to raise such things as would enable him to live from day to day. Here a handful of carrots had been torn out, there a mess of cabbage or potatoes, and the rest had fared on for good or ill, and much of it lay rotting on the ground. Everybody, too, had been in the habit of treading around and in it all, just as he listed, and the one broad field now presented nearly the desolate appearance of the once ownerless field whence had grown all the mischief that had wrought havoc and brought the two neighbors of old down so low. About the house itself there was no visible sign at all of farm work. The stable stood vacant, its door hung loosely from the broken staples, and innumerable spider's webs, grown thick and large during the summer, were shimmering in the sunshine. Against the broad door of a barn, where once were housed the fruits of the field, hung untidy fishermen's nets and other sporting apparatus, in grim token of abandoned farming. In the farmyard was to be seen not a single chicken, pigeon or turkey, no dog or cat. The well only was the sole live thing. But even its clear water no longer flowed in a regular gush through the spout, but trickled through the broken tube, wasting itself on the ground and forming dark pools on the soggy earth, a perfect symbol of neglect. For while it would not have taken much time or trouble to mend the broken tube, now Vreni was forced to use the water she needed for her domestic tasks, for cooking and laundry work, from the tricklings that escaped. The house itself, too, was a sad thing to see. The window panes were all broken and pasted over with paper. Yet the windows, after all, were the most cheerful-looking objects, for Vreni kept them clean and shiny with soap and water, as shiny, in fact, as her own eyes, and the latter, too, had to make up for all lack of finery. And as the curly hair and the bright kerchiefs made amends for much in her, so the wild growths stretching up toward windows and along the jamb of the doorsills, and almost covering the very broken panes on the windows, gave a charm to this tumbledown homestead. A wilderness of scarlet bean blossoms, of portulac and

diesen blinkenden Fenstern das wilde grüne Gewächs, was da durcheinander rankte um das Haus, flatternde Bohnenwäldchen und eine ganze duftende Wildnis von rotgelbem Goldlack. Die Bohnen hielten sich, so gut sie konnten, hier an einem Harkenstiel oder an einem verkehrt in die Erde gesteckten Stumpfbesen, dort an einer von Rost zerfressenen Helbarte oder Sponton, wie man es nannte, als Vrenchens Großvater das Ding als Wachtmeister getragen, welches es jetzt aus Not in die Bohnen gepflanzt hatte; dort kletterten sie wieder lustig eine verwitterte Leiter empor, die am Hause lehnte seit undenklichen Zeiten, und hingen von da in die klaren Fensterchen hinunter wie Vrenchens Kräuselhaare in seine Augen. Dieser mehr malerische als wirkliche Hof lag etwas beiseit und hatte keine näheren Nachbarhäuser, auch ließ sich in diesem Augenblicke nirgends eine lebendige Seele wahrnehmen; Sali lehnte daher in aller Sicherheit an einem alten Scheunchen, etwa dreißig Schritte entfernt, und schaute unverwandt nach dem stillen wüsten Hause hinüber. Eine geraume Zeit lehnte und schaute er so, als Vrenchen unter die Haustür kam und lange vor sich hin blickte, wie mit allen ihren Gedanken an einem Gegenstande hängend. Sali rührte sich nicht und wandte kein Auge von ihr. Als sie endlich zufällig in dieser Richtung hinsah, fiel er ihr in die Augen. Sie sahen sich eine Weile an, herüber und hinüber, als ob sie eine Lufterscheinung betrachteten, bis sich Sali endlich aufrichtete und langsam über die Straße und über den Hof ging auf Vrenchen los. Als er dem Mädchen nahe war, streckte es seine Hände gegen ihn aus und sagte: »Sali!« Er ergriff die Hände und sah ihr immerfort ins Gesicht. Tränen stürzten aus ihren Augen, während sie unter seinen Blicken vollends dunkelrot wurde, und sie sagte: »Was willst du hier?« – »Nur dich sehen!« erwiderte er, »wollen wir nicht wieder gute Freunde sein?« – »Und unsere Eltern?« fragte Vrenchen, sein weinendes Gesicht zur Seite neigend, da es die Hände nicht frei hatte, um es zu bedecken. »Sind wir schuld an dem, was sie getan und geworden sind?« sagte Sali, »vielleicht können wir das Elend nur gutmachen, wenn wir zwei zusammenhalten und uns recht lieb sind!« – »Es wird nie gut kommen«, antwortete Vrenchen mit einem tiefen Seufzer, »geh in Gottes Namen deiner Wege, Sali!« – »Bist du allein?« fragte dieser, »kann ich einen Augenblick hineinkommen?« – »Der Vater ist zur Stadt, wie er sagte, um deinem

sweet-scented flowers ran riot along the house front, and these in their vivid colors clambered along anything that would give them a hold, such as the handle of a rake, a stake or broken rod. Vreni's grandfather had left behind a rusty halberd or spontoon, such as were weapons much in vogue in his days, for he had fought as a mercenary abroad. Now this rusty implement had been stuck into the ground, and the willowy tendrils of the beanstalk embraced it tightly. More bean plants groped their way up a shattered ladder which had leaned against the house for ages, and thence their blossoms hung into the windows as Vreni's curls hung into her pretty face. This farmyard, so much more picturesque than prosperous, lay somewhat apart from its neighbors, and therefore was not exposed so much to their inspection. But for the moment as Sali stared and watched nothing human at all was visible. Sali thus was undisturbed in his reflections as he leaned with his back against the barndoor, about thirty paces away, and studied with attentive mien the deserted yard. He had been doing this for some time when Vreni at last appeared under the housedoor and gazed calmly and thoughtfully before her as if thinking deeply of only one matter. Sali himself did not stir but contemplated her as he would have done a fine painting. But after a brief while her eyes traveled towards him, and she perceived him. Then she and he stood without motion and looked, looked just as if they did not see living beings but aerial phenomena. But at last Sali slowly stood upright, and just as slowly went across the farmyard and towards Vreni. When he was but a step or so from her, she stretched out her hands toward him and pronounced only the one word: "Sali!" He seized her hands speechlessly, and then continued gazing into her face which had suddenly grown pale. Tears filled her eyes, and gradually under his gaze she flushed painfully, and at last she said in a very low voice: "What do you want here, Sali?" "Only to see you," he replied. "Will we not become good friends again?" "And our fathers, Sali?" asked Vreni, turning her weeping face aside, since her hands had been imprisoned by him. "Must we bear the burden of what they have done and have become?" answered Sali. "It may be that we ourselves can redeem the evil they have wrought, if we only love each other well enough and stand together against the future." "No, Sali, no good will ever come of it all," replied Vreni sobbingly; "therefore better go your ways, Sali, in God's name." "Are you alone, Vreni?" he asked. "May I come in a minute?" "Father has gone to town for a spell, as he told me before leaving," remarked Vreni, "to do your father a bad turn. But I cannot let you in here, because it may be that later on you would not be able to leave again without attracting notice. As yet everything around here

Vater irgend etwas anzuhängen; aber hereinkommen kannst du nicht, weil du später vielleicht nicht so ungesehen weggehen kannst wie jetzt. Noch ist alles still und niemand um den Weg, ich bitte dich, geh jetzt!« – »Nein, so geh ich nicht! Ich mußte seit gestern immer an dich denken, und ich geh nicht so fort, wir müssen miteinander reden, wenigstens eine halbe Stunde lang oder eine Stunde, das wird uns guttun!« Vrenchen besann sich ein Weilchen und sagte dann: »Ich geh gegen Abend auf unsern Acker hinaus, du weißt welchen, wir haben nur noch den, und hole etwas Gemüse. Ich weiß, daß niemand weiter dort sein wird, weil die Leute anderswo schneiden; wenn du willst, so komm dorthin, aber jetzt geh und nimm dich in acht, daß dich niemand sieht! Wenn auch kein Mensch hier mehr mit uns umgeht, so würden sie doch ein solches Gerede machen, daß es der Vater sogleich vernähme!« Sie ließen sich jetzt die Hände frei, ergriffen sie aber auf der Stelle wieder, und beide sagten gleichzeitig: »Und wie geht es dir auch?« Aber statt sich zu antworten, fragten sie das gleiche aufs neue, und die Antwort lag nur in den beredten Augen, da sie nach Art der Verliebten die Worte nicht mehr zu lenken wußten und, ohne sich weiter etwas zu sagen, endlich halb selig und halb traurig auseinanderhuschten. »Ich komme recht bald hinaus, geh nur gleich hin!« rief Vrenchen noch nach.

Sali ging auch alsobald auf die stille schöne Anhöhe hinaus, über welche die zwei Äcker sich erstreckten, und die prächtige stille Julisonne, die fahrenden weißen Wolken, welche über das reife wallende Kornfeld wegzogen, der glänzende blaue Fluß, der unten vorüberwallte, alles dies erfüllte ihn zum ersten Male seit langen Jahren wieder mit Glück und Zufriedenheit statt mit Kummer, und er warf sich der Länge nach in den durchsichtigen Halbschatten des Kornes, wo dasselbe Martis wilden Acker begrenzte, und guckte glückselig in den Himmel.

Obgleich es kaum eine Viertelstunde währte, bis Vrenchen nachkam, und er an nichts anderes dachte als an sein Glück und dessen Namen, stand es doch plötzlich und unverhofft vor ihm, auf ihn niederlächelnd, und froh erschreckt sprang er auf. »Vreeli!« rief er, und dieses gab ihm still und lächelnd beide Hände, und Hand in Hand gingen sie nun das flüsternde Korn

is still and nobody about. Therefore, I beg of you, go before it is too late." "No, I could not leave you without speaking," was his answer, and his voice shook with emotion. "Since yesterday I have had to think of you constantly, and I cannot go. We must speak to each other, at least for half an hour or an hour; that will be a relief to both of us." Vreni reflected a minute. Then she said thoughtfully: "Toward sundown I shall walk out toward our field. You know the one I mean--we have but the one left. I must pick some vegetables. I feel sure that nobody else will be there, because they are mowing all of them in a different direction. If you insist on coming, you may come there, but for the present go and take care nobody else sees you. Even if nobody at all bothers any longer about us, they would nevertheless gossip so much about it that father could not fail to hear it." They now dropped their hands, but once more seized them, and both also asked: "How do you do?" But instead of answering each other they repeated the same phrase over and over again, since they, after the manner of lovers, no longer were able to guide or control their words. Thus the only answer each received was given with the eyes, and without saying anything more to each other they finally separated, half sad, half joyful. "Go there at once," she called after him; "I shall be there almost as soon as yourself."

Sali followed this advice, and went at once up the steep path that led to the hill where the busy world seemed so far away and where the soul expanded, to the undulating fields that stretched out far on both sides, where the brooding July sun shone and the drifting white clouds sailed overhead, where the ripe corn in the gentle breeze bobbed up and down, where the river below glinted blue, and all these scenes of past happiness filled his soul after a long dearth with peace and gentle joy, and his griefs and fears were left below. At full length he threw himself down amid the half-shade of the upstanding wheat, there where it marked the boundary of Marti's waste acres, and peered with unblinking eyes into the gold-rimmed clouds.

Although scarcely a quarter hour elapsed until Vreni followed him, and although he had thought of nothing but his bliss and his love, dreaming of it and building castles in the air, he was yet surprised when Vreni suddenly stood at his side, smiling down at him, and with a start he rose. "Vreni," he exclaimed in a voice that trembled with love, and she, still and smiling, tendered both her hands to him. Hand in hand they then paced

entlang bis gegen den Fluß hinunter und wieder zurück, ohne viel zu reden; sie legten zwei- und dreimal den Hin- und Herweg zurück, still, glückselig und ruhig, so daß dieses einige Paar nun auch einem Sterntilde glich, welches über die sonnige Rundung der Anhöhe und hinter derselben niederging, wie einst die sicher gehenden Pflugzüge ihrer Väter. Als sie aber einsmals die Augen von den blauen Kornblumen aufschlugen, an denen sie gehaftet, sahen sie plötzlich einen andern dunklen Stern vor sich her gehen, einen schwärzlichen Kerl, von dem sie nicht wußten, woher er so unversehens gekommen. Er mußte im Korne gelegen haben; Vrenchen zuckte zusammen, und Sali sagte erschreckt: »Der schwarze Geiger!« In der Tat trug der Kerl, der vor ihnen herstrich, eine Geige mit dem Bogen unter dem Arm und sah übrigens schwarz genug aus; neben einem schwarzen Filzhütchen und einem schwarzen rußigen Kittel, den er trug, war auch sein Haar pechschwarz, so wie der ungeschorene Bart, das Gesicht und die Hände aber ebenfalls geschwärzt; denn er trieb allerlei Handwerk, meistens Kesselflicken, half auch den Kohlenbrennern und Pechsiedern in den Wäldern und ging mit der Geige nur auf einen guten Schick aus, wenn die Bauern irgendwo lustig waren und ein Fest feierten. Sali und Vrenchen gingen mäuschenstill hinter ihm drein und dachten, er würde vom Felde gehen und verschwinden, ohne sich umzusehen, und so schien es auch zu sein, denn er tat, als ob er nichts von ihnen merkte. Dazu waren sie in einem seltsamen Bann, daß sie nicht wagten, den schmalen Pfad zu verlassen, und dem unheimlichen Gesellen unwillkürlich folgten bis an das Ende des Feldes, wo jener ungerechte Steinhaufen lag, der das immer noch streitige Ackerzipfelchen bedeckte. Eine zahllose Menge von Mohnblumen oder Klatschrosen hatte sich darauf angesiedelt, weshalb der kleine Berg feuerrot aussah zurzeit. Plötzlich sprang der schwarze Geiger mit einem Satze auf die rotbekleidete Steinmasse hinauf, kehrte sich und sah ringsum. Das Pärchen blieb stehen und sah verlegen zu dem dunklen Burschen hinauf; denn vorbei konnten sie nicht gehen, weil der Weg in das Dorf führte, und umkehren mochten sie auch nicht vor seinen Augen. Er sah sie scharf an und rief: »Ich kenne euch, ihr seid die Kinder derer, die mir den Boden hier gestohlen haben! Es freut mich zu sehen, wie gut ihr gefahren seid, und werde gewiß noch erleben,

along the whispering corn, slowly down towards the river, and then as slowly back again, with scarcely any words. This short walk they repeated twice or thrice, back and forth, still, blissful, and quiet, so that this young pair now resembled likewise a pair of stars, coming and going across the gentle curve of the hillock and adown the declivity beyond, just as had once, years and years ago, the accurately measuring plows of the two rustic neighbors. But as they once on this pilgrimage lifted their eyes from the blue cornflowers along the edge of the field where they had rested, they suddenly saw a swarthy fellow, like a darksome star, precede them on their path, a fellow of whom they could not tell whence he had appeared so entirely without warning. Probably he had been lying in the corn, and Vreni shuddered, while Sali murmured with affright: "It's the black fiddler!" And indeed, the fellow ambling along before them carried under his arm a violin, and truly, too, he looked swarthy enough. A black crushed felt hat, a black blouse and hair and beard pitchdark, even his unwashed hands of that hue, he made the impression of a man carrying along an evil omen. This man led a wandering life. He did all sorts of jobs: mended kettles and pans, helped charcoal burners, aided in pitching in the woods, and only used his fiddle and earned money that way when the peasants somewhere were celebrating a festival or holiday, a wedding or big dance, and such like. Sali and Vreni meant to leave the fiddler by himself. Quiet as mice they slowly walked behind him, thinking that he would probably turn off the road soon. He seemed to pay no attention to the two, never turning around and keeping perfect silence. With that they felt a weird influence coming from the fellow, so that they had not the courage to openly avoid him and turning aside unconsciously they followed in his tracks to the very end of the field, the spot where that unjust heap of stone and rock lay, the one that had started the two families on their downward road. Innumerable poppies and wild roses had grown there and were now in full bloom, wherefore this stony desert lay like an enormous splotch of blood along the road. All at once the black fiddler sprang with one jump on top one of the irregular ramparts of stone, the rim of which was also scarlet with wild blossoms, then turned himself around, and threw a glance in every direction. The young couple stopped and looked up at him shamefaced. For turn they would not in face of him, and to proceed along on the same path would have taken them into the village, which they also wished to avoid. He looked at them keenly, and then he shouted: "I know you two. You are the children of those who have stolen from me this soil. I am glad to see you here, and to notice how the theft has benefited you. Surely, I shall also live to see you two

daß ihr vor mir den Weg alles Fleisches geht! Seht mich nur an, ihr zwei Spatzen! Gefällt euch meine Nase, wie?« In der Tat besaß er eine schreckbare Nase, welche wie ein großes Winkelmaß aus dem dürren schwarzen Gesicht ragte oder eigentlich mehr einem tüchtigen Knebel oder Prügel glich, welcher in dies Gesicht geworfen worden war und unter dem ein kleines rundes Löchelchen von einem Munde sich seltsam stutzte und zusammenzog, aus dem er unaufhörlich pustete, pfiff und zischte. Dazu stand das kleine Filzhütchen ganz unheimlich, welches nicht rund und nicht eckig und so sonderlich geformt war, daß es alle Augenblicke seine Gestalt zu verändern schien, obgleich es unbeweglich saß, und von den Augen des Kerls war fast nichts als das Weiße zu sehen, da die Sterne unaufhörlich auf einer blitzschnellen Wanderung begriffen waren und wie zwei Hasen im Zickzack umhersprangen. »Seht mich nur an«, fuhr er fort, »eure Väter kennen mich wohl, und jedermann in diesem Dorfe weiß, wer ich bin, wenn er nur meine Nase ansieht. Da haben sie vor Jahren ausgeschrieben, daß ein Stück Geld für den Erben dieses Ackers bereitliege; ich habe mich zwanzigmal gemeldet, aber ich habe keinen Taufschein und keinen Heimatschein, und meine Freunde, die Heimatlosen, die meine Geburt gesehen, haben kein gültiges Zeugnis, und so ist die Frist längst verlaufen, und ich bin um den blutigen Pfennig gekommen, mit dem ich hätte auswandern können! Ich habe eure Väter angefleht, daß sie mir bezeugen möchten, sie müßten mich nach ihrem Gewissen für den rechten Erben halten; aber sie haben mich von ihren Höfen gejagt, und nun sind sie selbst zum Teufel gegangen! Item, das ist der Welt Lauf, mir kann's recht sein, ich will euch doch geigen, wenn ihr tanzen wollt!« Damit sprang er auf der anderen Seite von den Steinen hinunter und machte sich dem Dorfe zu, wo gegen Abend der Erntesegen eingebracht wurde und die Leute guter Dinge waren. Als er verschwunden, ließ sich das Paar ganz mutlos und betrübt auf die Steine nieder; sie ließen ihre verschlungenen Hände fahren und stützten die traurigen Köpfe darauf; denn die Erscheinung des Geigers und seine Worte hatten sie aus der glücklichen Vergessenheit gerissen, in welcher sie wie zwei Kinder auf und ab gewandelt, und wie sie nun auf dem harten Grund ihres Elendes saßen, verdunkelte sich das heitere Lebenslicht, und ihre Gemüter wurden so schwer wie Steine.

go before me the way of all flesh. Yes, look at me, you little fools. Do you like my nose, eh?" And indeed, he had a terrible nose, one which broke forth from his emaciated swarthy face like a beak, or rather more like a good-sized club. As if it had been pasted on to his bony face it looked and below that the tiny mouth, in the shape of a small round hole, singularly contracted and expanded, and out of this hole his words constantly tumbled, whistling or buzzing or hissing. His small twisted felt hat, shapeless and shabby, pushed over his left ear, heightened the uncanny effect. This piece of his apparel seemed to change its form with every motion of the queer-looking head, although in reality it sat immovable on his pate. And of the eyes of this strange fellow nothing was to be noticed but their whites, since the pupils were flashing around all the time, just as though they were two hares jumping about to escape being seized. "Look at me well," he then continued. "Your two fathers know all about me, and everybody in the village can identify me by my nose. Years ago they were spreading the rumor that a good piece of money was awaiting the heir to these fields here. I have called at court twenty times. But since I had no baptismal certificate and since my friends, the vagrants, who witnessed my birth, have no voice that the law will recognize, the time set has elapsed, and they have cheated me out of the little sum, large enough all the same to permit my emigrating to a better country. I have implored your fathers at that time, again and again, to testify for me to the effect that they at least believed me, according to their conscience, to be the rightful heir. But they drove me from their farms, and now, ha! ha! ha! they themselves have gone to the devil. Well and good, that is the way things turn out in this world, and I don't care a rap. And now I will just the same fiddle if you want to dance." With that he was down again on the ground beside them, at a mighty bound, and seeing they did not want to dance he quickly disappeared in the direction of the village; there the crop was to be brought in towards nightfall, and there would be gay doings. When he was gone the young couple sat down, discouraged and out of spirits, among the wilderness of stone. They let their hands drop and hung their poor heads too. For the sudden appearance of the vagrant fiddler had wiped out the happy memories of their childhood, and their joyous mood in which they, like they used in their younger days, had wandered about in the green and among the corn, had gone with him. They sat once more on the hard soil of their misery, and the happy gleam of childhood had vanished, and their minds were oppressed and darkened.

Da erinnerte sich Vrenchen unversehens der wunderlichen Gestalt und der Nase des Geigers, es mußte plötzlich hell auflachen und rief: »Der arme Kerl sieht gar zu spaßhaft aus! Was für eine Nase!« und eine allerliebste sonnenhelle Lustigkeit verbreitete sich über des Mädchens Gesicht, als ob sie nur geharrt hätte, bis des Geigers Nase die trüben Wolken wegstieße. Sali sah Vrenchen an und sah diese Fröhlichkeit. Es hatte die Ursache aber schon wieder vergessen und lachte nur noch auf eigene Rechnung dem Sali ins Gesicht. Dieser, verblüfft und erstaunt, starrte unwillkürlich mit lachendem Munde auf die Augen, gleich einem Hungrigen, der ein süßes Weizenbrot erblickt, und rief: »Bei Gott, Vreeli! wie schön bist du!« Vrenchen lachte ihn nur noch mehr an und hauchte dazu aus klangvoller Kehle einige kurze mutwillige Lachtöne, welche dem armen Sali nicht anders dünkten als der Gesang einer Nachtigall. »O du Hexe!« rief er, »wo hast du das gelernt? Welche Teufelskünste treibst du da?« – »Ach du lieber Gott!« sagte Vrenchen mit schmeichelnder Stimme und nahm Salis Hand, »das sind keine Teufelskünste! Wie lange hätte ich gern einmal gelacht! Ich habe wohl zuweilen, wenn ich ganz allein war, über irgend etwas lachen müssen, aber es war nichts Rechts dabei; jetzt aber möchte ich dich immer und ewig anlachen, wenn ich dich sehe, und ich möchte dich wohl immer und ewig sehen! Bist du mir auch ein bißchen recht gut?« – »O Vreeli!« sagte er und sah ihr ergeben und treuherzig in die Augen, »ich habe noch nie ein Mädchen angesehen, es war mir immer, als ob ich dich einst liebhaben müßte, und ohne daß ich wollte oder wußte, hast du mir doch immer im Sinn gelegen!« – »Und du mir auch«, sagte Vrenchen, »und das noch viel mehr; denn du hast mich nie angesehen und wußtest nicht, wie ich geworden bin; ich aber habe dich zuzeiten aus der Ferne und sogar heimlich aus der Nähe recht gut betrachtet und wußte immer, wie du aussiehst! Weißt du noch, wie oft wir als Kinder hierher gekommen sind? Denkst du noch des kleinen Wagens? Wie kleine Leute sind wir damals gewesen, und wie lang ist es her! Man sollte denken, wir wären recht alt?« – »Wie alt bist du jetzt?« fragte Sali voll Vergnügen und Zufriedenheit, »du mußt ungefähr siebzehn sein?« – »Siebzehn und ein halbes Jahr bin ich alt!« erwiderte Vrenchen, »und wie alt bist du? Ich weiß aber schon, du bist bald zwanzig!« – »Woher weißt du das?« fragte Sali. »Gelt, wenn

But all at once Vreni remembered the fiddler's nose, and his whole odd figure, and she burst out laughing loud and merry. She exclaimed: "The poor fellow surely looks too queer. What a nose he had!" And with that a charmingly careless merriment flashed out of her brown eyes, just as though she had only been waiting for the fiddler's nose to chase away all the sad clouds from her mind. Sali, too, regarded the girl, and noticed this sunny gaiety. But by that time Vreni had already forgotten the immediate cause of her gleefulness, and now she laughed on her own account into Sali's face. Sali, dazed and astonished, involuntarily gazed at the girl with laughing mouth, like a hungry man who suddenly is offered sweetened wheat bread, and he said: "Heavens, Vreni, how pretty you are!" And Vreni, for sole answer, laughed but the more, and out of the mere enjoyment of her sweet temper she gurgled a few melodious notes that sounded to the boy like the warblings of a nightingale. "Oh, you little witch," he exclaimed enraptured, "where have you learned such tricks? What sorcery are you applying to me?" "Sorcery?" she murmured astonished, in a voice of sweet enchantment, and she seized Sali's hand anew. "There's no sorcery about this. How gladly I should have laughed now and then, with reason or without. Now and then, indeed, all by myself, I have laughed a bit, because I couldn't help it, but my heart was not in it. But now it's different. Now I should like to laugh all the time, holding your hand and feeling happy. I should like to hold your hand forever, and look into your eyes. Do you too love me a little bit?" "Ah, Vreni," he answered, and looked full and affectionately into her eyes, "I never cared for any girl before. And I have never until now taken a good look at another girl. It always seemed to me as though some time or other I should have to love you, and without knowing it, I think, you have always been in my thoughts." "And so it was in my case," said Vreni, "only more so. For you never would look at me and did not know what had become of me and what I had grown into. But as for me, I have from time to time, secretly, of course, and from afar, cast a glance at you, and knew well enough what you were like. Do you still remember how often as children we used to come here? You know in the little baby cart? What small folk we were those days, and how long, long ago that all is! One would think we were old, real old now. Eh?" Sali became thoughtful. "How old are you, Vreni?" he asked. "I should think you must be about seventeen?" "I am seventeen and a half," answered she. "And you?" "Guess!" "Oh, I know, you are going on twenty." "How do you know?" he asked. "I won't tell you," she laughed. "Won't tell me?" "No, no," and she giggled merrily. "But I want to know." "Will you compel me?" "We'll see about that." These silly remarks Sali made

ich es sagen wollte!« – »Du willst es nicht sagen?« – »Nein!« – »Gewiß nicht?« – »Nein, nein!« – »Du sollst es sagen!« – »Willst du mich etwa zwingen?« – »Das wollen wir sehen!« Diese einfältigen Reden führte Sali, um seine Hände zu beschäftigen und mit ungeschickten Liebkosungen, welche wie eine Strafe aussehen sollten, das schöne Mädchen zu bedrängen. Sie führte auch, sich wehrend, mit vieler Langmut den albernen Wortwechsel fort, der trotz seiner Leerheit beide witzig und süß genug dünkte, bis Sali erbost und kühn genug war, Vrenchens Hände zu bezwingen und es in die Mohnblumen zu drücken. Da lag es nun und zwinkerte in der Sonne mit den Augen; seine Wangen glühten wie Purpur, und sein Mund war halb geöffnet und ließ zwei Reihen weiße Zähne durchschimmern. Fein und schön flossen die dunklen Augenbrauen ineinander, und die junge Brust hob und senkte sich mutwillig unter sämtlichen vier Händen, welche sich kunterbunt darauf streichelten und bekriegten. Sali wußte sich nicht zu lassen vor Freuden, das schlanke schöne Geschöpf vor sich zu sehen, es sein eigen zu wissen, und es dünkte ihm ein Königreich. »Alle deine weißen Zähne hast du noch!« lachte er, »weißt du noch, wie oft wir sie einst gezählt haben? Kannst du jetzt zählen?« – »Das sind ja nicht die gleichen, du Kind!« sagte Vrenchen, »jene sind längst ausgefallen!« Sali wollte nun in seiner Einfalt jenes Spiel wieder erneuern und die glänzenden Zahnperlen zählen; aber Vrenchen verschloß plötzlich den roten Mund, richtete sich auf und begann einen Kranz von Mohnrosen zu winden, den es sich auf den Kopf setzte. Der Kranz war voll und breit und gab der bräunlichen Birne ein fabelhaftes reizendes Ansehen, und der arme Sali hielt in seinem Arm, was reiche Leute teuer bezahlt hätten, wenn sie es nur gemalt an ihren Wänden hätten sehen können. Jetzt sprang sie aber empor und rief: »Himmel, wie heiß ist es hier! Da sitzen wir wie die Narren und lassen uns versengen! Komm, mein Lieber! laß uns ins hohe Korn sitzen!« Sie schlüpften hinein so geschickt und sachte, daß sie kaum eine Spur zurückließen, und bauten sich einen engen Kerker in den goldenen Ähren, die ihnen hoch über den Kopf ragten, als sie drinsaßen, so daß sie nur den tiefblauen Himmel über sich sahen und sonst nichts von der Welt. Sie umhalsten sich und küßten sich unverweilt und so lange, bis sie einstweilen müde waren, oder wie man es nennen will, wenn das Küssen

because he wanted to keep his hands busy and to have a pretext for the awkward caresses he attempted and which his love for the beautiful girl hungered for. But she continued the childish dialogue willingly enough for some time longer, showing plenty of patience the while, feeling instinctively her lover's mood. And the simple sallies on both sides seemed to them the height of wisdom, so soft and sweet and full of their mutual feelings they were. At last, however, Sali waxed bold and aggressive, and seized Vreni and pressed her down into the scarlet bed of poppies by main strength. There she lay panting, blinking at the sun with eyes half-closed. Her softly rounded cheeks glowed like ripe apples and her mouth was breathing hard so that the snow-white rows of teeth became visible. Daintily as if penciled her eyebrows were defined above those flashing eyes, and her young bosom rose and fell under the working four hands which mutually caressed and fought each other. Sali was beyond himself with delight, seeing this wonderful young creature before him, knowing her to be his own, and he deemed himself wealthier than a monarch. "I see you still have all your teeth," he said. "Do you recall how often we tried to count them? Do you now know how to count?" "Oh, you silly," smilingly rejoined Vreni, "these are not the same. Those I lost long ago." So Sali in the simplicity of his soul wanted to renew the game, and prepared to count them over once more. But Vreni abruptly rose and closed her mouth. Then she began to form a wreath of poppies and to place it on her head. The wreath was broad and long, and on the brow of the nut-brown maid it was an ornament so bewitching as to lend her an enchanting air. Sali held in his arms what rich people would have dearly paid for if merely they had had it painted on their walls. But at last she sprang up. "Goodness, how hot it is here! Here we remain like ninnies and allow ourselves to be roasted alive. Come, dear, and let us sit among the corn!" And they got up and looked for a suitable hiding-place among the tall wheat. When they had found it, they slipped into the furrows of the field so that nobody would have discovered them without regular search, leaving no trace behind, and they built for themselves a narrow nest among the golden ears that topped their heads when they were seated, so that they only saw the deep azure of the sky above and nothing else in the world. They clung to each other tightly, and showered kisses on cheeks and hair and mouth, until at last they desisted from sheer exhaustion, or whatever one wishes to call it when the caresses of two lovers for one or two minutes cease and thus, right in the ecstasy of the blossom tide of life, there is the hint of the perishableness of everything mundane. They heard the larks singing high overhead, and sought

zweier Verliebter auf eine oder zwei Minuten sich selbst überlebt und die Vergänglichkeit alles Lebens mitten im Rausche der Blütezeit ahnen läßt. Sie hörten die Lerchen singen hoch über sich und suchten dieselben mit ihren scharfen Augen, und wenn sie glaubten, flüchtig eine in der Sonne aufblitzen zu sehen, gleich einem plötzlich aufleuchtenden oder hinschießenden Stern am blauen Himmel, so küßten sie sich wieder zur Belohnung und suchten einander zu übervorteilen und zu täuschen, soviel sie konnten. »Siehst du, dort blitzt eine!« flüsterte Sali, und Vrenchen erwiderte ebenso leise: »Ich höre sie wohl, aber ich sehe sie nicht!« – »Doch, paß nur auf, dort wo das weiße Wölkchen steht, ein wenig rechts davon!« Und beide sahen eifrig hin und sperrten vorläufig ihre Schnäbel auf, wie die jungen Wachteln im Neste, um sie unverzüglich aufeinander zu heften, wenn sie sich einbildeten, die Lerche gesehen zu haben. Auf einmal hielt Vrenchen inne und sagte: »Dies ist also eine ausgemachte Sache, daß jedes von uns einen Schatz hat, dünkt es dich nicht so?« – »Ja«, sagte Sali, »es scheint mir auch so!« – »Wie gefällt dir denn dein Schätzchen«, sagte Vrenchen, »was ist es für ein Ding, was hast du von ihm zu melden?« – »Es ist ein gar feines Ding«, sagte Sali, »es hat zwei braune Augen, einen roten Mund und läuft auf zwei Füßen; aber seinen Sinn kenn ich weniger als den Papst zu Rom! Und was kannst du von deinem Schatz berichten?« – »Er hat zwei blaue Augen, einen nichtsnutzigen Mund und braucht zwei verwegene starke Arme; aber seine Gedanken sind mir unbekannter als der türkische Kaiser!« – »Es ist eigentlich wahr«, sagte Sali, »daß wir uns weniger kennen, als wenn wir uns nie gesehen hätten, so fremd hat uns die lange Zeit gemacht, seit wir groß geworden sind! Was ist alles vorgegangen in deinem Köpfchen, mein liebes Kind?« – »Ach, nicht viel! Tausend Narrenspossen haben sich wollen regen, aber es ist mir immer so trübselig ergangen, daß sie nicht aufkommen konnten!« – »Du armes Schätzchen«, sagte Sali, »ich glaube aber, du hast es hinter den Ohren, nicht?« – »Das kannst du ja nach und nach erfahren, wenn du mich recht liebhast!« – »Wenn du einst meine Frau bist?« Vrenchen zitterte leis bei diesem letzten Worte und schmiegte sich tiefer in Salis Arme, ihn von neuem lange und zärtlich küssend. Es traten ihr dabei Tränen in die Augen, und beide wurden auf einmal traurig, da ihnen ihre hoffnungsarme

them with their sharp young eyes, and when they thought they saw one flashing along in the sunlight like shooting stars along the firmament, they kissed again, in token of reward, and tried to cheat and to overreach each other at this game just as much as they could. "Do you see, there is one flitting now," whispered Sali, and Vreni replied just as low: "I can hear it, but I do not see it." "Oh, but watch now," breathed Sali, "right there, where the small white cloud is floating, a hand's breadth to the right." And then both stared with all their might, and meanwhile opened their lips, thirsty and hungry for more nourishment, like young birds in their nest, in order to fasten these same lips upon the other if perchance they both felt convinced of the existence of that lark. But now Vreni made a stop, in order to say, very seriously and importantly: "Let us not forget; this, then, is agreed, that each of us loves the other. Now, I wish to know, what do you have to say about your sweetheart?" "This," said Sali, as though in a dream, "that it is a thing of beauty, with two brown eyes, a scarlet mouth, and with two swift feet. But how it really is thinking and believing I have no more idea than the Pope in Rome. And what can you tell me about your lover? What is he like?" "That he has two blue eyes, a bold mouth and two stout arms which he is swift to use. But what his thoughts are I know no more than the Turkish sultan." "True," said Sali, "it is singular, but we really do not know what either is thinking. We are less acquainted than if we had never seen each other before. So strange towards each other the long time between has made us. What really has happened during the long interval since we grew up in your dear little head, Vreni?" "Not much," whispered Vreni, "a thousand foolish things, but my life has been so hard that none of them could stay there long." "You poor little dear," said Sali in a very low voice, "but nevertheless, Vreni, I believe you are a sly little thing, are you not?" "That you may learn, by and by, if you really are fond of me, as you say," the young girl murmured. "You mean when you are my wife," whispered Sali. At these last words Vreni trembled slightly, and pressed herself more tightly into his arms, kissing him anew long and tenderly. Tears gathered in her eyes, and both of them all at once became sad, since their future, so devoid of hope, came into their minds, and the enmity of their fathers. Vreni now sighed deeply and murmured: "Come, Sali, I must be going now." And both rose and left the cornfield hand in hand, but at the same instant they spied Vreni's father. With the idle curiosity of the person without useful employment he had been speculating, from the moment he had met Sali hours before, what the young man might be wanting all alone in the village. Remembering the occurrence of the previous day, he fi-

Zukunft in den Sinn kam und die Feindschaft ihrer Eltern. Vrenchen seufzte und sagte: »Komm, ich muß nun gehen!« und so erhoben sie sich und gingen Hand in Hand aus dem Kornfeld, als sie Vrenchens Vater spähend vor sich sahen. Mit dem kleinlichen Scharfsinn des müßigen Elendes hatte dieser, als er dem Sali begegnet, neugierig gegrübelt, was der wohl allein im Dorfe zu suchen ginge, und sich des gestrigen Vorfalles erinnernd, verfiel er, immer nach der Stadt zu schlendernd, endlich auf die richtige Spur, rein aus Groll und unbeschäftigter Bosheit, und nicht so bald gewann der Verdacht eine bestimmte Gestalt, als er mitten in den Gassen von Seldwyla umkehrte und wieder in das Dorf hinaustrollte, wo er seine Tochter in Haus und Hof und rings in den Hecken vergeblich suchte. Mit wachsender Neugier rannte er auf den Acker hinaus, und als er da Vrenchens Korb liegen sah, in welchem es die Früchte zu holen pflegte, das Mädchen selbst aber nirgends erblickte, spähte er eben am Korne des Nachbars herum, als die erschrockenen Kinder herauskamen.

Sie standen wie versteinert, und Marti stand erst auch da, und beschaute sie mit bösen Blicken, bleich wie Blei; dann fing er fürchterlich an zu toben in Gebärden und Schimpfworten und langte zugleich grimmig nach dem jungen Burschen, um ihn zu würgen; Sali wich aus und floh einige Schritte zurück, entsetzt über den wilden Mann, sprang aber sogleich wieder zu, als er sah, daß der Alte statt seiner nun das zitternde Mädchen faßte, ihm eine Ohrfeige gab, daß der rote Kranz herunterflog, und seine Haare um die Hand wickelte, um es mit sich fortzureißen und weiter zu mißhandeln. Ohne sich zu besinnen, raffte er einen Stein auf und schlug mit demselben den Alten gegen den Kopf, halb in Angst um Vrenchen und halb im Jähzorn. Marti taumelte erst ein wenig, sank dann bewußtlos auf den Steinhaufen nieder und zog das erbärmlich aufschreiende Vrenchen mit. Sali befreite noch dessen Haare aus der Hand des Bewußtlosen und richtete es auf; dann stand er da wie eine Bildsäule, ratlos und gedankenlos. Das Mädchen, als es den wie tot daliegenden Vater sah, fuhr sich mit den Händen über das erbleichende Gesicht, schüttelte sich und sagte: »Hast du ihn erschlagen?« Sali nickte lautlos, und Vrenchen schrie: »O Gott, du lieber Gott! Es ist mein Vater! der arme Mann!« und sinnlos warf es sich über ihn und hob seinen Kopf auf, an

nally, strolling slowly towards the town, had hit upon the right cause, merely as the result of venom and suspicion. And no sooner had his suspicion taken on a definite shape, when he, in the middle of a Seldwyla street, turned back and reached the village. There he had vainly searched for Vreni everywhere, at home and in the meadow and all around in the hedges. With increasing restlessness he had now sought her right near by in the cornfield, and when picking up there Vreni's small vegetable basket, he had felt sure of being on the right track, spying about, when suddenly he perceived the two children issuing from the corn itself.

They stood there as if turned to stone. Marti himself also for a moment did not move, and stared at them with evil looks, pale as lead. But then he started to curse them like a fiend, and used the vilest language toward the young man. He made a vicious grab at him, attempting to throttle him. Sali instantly wrested himself loose, and sprang back a few paces, so as to be out of the reach of the old man, who acted like one demented. But when he perceived that Marti instead of himself now took hold of the trembling girl, dealing her a violent blow in the face, then seizing her by the back of her hair, trying to drag her along and mistreat her further, he stepped up once more. Without reflecting at all he picked up a rock and struck the old man with it against the side of the head, half in fear of what the maniac meant to do to Vreni, and half in self-defense. Marti after the blow stumbled a step or two, and then fell in a heap on a pile of stones, pulling his daughter down with him in so doing. Sali freed her hair from the rough grasp of the unconscious man, and helped the girl to her feet. But then he stood lifeless, not knowing what to say or do. The girl seeing her father lying prone on the ground like dead, put her hands to her face, shuddered and whispered: "Have you killed him?" Sali silently nodded his head, and Vreni shrieked: "Oh, God, oh, God! It is my father! The poor man!" And quite out of her senses she knelt down alongside of him, lifted up his head and began to examine his hurt. But there was no flow of blood, nor any other trace of injury. She let the limp body drop to

welchem indessen kein Blut floß. Es ließ ihn wieder sinken; Sali ließ sich auf der anderen Seite des Mannes nieder, und beide schauten still wie das Grab und mit erlahmten reglosen Händen, in das leblose Gesicht. Um nur etwas anzufangen, sagte endlich Sali: »Er wird doch nicht gleich tot sein müssen? das ist gar nicht ausgemacht!« Vrenchen riß ein Blatt von einer Klatschrose ab und legte es auf die erblaßten Lippen, und es bewegte sich schwach. »Er atmet noch«, rief es, »so lauf doch ins Dorf und hol Hilfe!« Als Sali aufsprang und laufen wollte, streckte es ihm die Hand nach und rief ihn zurück: »Komm aber nicht mit zurück und sage nichts, wie es zugegangen, ich, werde auch schweigen, man soll nichts aus mir herausbringen!« sagte es, und sein Gesicht, das es dem armen ratlosen Burschen zuwandte, überfloß von schmerzlichen Tränen. »Komm, küß mich noch einmal! Nein, geh, mach dich fort! Es ist aus, es ist ewig aus, wir können nicht zusammenkommen!« Es stieß ihn fort, und er lief willenlos dem Dorfe zu. Er begegnete einem Knäbchen, das ihn nicht kannte; diesem trug er auf, die nächsten Leute zu holen, und beschrieb ihm genau, wo die Hilfe nötig sei. Dann machte er sich verzweifelt fort und irrte die ganze Nacht im Gehölze herum. Am Morgen schlich er in die Felder, um zu erspähen, wie es gegangen sei, und hörte von frühen Leuten, welche miteinander sprachen, daß Marti noch lebe, aber nichts von sich wisse, und wie das eine seltsame Sache wäre, da kein Mensch wisse, was ihm zugestoßen. Erst jetzt ging er in die Stadt zurück und verbarg sich in dem dunklen Elend des Hauses.

Vrenchen hielt ihm Wort; es war nichts aus ihm herauszufragen, als daß es selbst den Vater so gefunden habe, und da er am andern Tage sich wieder tüchtig regte und atmete, freilich ohne Bewußtsein, und überdies kein Kläger da war, so nahm man an, er sei betrunken gewesen und auf die Steine gefallen, und ließ die Sache auf sich beruhen. Vrenchen pflegte ihn und ging nicht von seiner Seite, außer um die Arzneimittel zu holen beim Doktor und etwa für sich selbst eine schlechte Suppe zu kochen; denn es lebte beinahe von nichts, obgleich es Tag und Nacht wach sein mußte und niemand ihm half. Es dauerte beinahe sechs Wochen, bis der Kranke allmählich zu seinem Bewußtsein kam, obgleich er vorher schon wieder aß und in seinem Bette ziemlich munter

the ground again. Sali put himself on the other side of the unconscious old man, and both of them stared helplessly at the pale and motionless face of Marti. They were silent and their hands dropped. At last Sali remarked: "Perhaps he is not dead at all. I don't think he is dead. That blow can never have killed him." Vreni tore a leaf off one of the wild roses near her, and held it before the mouth of her father. The leaf fluttered a little. "He is still alive," she cried, "Run to the village, Sali, and get assistance." When Sali sprang up and was about to run off, she stretched out her hand towards him, and cried: "Don't come back with the others and say nothing as to how he came by his injury. I shall keep silent and betray nothing." In saying which the poor girl showed him a face streaming with tears of distress, and she looked at her lover as though parting from him forever. "Come and kiss me once more," she murmured. "But no, get along with you. Everything is over between us. We can never belong to each other." And she gave him a gentle push, and he ran with a heavy heart down the path to the village. On his way he met a small boy, one he did not know, and him he bade to get some people and described in detail where and what assistance was required. Then he drifted off in despair, wandering at random all night about the woods near the village. In the early morning he cautiously crept forth, in order to spy out how things had gone during the night. From several persons early astir he heard the news. Marti was alive, but out of his senses, and nobody, it seemed, knew what really had happened to him. And only after learning this his mind was so far at ease that he found the way back to town and to his father's tavern, where he buried himself in the family misery.

Vreni had kept her word. Nothing could be learned of her but that she had found her father in this condition, and as he on the next day became again quite active, breathed normally and began to move about, although still without his full senses, and since, besides, there was no one to frame a complaint, it was assumed that he had met with some accident while under the influence of drink, probably had had a bad fall on the stones, and matters were left as they were. Vreni nursed him very carefully, never left his side, except to get medicine and remedies from the shop of the village doctor, and also to pick in the vegetable patch something wherewith to cook him and herself a simple stew or soup. Those days she lived almost on air, although she had to be about and busy day and night and nobody came to help her. Thus nearly six weeks elapsed until the old man recover-

war. Aber es war nicht das alte Bewußtsein, das er jetzt erlangte, sondern es zeigte sich immer deutlicher, je mehr er sprach, daß er blödsinnig geworden, und zwar auf die wunderlichste Weise. Er erinnerte sich nur dunkel an das Geschehene und wie an etwas sehr Lustiges, was ihn nicht weiter berühre, lachte immer wie ein Narr und war guter Dinge. Noch im Bette liegend, brachte er hundert närrische, sinnlos mutwillige Redensarten und Einfälle zum Vorschein, schnitt Gesichter und zog sich die schwarzwollene Zipfelmütze in die Augen und über die Nase herunter, daß diese aussah wie ein Sarg unter einem Bahrtuch. Das bleiche und abgehärmte Vrenchen hörte ihm geduldig zu, Tränen vergießend über das törichte Wesen, welches die arme Tochter noch mehr ängstigte als die frühere Bosheit; aber wenn der Alte zuweilen etwas gar zu Drolliges anstellte, so mußte es mitten in seiner Qual laut auflachen, da sein unterdrücktes Wesen immer zur Lust aufzuspringen bereit war, wie ein gespannter Bogen, worauf dann eine um so tiefere Betrübnis erfolgte. Als der Alte aber aufstehen konnte, war gar nichts mehr mit ihm anzustellen; er machte nichts als Dummheiten, lachte und stöberte um das Haus herum, setzte sich in die Sonne und streckte die Zunge heraus oder hielt lange Reden in die Bohnen hinein.

Um die gleiche Zeit aber war es auch aus mit den wenigen Überbleibseln seines ehemaligen Besitzes und die Unordnung so weit gediehen, daß auch sein Haus und der letzte Acker, seit geraumer Zeit verpfändet, nun gerichtlich verkauft wurden. Denn der Bauer, welcher die zwei Acker des Manz gekauft, benutzte die gänzliche Verkommenheit Martis und seine Krankheit und führte den alten Streit wegen des strittigen Steinfleckes kurz und entschlossen zu Ende, und der verlorene Prozeß trieb Martis Faß vollends den Boden aus, indessen er in seinem Blödsinne nichts mehr von diesen Dingen wußte. Die Versteigerung fand statt; Marti wurde von der Gemeinde in einer Stiftung für dergleichen arme Tröpfe auf öffentliche Kosten untergebracht. Diese Anstalt befand sich in der Hauptstadt des Ländchens; der gesunde und eßbegierige Blödsinnige wurde noch gut gefüttert, dann auf ein mit

ed sufficiently to take care of himself, though long before that he had been sitting up in bed and had babbled about one thing or another. But he had not recovered his mind, and the things he was now saying and doing seemed to show plainly that he had become weak-minded, and this in the strangest manner. He could recall what had happened but darkly, and to him it seemed something very enjoyable and laughable. Something, too, which did not touch him in any way, and he laughed and laughed all day long, and was in the best of humor, very different from what he had been before his accident. While still abed he had a hundred foolish, senseless ideas, cut capers and made faces, pulled his black peaked woollen cap over his ears, down to his nose and his mouth, and then he would mumble something which seemed to amuse him highly. Vreni, pale and sorrowful, listened patiently to all his stories, shedding tears about his idiotic behavior, which grieved her even more than his former malicious and wicked tricks had. But it would nevertheless happen now and then, that the old man would perform some particularly ludicrous antics, and then Vreni, tortured as she was by all these scenes, would be unable to help bursting into laughter, as her joyous disposition, suppressed by all these sad events, would sometimes rend the bounds which confined her, just like a bow too tightly strung that would break. But as soon as the old man could once more get out of bed, there was nothing more to be done. All day long he did nothing but silly things, was grinning, smirking and laughing to himself constantly, turned everything in the house topsy-turvy, sat down in the sunshine and blared at the world, put out his tongue at everybody that passed, and made long monologues while standing in the midst of the bean field.

Simultaneous with all this there came also the end of his ownership in the farm. Everything upon it had, of course, gone to wrack and ruin, and disorder reigned supreme. Not only his house, but also the last bit of land left him, pledged in court some time before, were now seized and the day of forced sale was named. For the peasant who had claims to these pieces of property, very naturally made use of the opportunities now afforded him by the illness and the failing powers of Marti to bring about a quick decision. These last proceedings in court used up the bit of cash still left to Marti, and all this was done while he in his weakness of mind had not even a notion what it was all about. The forced sale took place, and at its close, Marti being penniless and bereft of sense, by the action of the village council, it was decided to make him an inmate of the community asylum that had been founded many years before for the precise benefit of just such poor devils as himself. This asylum was located in the cantonal capital. Before he started for

Ochsen bespanntes Wägelchen geladen, das ein ärmlicher Bauersmann nach der Stadt führte, um zugleich einen oder zwei Säcke Kartoffeln zu verkaufen, und Vrenchen setzte sich zu dem Vater auf das Fuhrwerk, um ihn auf diesem letzten Gange zu dem lebendigen Begräbnis zu begleiten. Es war eine traurige und bittere Fahrt, aber Vrenchen wachte sorgfältig über seinen Vater und ließ es ihm an nichts fehlen, und es sah sich nicht um und ward nicht ungeduldig, wenn durch die Kapriolen des Unglücklichen die Leute aufmerksam wurden und dem Wägelchen nachliefen, wo sie durchfuhren. Endlich erreichten sie das weitläufige Gebäude in der Stadt, wo die langen Gänge, die Höfe und ein freundlicher Garten von einer Menge ähnlicher Tröpfe belebt waren, die alle in weiße Kittel gekleidet waren und dauerhafte Lederkäppchen auf den harten Köpfen trugen. Auch Marti wurde noch vor Vrenchens Augen in diese Tracht gekleidet, und er freute sich wie ein Kind darüber und tanzte singend umher. »Gott grüß euch, ihr geehrten Herren!« rief er seine neuen Genossen an, »ein schönes Haus habt ihr hier! Geh heim, Vrenggel, und sag der Mutter, ich komme nicht mehr nach Haus, hier gefällt's mir bei Gott! Juchhei! Es kreucht ein Igel über den Hag, ich hab ihn hören bellen! O Meitli, küß kein alten Knab, küß nur die jungen Gesellen! Alle die Wässerlein laufen in Rhein, die mit dem Pflaumenaug, die muß es sein! Gehst du schon, Vreeli? Du siehst ja aus wie der Tod im Häfelein, und geht es mir doch so erfreulich! Die Füchsin schreit im Felde: Halleo, halleo! das Herz tut ihr weho! hoho!« Ein Aufseher gebot ihm Ruhe und führte ihn zu einer leichten Arbeit, und Vrenchen ging, das Fuhrwerk aufzusuchen. Es setzte sich auf den Wagen, zog ein Stückchen Brot hervor und aß dasselbe, dann schlief es, bis der Bauer kam und mit ihm nach dem Dorfe zurückfuhr. Sie kamen erst in der Nacht an. Vrenchen ging nach dem Hause, in dem es geboren und nur zwei Tage bleiben durfte, und es war jetzt zum ersten Mal in seinem Leben ganz allein darin. Es machte ein Feuer, um das letzte Restchen Kaffee zu kochen, das es noch besaß, und setzte sich auf den Herd, denn es war ihm ganz elendiglich zu Mut. Es sehnte sich und härmte sich ab, den Sali nur ein einziges Mal zu sehen, und dachte inbrünstig an ihn; aber die Sorgen und der Kummer verbitterten seine Sehnsucht, und diese machte die Sorgen wieder viel schwerer. So saß es und stützte den Kopf in

his destination he was well fed for a day or two, to the eminent satisfaction of the idiot, who had developed an enormous appetite of late, and then was put on a cart drawn by a phlegmatic ox and driven by a poor peasant who besides attending to this community errand wanted to sell also a sack of potatoes at the town. Vreni sat down on the same vehicle alongside of her father in order to accompany him on this day of his being buried alive, so to speak. It was a sad and bitter drive, but Vreni watched lovingly over her father, and let him want for nothing; neither did she grow impatient when passers-by, attracted by the ridiculous behavior of the old man, would follow the cart and make all sorts of audible remarks on its inmates. Finally they did reach the asylum, a complex of buildings connected by courts and corridors, and where a big garden was seen alive with similarly unfortunate beings as Marti himself, all dressed in a sort of uniform consisting of white coarse linen blouses and vests, with stiff caps of leather on their foolish old heads. Marti, too, was put into such a uniform, even before Vreni's departure, and her father evinced a childish joy at his new clothes, dancing about in them and singing snatches of wicked drinking songs. "God be with you, my lords and honored fellow-inmates," he harangued a knot of them, "you surely have a palace-like home here. Go away, Vreni, and tell mother that I won't come home any more. I like it here splendidly. Goodness me, what a palace! There runs a spider across the road, and I have heard him barking! Oh, maiden mine, oh, maiden mine, don't kiss the old, kiss but the young! All the waters in the world are running into the Rhine! She with the darkest eye, she is not mine. Already going, little Vreni? Why, thou lookest as though death were in thy pot. And yet things are looking up with me. I am doing fine. Am getting wealthy in my old days. The she-fox cries with him: Halloo! Halloo! Her heart pains her. Why--oh, why? Halloo! Halloo!" An official of the institution bade him hold his infernal noise, and then he led him away to do some easy work. Vreni took her leave sadly and then began to look up her ox cart with the peasant. When she had found it she climbed in and sat down and ate a slice of bread she had brought with her. Then she lay down and fell asleep, and a couple of hours later the peasant came and woke her, and then they drove home to the village. They arrived there in the middle of the night. Vreni went to her father's house, the one where she had been born and had spent all her days. For the first time she was all alone in it. Two days' grace she had to get out and find some other shelter. She made a fire and prepared a cup of coffee for herself, using the last remnants she still had. Then she sat down on the edge of the hearth, and wept bitterly. She was longing with all

die Hände, als jemand durch die offenstehende Tür hereinkam. »Sali!« rief Vrenchen, als es aufsah, und fiel ihm um den Hals; dann sahen sich aber beide erschrocken an und riefen: »Wie siehst du elend aus!« Denn Sali sah nicht minder als Vrenchen bleich und abgezehrt aus. Alles vergessend, zog es ihn zu sich auf den Herd und sagte: »Bist du krank gewesen, oder ist es dir auch so schlimm gegangen?« Sali antwortete: »Nein, ich bin gerade nicht krank, außer vor Heimweh nach dir! Bei uns geht es jetzt hoch und herrlich zu; der Vater hat einen Einzug und Unterschleif von auswärtigem Gesindel, und ich glaube, soviel ich merke, ist er ein Diebshehler geworden. Deshalb ist jetzt einstweilen Hülle und Fülle in unserer Taverne, solang es geht und bis es ein Ende mit Schrecken nimmt. Die Mutter hilft dazu, aus bitterlicher Gier, nur etwas im Hause zu sehen, und glaubt den Unfug noch durch eine gewisse Aufsicht und Ordnung annehmlich und nützlich zu machen! Mich fragt man nicht, und ich konnte mich nicht viel darum kümmern; denn ich kann nur an dich denken Tag und Nacht. Da allerlei Landstreicher bei uns einkehren, so haben wir alle Tage gehört, was bei euch vorgeht, worüber mein Vater sich freut wie ein kleines Kind. Daß dein Vater heute nach dem Spittel gebracht wurde, haben wir auch vernommen; ich habe gedacht, du werdest Jetzt allein sein, und bin gekommen, um dich zu sehen!« Vrenchen klagte ihm jetzt auch alles, was sie drückte und was sie erlitt, aber mit so leichter zutraulicher Zunge, als ob sie ein großes Glück beschriebe, weil sie glücklich war, Sali neben sich zu sehen. Sie brachte inzwischen notdürftig ein Becken voll warmen Kaffee zusammen, welchen mit ihr zu teilen sie den Geliebten zwang. »Also übermorgen mußt du hier weg?« sagte Sali, »was soll denn ums Himmels willen werden?« – »Das weiß ich nicht«, sagte Vrenchen, »ich werde dienen müssen und in die Welt hinaus! Ich werde es aber nicht aushalten ohne dich, und doch kann ich dich nie bekommen, auch wenn alles andere nicht wäre, bloß weil du meinen Vater geschlagen und um den Verstand gebracht hast! Dies würde immer ein schlechter Grundstein unserer Ehe sein und wir beide nie sorglos werden, nie!« Sali seufzte und sagte: »Ich wollte auch schon hundertmal Soldat werden oder mich in einer fremden Gegend als Knecht verdingen, aber ich kann noch nicht fortgehen, solange du hier bist, und hernach wird es mich aufreiben. Ich glaube, das

her soul to see and talk once more to Sali, and she was thinking and thinking of him. But mingling with these desires of hers were her anxieties and her fears of the future. Thus sat the poor thing, holding her head in her hand, when somebody entered at the door. "Sali!" cried Vreni, when she looked up and saw the face dearest to her in the world. And she fell on his neck, but then they both looked at one another, and they shouted: "How poorly you look!" For Sali was as pale and sorrowful as the girl herself. Forgetting everything she drew him to her on the hearth, and questioned him: "Have you been ill, or have you also fared badly?" "No, not ill," said Sali, "but longing for you. At home things are going fine. My father now has rare guests, and as I believe, he has become a receiver of stolen goods. And that is why there are big doings at our place, both day and night, until, I suppose, there will come a bad end to it all. Mother is helping along, eager to have guests of any kind at all, guests that fetch money into the house, and she tries to bring some order out of all this disorder, and also to make it profitable. I am not questioned about the matter at all, neither do I care. For I have only been thinking of you all along. Since all sorts of vagrants come and go in our place, we have heard of everything concerning you, and my father is beside himself with joy, and that your father has been taken to-day to the asylum has delighted him immensely. Since he has now left you I have come, thinking you might be lonesome, and maybe in trouble." Then Vreni told him all her sorrows in detail, but she did this with such fluency and described the intimate details in such an almost happy tone of voice as if what she was saying did not disturb her in the least. All this because the presence of her lover and his solicitude about her really rendered her happy and minimized her anxieties. She had Sali at her side. And what more did she want? Soon she had a vessel with the steaming coffee which she forced Sali to share with her. "Day after to-morrow, then, you must leave here?" said Sali. "What is to become of you now?" "I don't know," answered Vreni. "I suppose I shall have to seek some service and go away from here, somewhere in the wide world. But I know I won't be able to endure that without you, Sali, and yet we cannot come together. If there were no other reason it would not do because you hurt my father and made him lose his mind. That would always be a bad foundation for our wedded state, would it not? And neither of us would ever be able to forget that, never!" Sali sighed deeply, and rejoined: "I myself wanted a hundred times to become a soldier or else go far away and hire out on a farm, but I cannot do it, I cannot leave you here, and after we are separated it will kill me, I feel sure of it, for longing for you will not let me rest day or

Elend macht meine Liebe zu dir stärker und schmerzhafter, so daß es um Leben und Tod geht! Ich habe von dergleichen keine Ahnung gehabt!« Vrenchen sah ihn liebevoll lächelnd an; sie lehnten sich an die Wand zurück und sprachen nichts mehr, sondern gaben sich schweigend der glückseligen Empfindung hin, die sich über allen Gram erhob, daß sie sich im größten Ernste gut wären und geliebt wüßten. Darüber schliefen sie friedlich ein auf dem unbequemen Herde, ohne Kissen und Pfühl, und schliefen so sanft und ruhig wie zwei Kinder in einer Wiege. Schon graute der Morgen, als Sali zuerst erwachte; er weckte Vrenchen, so acht er konnte; aber es duckte sich immer wieder an ihn, schlaftrunken, und wollte sich nicht ermuntern. Da küßte er es heftig ruf den Mund, und Vrenchen fuhr empor, machte die Augen weit auf, und als es Sali erblickte, rief es: »Herrgott! ich habe eben noch von dir geträumt! Es träumte mir, wir tanzten miteinander auf unserer Hochzeit, lange, lange Stunden! Und waren so glücklich, sauber geschmückt, und es fehlte uns an nichts. Da wollten wir uns endlich küssen und dürsteten danach, aber immer zog uns etwas auseinander, und nun bist du es selbst gewesen, der uns gestört und gehindert hat! Aber wie gut, laß du gleich da bist!« Gierig fiel es ihm um den Hals und küßte ihn, als ob es kein Ende nehmen sollte. »Und was hast du denn geträumt?« fragte es und streichelte ihm Wangen und Kinn. »Mir träumte, ich ginge endlos auf einer langen Straße durch einen Wald und du in der Ferne immer vor mir her; zuweilen sahest du nach mir um, winktest mir und lachtest, und dann war ich wie im Himmel. Das ist alles!« Sie traten unter die offengebliebene Küchentüre, die unmittelbar ins Freie führte, und mußten lachen, als sie sich ins Gesicht sahen. Denn die rechte Wange Vrenchens und die linke Salis, welche im Schlafe aneinander gelehnt hatten, waren von dem Drucke ganz rot gefärbt, während die Blässe der anderen durch die kühle Nachtluft noch erhöht war. Sie rieben sich zärtlich die kalte bleiche Seite ihrer Gesichter, um sie auch rot zu machen; die frische Morgenluft, der traurige stille Frieden, der über der Gegend lag, das junge Morgenrot machten sie fröhlich und selbstvergessen, und besonders in Vrenchen schien ein freundlicher Geist der Sorglosigkeit gefahren zu sein. »Morgen abend muß ich also aus diesem Hause fort«, sagte es, »und ein anderes Obdach suchen. Vorher aber möchte ich,

night. I really believe, Vreni, that all this misery makes my love for you only the stronger and the more painful, so that it becomes a matter of life or death. Never did I dream that this should ever be my end." But Vreni, while he was thus pouring out his burdened mind, gazed at him smilingly and with a face that shone with joy. They were leaning against the chimney corner, and silently they felt to the full the intense ecstasy of communion of spirits. Over and above all their troubles, high above them all, there was hovering the genius of their love, that each felt loving and beloved. And in this beatitude they both fell asleep on this cold hearth with its feathery ashes, without cover or pillow, and slept just as peacefully and softly as two little children in their cradle. Dawn was breaking in the eastern sky when Sali awoke the first. Gently he woke Vreni, but she again and again snuggled near to him and would not rouse herself. At last he kissed her with vehemence on her mouth, and then Vreni did awaken, opened her eyes wide, and when she saw Sali she exclaimed: "Zounds, I've just been dreaming of you. I was dreaming I danced on our wedding-day, many, many hours, and we were both so happy, both so finely dressed, and nothing was lacking to our joy. And then we wanted to kiss each other, and we both longed for it, oh, so much, but always something was dragging us apart, and now it appears that it was you yourself that was interfering, that it was you who disturbed and hindered us. But how nice, how nice, that you are at least close by now." And she fell around his neck and kissed him wildly, kissed him as if there were to be no end to it. "And now confess, my dear, what have you been dreaming?" and she tenderly caressed his cheeks and chin. "I was dreaming," he said, "that I was walking endlessly along a lengthy street, and through a forest, and you in the distance always ahead of me. Off and on you turned around for me, and were beckoning and smiling at me, and then it seemed to me I were in heaven. And that is all." They stepped on the threshold of the kitchen door left open the whole night and which led direct into the open, and they had to laugh as they now saw each other plainly. For the right cheek of Vreni and the left one of Sali, which in their sleep had been resting against each other, were both quite red from the pressure, while the pallor of the opposite cheeks was engrossed by the coolth of early morning. So then they rubbed vigorously the pale cheeks to bring them into consonance with the others, each performing that service for the other. The fresh morning air, the dewy peace lying over the whole landscape, and the ruddy tints of coming sunrise, all this together made them forget their griefs and made them merry and playful, and into Vreni especially a gay spirit of carelessness seemed to have passed.

einmal nur *einmal* recht lustig sein, und zwar mit dir; ich möchte recht herzlich und fleißig mit dir tanzen irgendwo, denn das Tanzen aus dem Traume steckt mir immerfort im Sinn!« – »Jedenfalls will ich dabeisein und sehen, wo du unterkommst«, sagte Sali, »und tanzen wollte ich, auch gerne mit dir, du herziges Kind! aber wo?« – »Es ist morgen Kirchweih an zwei Orten nicht sehr weit von hier«, erwiderte Vrenchen, »da kennt und beachtet man uns weniger; draußen am Wasser will ich auf dich warten, und dann können wir gehen, wohin es uns gefällt, um uns lustig zu machen, einmal, *einmal* nur! Aber je, wir haben ja gar kein Geld!« setzte es traurig hinzu, »da kann nichts daraus werden!« – »Laß nur«, sagte Sali, »ich will schon etwas mitbringen!« – »Doch nicht von deinem Vater, von – von dem Gestohlenen?« – »Nein, sei nur ruhig! Ich habe noch meine silberne Uhr bewahrt bis dahin, die will ich verkaufen!« – »Ich will dir nicht abraten«, sagte Vrenchen errötend, »denn ich glaube, ich müßte sterben, wenn ich nicht morgen mit dir tanzen könnte.« – »Es wäre das beste, wir beide könnten sterben!« sagte Sali; sie umarmten sich wehmütig und schmerzlich zum Abschied, und als sie voneinander ließen, lachten sie sich doch freundlich an in der sicheren Hoffnung auf den nächsten Tag. »Aber wann willst du denn kommen?« rief Vrenchen noch. »Spätestens um eilf Uhr mittags«, erwiderte er, »wir wollen recht ordentlich zusammen Mittag essen!« – »Gut, gut! komm lieber um halb eilf schon!« Doch als Sali schon im Gehen war, rief sie ihn noch einmal zurück und zeigte ein plötzlich verändertes verzweiflungsvolles Gesicht. »Es wird doch nichts daraus«, sagte sie bitterlich weinend, »ich habe keine Sonntagsschuhe mehr! Schon gestern habe ich diese groben hier anziehen müssen, um nach der Stadt zu kommen! Ich weiß keine Schuhe aufzubringen!« Sali stand ratlos und verblüfft. »Keine Schuhe!« sagte er, »da mußt du halt in diesen kommen!« – »Nein, nein, in denen kann ich nicht tanzen!« – »Nun, so müssen wir welche kaufen?« – »Wo, mit was?« – »Ei, in Seldwyl, da gibt es Schuhläden genug! Geld werde ich in minder als zwei Stunden haben.« – »Aber ich kann doch nicht mit dir in Seldwyl herumgehen, und dann wird das Geld nicht langen, auch noch Schuhe zu kaufen!« – »Es muß! und ich will die Schuhe kaufen und morgen mitbringen!« – »O du Närrchen, sie werden ja nicht passen, die du kaufst!« – »So gib

"To-morrow night then, I must leave this house," she said, "and find some other shelter. But before that happens I should love to be merry, real merry, just once, only once. And it is with thee, dear, that I want to enjoy myself. I should like to dance with you, really and truly, for a long, long time, till I could no longer move a foot. For it is that dance in my dream that I have to think of steadily. That dream was too fine, let us realize it." "At all events I must be present when you dance," said Sali, "and see what becomes of you, and to dance with you as long as you like is just what I myself would love to do, you charming wild thing. But where?" "Ah, Sali, to-morrow there will be kermess in a number of places near by. Of two of these I know. On such occasions we should not be spied upon and could enjoy ourselves to our heart's content. Below at the river front I could await you, and then we can go wherever we like, to laugh and be merry--just once, only once. But stop--we have no money." And Vreni's face clouded with the sad thought, and she added blankly: "What a pity! Nothing can come of it." "Let be," smilingly said Sali, "I shall have money enough when I meet you." But Vreni flushed and said haltingly: "But how--not from your father, not stolen money?" "No, Vreni. I still have my silver watch, and I will sell that." "Then that is arranged," said Vreni, and she flushed once more. "In fact, I think I should die if I could not dance with you to-morrow." "Probably the best for us," said Sali, "if we both could die." They embraced with tearful smiles, and bade each other good-by, but at the moment of parting they again laughed at each other, in the sure hope of meeting again next day. "But when shall we meet?" asked Vreni. "At eleven at latest," answered Sali. "Then we can eat a good noon meal together somewhere." "Fine, fine," Vreni cried after him, "come half an hour earlier then." But the very moment of their parting Vreni summoned him back once more, and she showed suddenly a wholly changed and despairing face: "Nothing, after all, can come of our plans," she then said, weeping hard, "because I had forgotten I had no Sunday shoes any more. Even yesterday I had to put on these clumsy ones going to town, and I don't know where to find a pair I could wear." Sali stood undecided and amazed. "No shoes?" he repeated after her. "In that case you'll have to go in these." "But no, no," she remonstrated. "In these I should never be able to dance." "Well, all we can do then is to buy new ones," said Sali in a matter-of-fact tone. "Where and what with?" asked Vreni. "Why, in Seldwyla, where they have shoe stores enough. And money I shall have in less than two hours." "But, Sali, I cannot accompany you to all these shoe stores, and then there will not be money enough for all the other things as well." "It must. And I will buy the shoes

mir einen alten Schuh mit, oder halt, noch besser, ich will dir das Maß nehmen, das wird doch kein Hexenwerk sein!« – »Das Maß nehmen? Wahrhaftig, daran hab ich nicht gedacht! Komm, komm, ich will dir ein Schnürchen suchen!« Sie setzte sich wieder auf den Herd, zog den Rock etwas zurück: und streifte den Schuh vom Fuße, der noch von der gestrigen Reise her mit einem weißen Strumpfe bekleidet war. Sali kniete nieder und nahm, so gut er es verstand, das Maß, indem er den zierlichen Fuß der Länge und Breite nach umspannte mit dem Schnürchen und sorgfältig Knoten in dasselbe knüpfte. »Du Schuhmacher!« sagte Vrenchen und lachte errötend und freundschaftlich zu ihm nieder. Sali wurde aber auch rot und hielt den Fuß fest in seinen Händen, länger als nötig war, so daß Vrenchen ihn, noch tiefer errötend, zurückzog, den verwirrten Sali aber noch einmal stürmisch umhalste und küßte, dann aber fortschickte.

Sobald er in der Stadt war, trug er seine Uhr zu einem Uhrmacher, der ihm sechs oder sieben Gulden dafür gab; für die silberne Kette bekam er auch einige Gulden, und er dünkte sich nun reich genug, denn er hatte, seit er groß war, nie so viel Geld besessen auf einmal. Wenn nur erst der Tag vorüber und der Sonntag angebrochen wäre, um das Glück damit zu erkaufen, das er sich von dem Tage versprach, dachte er; denn wenn das Übermorgen auch um so dunkler und unbekannter hereinragte, so gewann die ersehnte Lustbarkeit von morgen nur einen seltsamern erhöhten Glanz und Schein. Indessen brachte er die Zeit noch leidlich hin, indem er ein Paar Schuhe für Vrenchen suchte, und dies war ihm das vergnügteste Geschäft, das er je betrieben. Er ging von einem Schuhmacher zum andern, ließ sich alle Weiberschuhe zeigen, die vorhanden waren, und endlich handelte er ein leichtes und feines Paar ein, so hübsch, wie sie Vrenchen noch nie getragen. Er verbarg die Schuhe unter seiner Weste und tat sie die übrige Zeit des Tages nicht mehr von sich; er nahm sie sogar mit ins Bett und legte sie unter das Kopfkissen. Da er das Mädchen heute früh noch gesehen und morgen wieder sehen sollte, so schlief er fest und ruhig, war aber in aller Frühe munter und begann seinen dürftigen Sonntagsstaat zurechtzumachen und auszuputzen, so gut es gelingen wollte. Es fiel seiner Mutter auf, und sie fragte verwundert, was er vorhabe, da er sich schon lange nicht mehr so sorglich, angezogen. Er wolle einmal

for you and bring them along to-morrow." "Oh, but, you silly, they would not fit me." "Then give me an old shoe of yours to take along, or, stop, better still, I will take your measure. Surely that will not be very difficult." "Take my measure, of course. I never thought of that. Come, come, I will find you a bit of tape." Then she sat down once more on the hearth, turned her skirt somewhat up and slipped her shoe off, and the little foot showed, from yesterday's excursion to town, yet covered with a white stocking. Sali knelt down, and then took, as well as he was able, the measure, using the tape daintily in encompassing the length and width with great care, and tying knots where wanted. "You shoemaker," said Vreni, bending down to him and laughingly flushing in embarrassment. But Sali also reddened, and he held the little foot firmly in the palm of his hand, really longer than was necessary, so that Vreni at last, blushing still a deeper red, withdrew it, embracing, however, Sali once more stormily and kissing him with ardor, but then telling him hastily to go.

As soon as Sali arrived in town he took his watch to a jeweler and received six or seven florins for it. For his silver watch chain he also got some money, and now he thought himself rich as Croesus, for since he had grown up he had never had as large a sum at once. If only the day were over, he was saying to himself, and Sunday come, so that he could purchase with his riches all the happiness which Vreni and himself were dreaming of. For though the awful day after seemed to loom darker and darker in comparison, the heavenly pleasures anticipated for Sunday shone with all the greater lustre. However, some of his remaining leisure time was spent agreeably by him in choosing the desired pair of shoes for Vreni. In fact this job to him was a most joyous diversion. He went from one shoestore to another, had them show him all the women's footwear they had in stock, and finally bought the prettiest pair he could find. They were of a finer quality and more ornate than any Vreni had ever owned. He hid them under his vest, and throughout the rest of the day did not leave them out of his sight; he even put them under his pillow at night when he went to bed. Since he had seen the girl that day and was to meet her again next day, he slept soundly and well, but was up early, and then began to pick out his Sunday finery, dressing with greater care than ever before in his life. When he was done he looked with satisfaction at his own image in his little broken mirror. And indeed it presented an enticing picture of youth and good looks. His mother was astonished when she saw him thus attired as though for his wedding, and she asked him the meaning of it. The son replied, with a mien of indifference, that he wanted to take a long stroll into the

über Land gehen und sich ein wenig umtun, erwiderte er, er werde sonst krank in diesem Hause. »Das ist mir die Zeit her ein merkwürdiges Leben«, murrte der Vater, »und ein Herumschleichen!« – »Laß ihn nur gehen«, sagte aber die Mutter, »es tut ihm vielleicht gut, es ist ja ein Elend, wie er aussieht!« – »Hast du Geld zum Spazierengehen? woher hast du es?« sagte der Alte. »Ich brauche keines!« sagte Sali. »Da hast du einen Gulden!« versetzte der Alte und warf ihm denselben hin, »du kannst im Dorf ins Wirtshaus gehen und ihn dort verzehren, damit sie nicht glauben, wir seien hier so übel dran.« – »Ich will nicht ins Dorf und brauche den Gulden nicht, behaltet ihn nur!« – »So hast du ihn gehabt, es wäre schad, wenn du ihn haben müßtest, du Starrkopf!« rief Manz und schob seinen Gulden wieder in die Tasche. Seine Frau aber, welche nicht wußte, warum sie heute ihres Sohnes wegen so wehmütig und gerührt war, brachte ihm ein großes schwarzes Mailänder Halstuch mit rotem Rande, das sie nur selten getragen und er schon früher gern gehabt hätte. Er schlang es um den Hals und ließ die langen Zipfel fliegen; auch stellte er zum ersten Mal den Hemdkragen, den er sonst immer umgeschlagen, ehrbar und männlich, in die Höhe, bis über die Ohren hinauf, in einer Anwandlung ländlichen Stolzes, und machte sich dann, seine Schuhe in der Brusttasche des Rockes, schon nach sieben Uhr auf den Weg. Als er die Stube verließ, drängte ihn ein seltsames Gefühl, Vater und Mutter die Hand zu geben, und auf der Straße sah er sich noch einmal nach dem Hause um. »Ich glaube am Ende«, sagte Manz, »der Bursche streicht irgendeinem Weibsbild nach; das hätten wir gerade noch, nötig!« Die Frau sagte: »O wollte Gott! daß er vielleicht ein Glück machte! das täte dem armen Buben gut!« – »Richtig!« sagte der Mann, »das fehlt nicht! das wird ein himmlisches Glück geben, wenn er nur erst an eine solche Maultasche zu geraten das Unglück hat! das täte dem armen Bübchen gut! natürlich!«

Sali richtete seinen Schritt erst nach dem Flusse zu, wo er Vrenchen erwarten wollte; aber unterwegs ward er andern Sinnes und ging gradezu ins Dorf, um Vrenchen im Hause selbst abzuholen, weil es ihm zu lang währte bis halb eilf. Was kümmern uns die Leute! dachte er. Niemand hilft uns, und ich bin ehrlich und fürchte niemand! So trat er unerwartet in Vrenchens Stube, und ebenso unerwartet fand er es

country, adding that he felt the effects of his constant confinement in the close house. "Queer doings, all the time," grumbled his father with ill-humor, "and forever skirmishing about." "Let him have his way," said the mother. "Perhaps a change of air and surroundings will do him good. I'm sure to look at him he needs it. He is as pale as a ghost." "Have you some money to spend for your outing?" now asked his father. "Where did you get it from?" "I don't need any," said Sali. "There is a florin for you," replied the old man, and threw him the coin. "You can turn in at the village and visit the tavern, so that they don't think we're so badly off." "I don't intend to go to the village, and I have no use for the money. You may keep it," replied Sali, with a show of indignation. "Well, you've had it, at any rate, and so I'll keep the money, you ill-conditioned fellow," muttered the father, and put the coin back in his pocket. But his wife who for some reason unknown to herself felt that day particularly distressed on account of her son, brought down for him a large handkerchief of Milan silk, with scarlet edges, which she herself had worn a few odd times before and of which she knew that he liked it. He wound it about his neck, and left the long ends of it dangling. And the flaps of his shirt collar, usually worn by him turned down, he this time let stand on end, in a fit of rustic coquetry, so that he offered altogether the appearance of a well-to-do young man. Then at last, Vreni's little shoes hid below his vest, he left the house at near seven in the morning. In leaving the room a singularly powerful sentiment urged him to shake hands once more with his parents, and having reached the street, he was impelled to turn and take a last glance at the house. "I almost believe," said Manz sententiously, "that the young fool is smitten with some woman. Nothing but that would be lacking in our present circumstances indeed." And the mother replied: "Would to God it were so. Perhaps the poor fellow might yet be happy in life." "Just so," growled the father. "That's it. What a heavenly lot you are picking for him. To fall in love and to have to take care of some penniless woman--yes indeed, that would be a great thing for him, would it not?" But Mother Manz only smiled slightly, and said never another word.

Sali at first directed his steps toward the shore of the river, to that trysting-place where he was to meet Vreni. But on the way he changed his mind and steered straight for the village itself, hoping to meet her there awaiting him, since the time till noon otherwise seemed lost to him. "What do we have to care about gossips now?" he said to himself. "And they dare not say anything against her anyway, nor am I afraid of anyone." So he stepped into Vreni's room without any ceremony, and to his de-

schon vollkommen angekleidet und geschmückt dasitzen und der Zeit harren, wo es gehen könne, nur die Schuhe fehlten ihm noch. Aber Sali stand mit offenem Munde still in der Mitte der Stube, als er das Mädchen erblickte, so schön sah es aus. Es hatte nur ein einfaches Kleid an von blaugefärbter Leinwand, aber dasselbe war frisch und sauber und saß ihm sehr gut um den schlanken Leib. Darüber trug es ein schneeweißes Mousselinehalstuch, und dies war der ganze Anzug. Das braune gekräuselte Haar war sehr wohl geordnet, und die sonst so wilden Löckchen lagen nun fein und lieblich um den Kopf; da Vrenchen seit vielen Wochen fast nicht aus dem Hause gekommen, so war seine Farbe zarter und durchsichtiger geworden, sowie auch vom Kummer; aber in diese Durchsichtigkeit goß jetzt die Liebe und die Freude ein Rot um das andere, und an der Brust trug es einen schönen Blumenstrauß von Rosmarin, Rosen und prächtigen Astern. Es saß am offenen Fenster und atmete still und hold die frisch durchsonnte Morgenluft; wie es aber Sali erscheinen sah, streckte es ihm beide hübsche Arme entgegen, welche vom Ellbogen an bloß waren, und rief: »Wie recht hast du, daß du schon jetzt und hierher kommst! Aber hast du mir Schuhe gebracht? Gewiß? Nun steh ich nicht auf, bis ich sie anhabe!« Er zog die ersehnten aus der Tasche und gab sie dem begierigen schönen Mädchen; es schleuderte die alten von sich, schlüpfte in die neuen, und sie paßten sehr gut. Erst jetzt erhob es sich vom Stuhl, wiegte sich in den neuen Schuhen und ging eifrig einigemal auf und nieder. Es zog das lange blaue Kleid etwas zurück und beschaute wohlgefällig die roten wollenen Schleifen, welche die Schuhe zierten, während Sali unaufhörlich die feine reizende Gestalt betrachtete, welche da in lieblicher Aufregung vor ihm sich regte und freute. »Du beschaust meinen Strauß?« sagte Vrenchen, »hab ich nicht einen schönen zusammengebracht? Du mußt wissen, dies sind die letzten Blumen, die ich noch aufgefunden in dieser Wüstenei. Hier war noch ein Röschen, dort eine Aster, und wie sie nun gebunden sind, würde man es ihnen nicht ansehen, daß sie aus einem Untergange zusammengesucht sind! Nun ist es aber Zeit, daß ich fortkomme, nicht ein Blümchen mehr im Garten und das Haus auch leer!« Sali sah sich um und bemerkte erst jetzt, daß alle Fahrhabe, die noch dagewesen, weggebracht war. »Du armes Vreeli!« sagte er, »haben sie dir schon alles ge-

light found her already completely dressed and bedecked, seated patiently on a stool, and awaiting her lover's coming. Nothing but the shoes was lacking. But Sali stopped right in the centre of the room and stood like one nailed to the spot, so beautiful and alluring Vreni looked in her holiday attire. Yet it was simple enough. She wore a plain skirt of blue linen, and above that a snow-white muslin kerchief. The dress fitted her slender body wonderfully, and the brown hair with its pretty curls had been well arranged, and the usually obstinate curls lay fine and dainty about head and neck. Since Vreni had scarcely left the house for so many weeks, her complexion had grown more delicate and almost transparent; her griefs also had contributed toward that result. But at that instant a rush of sudden joy and love poured over that pallor one scarlet layer after another, and on her bosom she wore a fine nosegay of roses, asters and rosemary. She was seated at the window, and was breathing still and quiet the fresh morning air perfumed by the sun. But when she saw Sali she at once stretched out her pretty arms, bare from the elbow. And with a voice melodious and tender she exclaimed: "How nice of you and how right to come already. But have you really brought me the shoes? Surely? Well, then I won't get up until I have them on." Sali without further ado produced the shoes and handed them to the eager maiden. Vreni instantly cast her old ones aside, slipped the new ones on, and indeed, they fitted excellently. Only now she rose quickly from her seat, dandled herself in the shoes, and walked up and down the room a few times, to be sure of their fit. She pulled up a bit her blue dress in order to admire them the better, and with extreme pleasure she examined the red loops in front, while Sali could not get his fill of the charming picture the girl presented-- the lovely excitement that beautified her the more, the willowy shape, the gently heaving bosom, the delicate oval of the face with its pretty features, animated with feminine enjoyment of the moment, eager with the mere joy of living, grateful to the giver of this last bit of finery that her childish soul had longed for. "You are looking at my posy," she said. "Have I not managed to pick a nice one? You must know these are the last ones I have managed to find in this wasted place. But there was, after all, still left a rosebud, over at the hedge in a sheltered spot a few of them and some other flowers, and the way they are now gathered up and arranged one would never think they came from a house decayed and fallen. But now it is high time for me to leave here, for not a single flower is there, and the whole house is bare." Then only Sali noticed that all the few movables still left were gone. "You poor little Vreni," he deplored, "have they already taken everything from you?" "Yes," she said with a ludic-

nommen?« – »Gestern«, erwiderte es, »haben sie's weggeholt, was sich von der Stelle bewegen ließ, und mir kaum mehr mein Bett gelassen. Ich hab's aber auch gleich verkauft und hab jetzt auch Geld, sieh!« Es holte einige neu glänzende Talerstücke aus der Tasche seines Kleides und zeigte sie ihm. »Damit«, fuhr es fort, »sagte der Waisenvogt, der auch hier war, solle ich mir einen Dienst suchen in einer Stadt, und ich solle mich heute gleich auf den Weg machen!« – »Da ist aber auch gar nichts mehr vorhanden«, sagte Sali, nachdem er in die Küche geguckt hatte, »ich sehe kein Hölzchen, kein Pfännchen, kein Messer! Hast du denn auch nicht zu Morgen gegessen?« – »Nichts!« sagte Vrenchen, »ich hätte mir etwas holen können, aber ich dachte, ich wolle lieber hungrig bleiben, damit ich recht viel essen könne mit dir zusammen, denn ich freue mich so sehr darauf, du glaubst nicht, wie ich mich freue!« – »Wenn ich dich nur anrühren dürfte«, sagte Sali, »so wollte ich dir zeigen, wie es mir ist, du schönes, schönes Ding!« – »Du hast recht, du würdest meinen ganzen Staat verderben, und wenn wir die Blumen ein bißchen schonen, so kommt es zugleich meinem armen Kopf zu gut, den du mir übel zuzurichten pflegst!« – »So komm, jetzt vollen wir ausrücken!« – »Noch müssen wir warten, bis das Bett abgeholt wird; denn nachher schließe ich das leere Haus zu und gehe nicht mehr hierher zurück! Mein Bündelchen gebe ich der Frau aufzuheben, die das Bett gekauft hat.« Sie setzten sich daher einander gegenüber und warteten; die Bäuerin kam bald, eine vierschrötige Frau mit lautem Mundwerk, und hatte einen Burschen bei sich, welcher die Bettstelle tragen sollte. Als diese Frau Vrenchens Liebhaber erblickte und das geputzte Mädchen selbst, sperrte sie Maul und Augen auf, stemmte die Arme unter und schrie: »Ei sieh da, Vreeli! Du treibst es ja schon gut! Hast einen Besucher und bist gerüstet wie eine Prinzeß?« – »Gelt aber!« sagte Vrenchen freundlich lachend, »wißt Ihr auch, wer das ist?« – »Ei, ich denke, das ist wohl der Sali Manz? Berg und Tal kommen nickt zusammen, sagt man, aber die Leute! Aber nimm dich doch in acht, Kind, und denk, wie es euren Eltern ergangen ist!« – »Ei, das hat sich jetzt gewendet, und alles ist gut geworden«, erwiderte Vrenchen lächelnd und freundlich, mitteilsam, ja beinahe herablassend, »seht, Sali ist mein Hochzeiter!« – »Dein Hochzeiter! was du sagst!« – »Ja, und er ist ein reicher Herr, er hat hundert-

rous attempt to be tragic, "yesterday, after you had left, they came and took everything of mine away that could be moved at all, and left me nothing but my bed. But that I have also sold at once, and here is the money for it--see!" And she hauled forth from the depths of an inside pocket a handful of bright new silver coins. "With this," she continued, "the orphan patron said to me, I was to find another service in town somewhere, and that I was to start out to-day." "Really," said Sali, after glancing about in the kitchen and the other rooms, "there is nothing at all left, no furniture, no sliver of fuel, no pot or kettle, no knife or fork. And have you had nothing to eat this morning?" "Nothing at all," answered Vreni, with a happy laugh. "I might have gone out and got myself something for breakfast, but I preferred to remain hungry, so I could eat a lot with you, for you cannot think how much I am going to enjoy my first meal with you--how awfully much I am going to eat with you present. I am almost dying with impatience for it." And she showed him a row of pearly teeth and a little red tongue to emphasize what she said. Sali stood like one enchanted. "If I only might touch you," murmured Sali, "I should soon show you how much I love you, you pretty, pretty thing." "No, no, you are right," quickly rejoined Vreni, "you would ruin all my finery, and if we also handle my flowers with some care my head and hair will profit from it, because ordinarily you disarrange all my curls." "Well, then," grumbled Sali, "let us go." "Not quite yet; we must wait till my bed has been fetched away. For as soon as that is gone I am going to lock up the house, and I am never to return to it. My little bundle I am going to give to the woman to keep, to the one who has bought my bed." So they sat down together and waited until the woman showed up, a peasant woman of squat shape and robust habit, one who loved to talk, who had a stout boy with her that was to carry the bedstead. When this woman got sight of Vreni's lover and of the girl herself in all her finery, she opened mouth and eyes to their fullest, squared herself and put her arms akimbo, shouting: "Why, look only, you're starting well, Vreni. With a lover and yourself dressed up like a princess." "Don't I?" laughed Vreni, in a friendly way. "And do you know who that is?" "I should think so," said the woman. "That is Sali Manz, or I am much mistaken. Mountains and valleys, they say, do not meet, but people most certainly do. But, child, let me warn you. Think how your parents have fared." "Ah, that is all changed now," smilingly replied Vreni. "Everything has been adjusted, and now things are smoothed out. See here, Sali is my promised husband." And the girl told this bit of news in a manner almost condescending, and bent toward the woman one of her bewitching glances. "Your promised husband, is

tausend Gulden in der Lotterie gewonnen! Denket einmal, Frau!« Diese tat einen Sprung, schlug ganz erschrocken die Hände zusammen und schrie: »Hund – hunderttausend Gulden!« – »Hunderttausend Gulden!« versicherte Vrenchen ernsthaft. »Herr du meines Lebens! Es ist aber nicht wahr, du lügst mich an, Kind!« – »Nun, glaubt, was Ihr wollt!« – »Aber wenn es wahr ist und du heiratest ihn, was wollt ihr denn machen mit dem Gelde? Willst du wirklich eine vornehme Frau werden?« – »Versteht sich, in drei Wochen halten wir die Hochzeit!« – »Geh mir weg, du bist eine häßliche Lügnerin!« – »Das schönste Haus hat er schon gekauft in Seldwyl, mit einem großen Garten und Weinberg; Ihr müßt mich auch besuchen, wenn wir eingerichtet sind, ich zähle darauf!« – »Allweg, du Teufelshexlein, was du bist!« – »Ihr werdet sehen, wie schön es da ist! einen herrlichen Kaffee werde ich machen und Euch mit feinem Eierbrot aufwarten, mit Butter und Honig!« – »O du Schelmenkind! zähl drauf, daß ich komme!« rief die Frau mit lüsternem Gesicht, und der Mund wässerte ihr. »Kommt Ihr aber um die Mittagszeit und seid ermüdet vom Markt, so soll Euch eine kräftige Fleischbrühe und ein Glas Wein immer parat stehen!« – »Das wird mir baß tun!« – »Und an etwas Zuckerwerk oder weißen Wecken für die lieben Kinder zu Hause soll es Euch auch nicht fehlen!« – »Es wird mir ganz schmachtend!« – »Ein artiges Halstüchelchen oder ein Restchen Seidenzeug oder ein hübsches altes Band für Eure Röcke oder ein Stück Zeug zu einer neuen Schürze wird gewiß auch zu finden sein, wenn wir meine Kisten und Kasten durchmustern in einer vertrauten Stunde!« Die Frau drehte sich auf den Hacken herum und schüttelte jauchzend ihre Röcke. »Und wenn Euer Mann ein vorteilhaftes Geschäft machen könnte mit einem Land- oder Viehhandel und er mangelt des Geldes, so wißt Ihr, wo Ihr anklopfen sollt. Mein lieber Sali wird froh sein, jederzeit ein Stück Bares sicher und erfreulich anzulegen! Ich selbst werde auch etwa einen Sparpfennig haben, einer vertrauten Freundin beizustehen!« Jetzt war der Frau nicht mehr zu helfen, sie sagte gerührt: »Ich habe immer gesagt, du seist ein braves und gutes und schönes Kind! Der Herr wolle es dir wohl ergehen lassen immer und ewiglich und es dir gesegnen, was du an mir tust!« – »Dagegen verlange ich aber auch, daß Ihr es gut mit mir meint!« – »Allweg kannst du das verlangen!« – »Und daß

he? Well, well, who would have thought it?" chattered the peasant woman, feeling highly honored at being the recipient of this interesting intelligence. "Yes, and he is now a wealthy gentleman," went on Vreni, "for he has just won a hundred thousand dollars in the lottery. Just think!" The woman gave a jump of surprise, threw up her hands, and shouted: "Hund--hundred thousand--Hund--" Vreni repeated it with a serious face. The woman grew still more excited. "Hundred thousand--well, well. But you are making fun of me, child. Hund--Is it possible?" "All right, as you choose," went on Vreni, still smiling. "But if it is true, and he gets all that money, what are you two going to do with it? Are you to become a stylish lady, or what?" "Of course, within three weeks our wedding takes place--such a wedding." "Oh, my goodness, is it possible? But no, you are telling me stories, I know." "Well, he has already bought the finest house in Seldwyla, with a fine vineyard and the biggest garden attached. And you must come and pay us a visit, after we're there--I count on it." "Why, what a witch you are," the woman went on between belief and unbelief. "You will see how nice it is there," continued Vreni unabashed. "A cup of coffee you'll get, such as you never drank before, and plenty of cake with it, of butter and honey." "Oh, you lucky duck!" shrieked the woman, "depend upon my coming, of course." And she made an eager face, as though she already saw spread before her all these dainties. "But if you should happen to come at noontime," went on Vreni in her fanciful tale, "and you would be tired from marketing, you shall have a bowl of strong broth and a bottle of our extra wine, the one with the blue seal." "That will certainly do me good," said the woman. "And there shall be no lack of some candy and white wheaten rolls, for your little ones at home." "I think I can taste it already," answered the woman, and she turned her eyes heavenwards. "Perhaps a pretty kerchief, or the remnant of a bolt of extra fine silk, or a costly ribbon or two for your skirts, or enough for an apron I suppose will be found, if we rummage in my drawers and trunks together sometime when we are talking things over." The woman turned completely on her heels and shook her skirts with a jubilant yodel. "And in case your husband could start in the cattle dealing way, and needed a bit of capital for it, you would know where to apply, would you not? My dear Sali will always be glad to invest some of his superfluous money in such a manner. And I myself might add a few pennies from my savings to help out a good and intimate gossip, you may be certain." By this time the last faint doubts had vanished. The woman wrung her uncouth hands, and said, with a great deal of sentiment: "That's what I have always been saying, you are a square and honest and beautiful girl! May the

Ihr jederzeit Eure Waren, sei es Obst, seien es Kartoffeln, sei es Gemüse, erst zu mir bringet und mir anbietet, ehe Ihr auf den Markt gehet, damit ich sicher sei, eine rechte Bäuerin an der Hand zu haben, auf die ich mich verlassen kann! Was irgendeiner gibt für die Ware, werde ich gewiß auch geben mit tausend Freuden, Ihr kennt mich ja! Ach, es ist nichts Schöneres, als wenn eine wohlhabende Stadtfrau, die so ratlos in ihren Mauern sitzt und doch so vieler Dinge benötigt ist, und eine rechtschaffene ehrliche Landfrau, erfahren in allem Wichtigen und Nützlichen, eine gute und dauerhafte Freundschaft zusammen haben! Es kommt einem zu gut in hundert Fällen, in Freud und Leid, bei Gevatterschaften und Hochzeiten, wenn die Kinder unterrichtet werden und konfirmiert, wenn sie in die Lehre kommen und wenn sie in die Fremde sollen! Bei Mißwachs und Überschwemmungen, bei Feuersbrünsten und Hagelschlag, wofür uns Gott behüte!« – »Wofür uns Gott behüte!« sagte die gute Frau schluchzend und trocknete mit ihrer Schürze die Augen; »welch ein verständiges und tiefsinniges Bräutlein bist du, ja, dir wird es gut gehen, da müßte keine Gerechtigkeit in der Welt sein! Schön, sauber, klug und weise bist du, arbeitsam und geschickt zu allen Dingen! Keine ist feiner und besser als du, in und außer dem Dorfe, und wer dich hat, der muß meinen, er sei im Himmelreich, oder er ist ein Schelm und hat es mit mir zu tun. Hör, Sali! daß du nur recht artlich bist mit meinem Vreeli, oder ich will dir den Meister zeigen, du Glückskind, das du bist, ein solches Röslein zu brechen!« – »So nehmt jetzt auch hier noch mein Bündel mit, wie Ihr mir versprochen habt, bis ich es abholen lassen werde! Vielleicht komme ich aber selbst in der Kutsche und hole es ab, wenn Ihr nichts dagegen habt! Ein Töpfchen Milch werdet Ihr mir nicht abschlagen alsdann, und etwa eine schöne Mandeltorte dazu werde ich schon selbst mitbringen!«– »Tausendskind! Gib her den Bündel!« Vrenchen lud ihr auf das zusammengebundene Bett, das sie schon auf dem Kopfe trug, einen langen Sack, in welchen es sein Plunder und Habseliges gestopft, so daß die arme Frau mit einem schwankenden Turme auf dem Haupte dastand. »Es wird mir doch fast zu schwer auf einmal«, sagte sie, »könnte ich nicht zweimal dran machen?« – »Nein nein! wir müssen jetzt augenblicklich gehen, denn wir haben einen weiten Weg, um vornehme Verwandte zu besuchen, die sich jetzt

Lord always be good to you and reward you for what you are going to do for me!" "But on my part, I must insist that you, too, treat me well." "Surely you have a right to expect that," said the woman. "And that you at all times offer me first all your produce, be it fruit or potatoes, or vegetables, and to do this before you take them to the public market, so that I may always be sure of having a real peasant woman on hand, one upon whom I may rely. Whatever anybody else is willing to pay you for your produce, I will also be willing to give. You know me. Why, there is nothing nicer than a wealthy city lady, one who sits within town walls and cannot know prices and conditions there, and yet needs so many things in her household, and an honest and well-posted woman from the country, experienced in all that concerns her, who are bound together by durable friendship and a community of interests. The city lady profits from it at all sorts of occasions, as for example at weddings and baptisms, at seasons of illness or crop failure, at holidays and famine time, or inundations, from which the Lord preserve us!" "From which the Lord preserve us!" repeated the woman solemnly, sobbing and wiping her wet face on her ample apron. "But what a sensible and well-informed little wife you'll make, to be sure! Without doubt you will live as happily as a mouse in the cheese, or there is no justice in this world. Handsome, clean, smart and wise, fit for and willing to tackle all work at any time. None is as good-looking and as fine as thou art, no, not in the whole village, and even some distance further away. And who has got you for wife can congratulate himself; he is bound to be in paradise, or he is a scoundrel, and he will have me to deal with. Listen, Sali, do not fail to be nice to Vreni, or you will hear a word from me, you lucky devil, to break such a rose without thorns as this one here!" "For to-day, my dear woman," concluded Vreni, "take this bundle along, as we agreed yesterday, and keep it till I send for it. But it may be that I myself come for it, in my own carriage, and get it, if you have no objection. A drink of milk you will not refuse me in that case, and a nice cake, such as perhaps an almond tart, I shall probably bring along myself." "You blessed child, give it here, your bundle," the peasant woman quavered, still completely under the influence of Vreni's eloquence. Vreni therefore deposited on top of the bedding which the woman had already tied up, a huge bag containing all the girl's belongings, so that the stout-limbed woman was bearing a perfect tower of shaking and trembling baggage on her head. "It is almost too much for me to carry at once," she complained. "Could I not come again and divide the load in halves?" she wanted to know. "No, no," answered Vreni, "we must leave here at once, for we have to visit a whole number

gezeigt haben, seit wir reich sind! Ihr wißt ja, wie es geht!« – »Weiß wohl! So behüt dich Gott, und denk an mich in deiner Herrlichkeit!«

Die Bäuerin zog ab mit ihrem Bündelturme, mit Mühe das Gleichgewicht behauptend, und hinter ihr drein ging ihr Knechtchen, das sich, in Vrenchens einst buntbemalte Bettstatt hineinstellte, den Kopf gegen den mit verblichenen Sternen bedeckten Himmel derselben stemmte und, ein zweiter Simson, die zwei vorderen zierlich geschnitzten Säulen faßte, welche diesen Himmel trugen. Als Vrenchen, an Sali gelehnt, dem Zuge nachschaute und den wandelnden Tempel zwischen den Gärten sah, sagte es: »Das gäbe noch ein artiges Gartenhäuschen oder eine Laube, wenn man's in einen Garten pflanzte, ein Tischchen und ein Bänklein dreinstellte und Winden drum herumsäete! Wolltest du mit darinsitzen, Sali?« – »Ja, Vreeli! besonders wenn die Winden aufgewachsen wären!« – »Was stehen wir noch?« sagte Vrenchen, »nichts hält uns mehr zurück!« – »So komm und schließ das Haus zu! Wem willst du denn den Schlüssel übergeben?« Vrenchen sah sich um. »Hier an die Helbart wollen wir ihn hängen; sie ist über hundert Jahr in diesem Hause gewesen, habe ich den Vater oft sagen hören, nun steht sie da als der letzte Wächter!« Sie hingen den rostigen Hausschlüssel an einen rostigen Schnörkel der alten Waffe, an welcher die Bohnen rankten, und gingen davon. Vrenchen wurde aber bleicher und verhüllte ein Weilchen die Augen, daß Sali es führen mußte, bis sie ein Dutzend Schritte entfernt waren. Es sah aber nicht zurück. »Wo gehen wir nun zuerst hin?« fragte es. »Wir wollen ordentlich über Land gehen«, erwiderte Sali, »wo es uns freut den ganzen Tag, uns nicht übereilen, und gegen Abend werden wir dann schon einen Tanzplatz finden!« – »Gut!« sagte Vrenchen, »den ganzen Tag werden wir beisammen sein und gehen, wo wir Lust haben. Jetzt ist mir aber elend, wir wollen gleich im andern Dorf einen Kaffee trinken!« – »Versteht sich!« sagte Sali, »mach nur, daß wir aus diesem Dorf wegkommen!«

Bald waren sie auch im freien Felde und gingen still nebeneinander durch die Fluren; es war ein schöner Sonntagmorgen im September, keine Wolke stand am Himmel, die Höhen und die Wälder waren mit einem zarten Duftgewebe be-

of wealthy relatives, and some of these are far away, the kind, you know, who have now recognized us since we have become rich ourselves. You know how the world wags." "Yes, indeed," said the woman, "I do know, and so God keep you, and think of me now and then in your glorious new state."

Then the peasant woman trundled off with her monstrously high tower of bundles, preserving its equilibrium by skillfully balancing the weight, and behind her trudged her boy, who stood up in the center of Vreni's gaily painted bedstead, his hard head braced against the baldaquin of it in which the eye beheld stars and suns in a firmament of multicolored muslin, and like another Samson, grasping with his red fists the two prettily carved slender pillars in front which supported the whole. As Vreni, leaning against Sali, watched the procession meandering down between the gardens of the nearer houses, and the aforesaid little temple forming part of her whilom bedstead, she remarked: "That would still make a fine little arbor or garden pavilion if placed in the midst of a sunny garden, with a small table and a bench inside, and quickly growing vines planted around. Eh, Sali, wouldn't you like to sit there with me in the shade?" "Why, yes, Vreni," said he, smiling, "especially if the vines once had grown to a size." "But why not go now?" continued she. "Nothing more is holding us here." "True," he assented. "Come, then, and lock up the house. But to whom will you deliver up the key?" Vreni looked around. "Here to this halberd let us hang it. For more than a century it has been in our house, as I've often heard father say. Now it stands at the door as the last sentinel." So they hung the rusty key of the housedoor to one of the rustier curves of the stout weapon, which was fairly overgrown with bean vines, and sallied forth. But after all Vreni grew faint, and Sali had to support her the first score steps, the parting with the place where her cradle had stood making her sad. But she did not look back. "Where are we bound for first?" she wanted to know. "Let us make a regular excursion across the country," said Sali, "and stop at a spot where we shall be comfortable all day long. And don't let us hurry. Towards evening we shall easily be able to find a dance going on." "Good," answered Vreni. "Thus we shall be together the whole day, and go where we like. But above all, I feel quite faint. Let us stop in the next village and get some coffee." "Of course," said the young man. "But let us first get away from here."

Soon they were in the open, fields of ripe, waving corn or else of fresh stubble around them, and went along, quietly and full of deep contentment, close to each other, breathing the pure air as though freed from prison walls. It was a delicious Sunday morning in September. There

kleidet, welches die Gegend geheimnisvoller und feierlicher machte, und von allen Seiten tönten die Kirchenglocken herüber, hier das harmonische tiefe Geläute einer reichen Ortschaft, dort die geschwätzigen zwei Bimmelglöcklein eines kleinen armen Dörfchens. Das liebende Paar vergaß, was am Ende dieses Tages werden sollte, und gab sich einzig der hoch aufatmenden wortlosen Freude hin, sauber gekleidet und frei, wie zwei Glückliche, die sich von Rechts wegen angehören, in den Sonntag hineinzuwandeln. Jeder in der Sonntagsstille verhallende Ton oder ferne Ruf klang ihnen erschütternd durch die Seele; denn die Liebe ist eine Glocke, welche das Entlegenste und Gleichgültigste widertönen läßt und in eine besondere Musik verwandelt. Obgleich sie hungrig waren, dünkte sie die halbe Stunde Weges bis zum nächsten Dorfe nur ein Katzensprung lang zu sein, und sie betraten zögernd das Wirtshaus am Eingang des Ortes. Sali bestellte ein gutes Frühstück, und während es bereitet wurde, sahen sie mäuschenstill der sicheren und freundlichen Wirtschaft in der großen reinlichen Gaststube zu. Der Wirt war zugleich ein Bäcker, das eben Gebackene durchduftete angenehm das ganze Haus, und Brot allerart wurde in gehäuften Körben herbeigetragen, da nach der Kirche die Leute hier ihr Weißbrot holten oder ihren Frühschoppen tranken. Die Wirtin, eine artige und saubere Frau, putzte gelassen und freundlich ihre Kinder heraus, und sowie eines entlassen war, kam es zutraulich zu Vrenchen gelaufen, zeigte ihm seine Herrlichkeiten und erzählte von allem, dessen es sich erfreute und rühmte. Wie nun der wohlduftende starke Kaffee kam, setzten sich die zwei Leutchen schüchtern an den Tisch, als ob sie da zu Gast gebeten wären. Sie ermunterten sich jedoch bald und flüsterten bescheiden, aber glückselig miteinander; ach, wie schmeckte dem aufblühenden Vrenchen der gute Kaffee, der fette Rahm, die frischen, noch warmen Brötchen, die schöne Butter und der Honig, der Eierkuchen und was alles noch für Leckerbissen da waren! Sie schmeckten ihm, weil es den Sali dazu ansah, und es aß so vergnügt, als ob es ein Jahr lang gefastet hätte. Dazu freute es sich über das feine Geschirr, über die silbernen Kaffeelöffelchen; denn die Wirtin schien sie für rechtliche junge Leutchen zu halten, die man anständig bedienen müsse, und setzte sich auch ab und zu plaudernd zu ihnen, und die beiden gaben ihr verständigen

was not a cloud to be seen in the sky of deep azure, and in the distance the hills and woods were enwrapped in a delicate haze, so that the whole landscape looked more solemn and mysterious. From everywhere the tolling of the church bells was heard, the harmonious deep tones of a big swinging bell belonging to a wealthy congregation, or the talkative two small bells of a poor village that made fast time to create any impression at all. The lovers forgot completely as to what was to become of them at the end of this rare day, forgot the disturbing uncertainties of their young lives, and gave themselves up completely to the intoxicating delights of the moment, sank their very souls in a calm joy that knew no words and no fears. Neatly clothed, free to come or go, like two happy ones who before God and men belong to each other by all rights, they went forth into the still Sunday country side. Each slight sound or call, reverberating and finally losing itself in the general silence, shook their hearts as though the strings of a harp had been touched by divine fingers. For Love is a musical instrument which makes resound the farthest and the most indifferent subjects and changes them into a music all its own. Though both were hungry and faint, the half hour's walk to the next village seemed to them but a step, and they entered slowly the little inn that stood at the entrance to the place. Sali ordered a substantial and appetizing breakfast, and while it was being prepared they observed, quiet as two mice, the interior of this homely place of entertainment, everything in it being scrupulously clean and orderly, from the walls and tables and napkins to the hearth and floor. The guest room itself was large and airy, and the window panes glittered in the furtive rays of the sun. The host of the inn was at the same time a baker, and his last baking, just out of the oven, spread a delicious odor through the whole house. Stacks of fresh loaves were carried past them in clean baskets, since after church service the members of the congregation were in the habit of getting here their white bread or to drink their noon shoppen. The hostess, a rather handsome and neat woman, dressed in their Sunday finery all her little brood of children, leisurely and pleasantly, and as she was done with one more of the little ones, the latter, proud and glad, would come running to Vreni, showing her all their finery, and innocently boasting and bragging of their belongings and of all else they held precious. When at last the fragrant coffee was brought and served for them, together with other good things, at a convenient table, the two young people sat down somewhat embarrassed, just as if they had been invited as honored guests to do so. But they got over this mood, and whispered to each other modestly but happily, feeling the joy of each other's presence. And oh, how Vreni enjoyed her break-

Bescheid, welches ihr gefiel. Es ward dem guten Vrenchen so wählig zu Mut, daß es nicht wußte, mochte es lieber wieder ins Freie, um allein mit seinem Schatz herumzuschweifen durch Auen und Wälder, oder mochte es lieber in der gastlichen Stube bleiben, um wenigstens auf Stunden sich an einem stattlichen Orte zu Hause zu träumen. Doch Sali erleichterte die Wahl, indem er ehrbar und geschäftig zum Aufbruch mahnte, als ob sie einen bestimmten und wichtigen Weg zu machen hätten. Die Wirtin und der Wirt begleiteten sie bis vor das Haus und entließen sie auf das wohlwollendste wegen ihres guten Benehmens, trotz der durchscheinenden Dürftigkeit, und das arme junge Blut verabschiedete sich mit den besten Manieren von der Welt und wandelte sittig und ehrbar von hinnen. Aber auch als sie schon wieder im Freien waren und einen stundenlangen Eichwald betraten, gingen sie noch in dieser Weise nebeneinander her, in angenehme Träume vertieft, als ob sie nicht aus zank- und elenderfüllten vernichteten Häusern herkämen, sondern guter Leute Kinder wären, welche in lieblicher Hoffnung wandelten. Vrenchen senkte das Köpfchen tiefsinnig gegen seine blumengeschmückte Brust und ging, die Hände sorglich an das Gewand gelegt, einher auf dem glatten feuchten Waldboden; Sali dagegen schritt schlank aufgerichtet, rasch und nachdenklich, die Augen auf die festen Eichenstämme geheftet, wie ein Bauer, der überlegt, welche Bäume er am vorteilhaftesten fällen soll. Endlich erwachten sie aus diesen vergeblichen Träumen, sahen sich an und entdeckten, daß sie immer noch in der Haltung gingen, in welcher sie das Gasthaus verlassen, erröteten und ließen traurig die Köpfe hängen. Aber Jugend hat keine Tugend; der Wald war grün, der Himmel blau und sie allein in der weiten Welt, und sie überließen sich alsbald wieder diesem Gefühle. Doch blieben sie nicht lange mehr allein, da die schöne Waldstraße sich belebte mit lustwandelnden Gruppen von jungen Leuten sowie mit einzelnen Paaren, welche schäkernd und singend die Zeit nach der Kirche verbrachten. Denn die Landleute haben so gut ihre ausgesuchten Promenaden und Lustwälder wie die Städter, nur mit dem Unterschied, daß dieselben keine Unterhaltung kosten und noch schöner sind; sie spazieren nicht nur mit einem besondern Sinn des Sonntags durch ihre blühenden und reifenden Felder, sondern sie machen sehr gewählte Gänge durch Gehölze und an

fast, the strong coffee, the cream, the fresh rolls still warm from the oven, the rich butter and the honey, the omelet, and all the other splendid things dished up for them. Delicious it all tasted, not only because she had been really hungry, but because she could look all the while at Sali, and she ate and ate, as if she had been fasting for a whole year. With that she also took pleasure in the pretty service, the fine cups and saucers and dishes, the dainty silver spoons, and the snowy linen. For the hostess seemed to have made up her mind about these two, and she evidently regarded them as young people of good family, who were to be waited upon in proper style, and several times she came and sat down by them, chatting most agreeably, and both Sali and Vreni answered her sensibly, whereat the woman became still more affable. And Vreni felt the wholesome influence of all this so strongly, and a sense of snug comfort coursed so pleasantly through her veins that she in her mind found it hard to choose between the delights of wandering about in the woods and fields, hand in hand with her lover, or remaining for some time longer here in this inn, in this haven of rest and creature comfort, honored and respected and dreaming herself into the illusion of owning such a nice home as this herself. But Sali himself rendered the choice easier, for in a perfectly proper and rather husbandlike manner he urged departure, just as though they had duties to fulfil elsewhere. Both host and hostess saw the young couple to the door, and bade them good-by in the most orthodox and well-meaning way, and Vreni, too, showed her manners and reciprocated their courtesy like one to the manner born, then following Sali in most decent and moral style. But even after reaching the open country once more and entering an oak forest a couple of miles long, both of them were still under the influence of the spell, and they went along in a dreamy mood, just as though they both did not come from homes destroyed and filled with hatred and discord, but from happy and harmonious homes, expecting from life the near fulfilment of all their rosy hopes. Vreni bent her pretty head down on her flower-bedecked bosom, deep in thought, and went along the smooth, damp woodpath with hands carefully held along her sides, while Sali stepped along elastic and upright, quick and thoughtful, his eyes fastened to the oak trunks ahead of him, like a well-to-do peasant reflecting on the problem which of these trees it would best pay to cut down and which to leave. But at last they awoke from these vain dreams, glanced at each other and discovered that they were still maintaining the attitude with which they had left the inn. Then they both blushed and their heads drooped in melancholy fashion. Youth, however, soon reasserted itself. The woods were green, the sky overhead faultlessly blue, and they

grünen Halden entlang, setzen sich hier auf eine anmutige fernsichtige Höhe, dort an einen Waldrand, lassen ihre Lieder ertönen und die schöne Wildnis ganz behaglich auf sich einwirken; und da sie dies offenbar nicht zu ihrer Pönitenz tun, sondern zu ihrem Vergnügen, so ist wohl anzunehmen, daß sie Sinn für die Natur haben, auch abgesehen von ihrer Nützlichkeit. Immer brechen sie was Grünes ab, junge Bursche wie alte Mütterchen, welche die alten Wege ihrer Jugend aufsuchen, und selbst steife Landmänner in den besten Geschäftsjahren, wenn sie über Land gehen, schneiden sich gern eine schlanke Gerte, sobald sie durch einen Wald gehen, und schälen die Blätter ab, von denen sie nur oben ein grünes Büschel stehenlassen. Solche Rute tragen sie wie ein Zepter vor sich hin; wenn sie in eine Amtsstube oder Kanzlei treten, so stellen sie die Gerte ehrerbietig in einen Winkel, vergessen aber auch nach, den ernstesten Verhandlungen nie, dieselbe säuberlich wieder mitzunehmen und unversehrt nach Hause zu tragen, wo es erst dem kleinsten Söhnchen gestattet ist, sie zugrunde zu richten. – Als Sali und Vrenchen die vielen Spaziergänger sahen, lachten sie ins Fäustchen und freuten sich, auch gepaart zu sein, schlüpften aber seitwärts auf engere Waldpfade, wo sie sich in tiefen Einsamkeiten verloren. Sie hielten sich auf, wo es sie freute, eilten vorwärts und ruhten wieder, und wie keine Wolke am reinen Himmel stand, trübte auch keine Sorge in diesen Stunden ihr Gemüt; sie vergaßen, woher sie kamen und wohin sie gingen, und benahmen sich so fein und ordentlich dabei, daß trotz aller frohen Erregung und Bewegung Vrenchens niedlicher einfacher Aufputz so frisch und unversehrt blieb, wie er am Morgen gewesen war. Sali betrug sich auf diesem Wege nicht wie ein beinahe zwanzigjähriger Landbursche oder der Sohn eines verkommenen Schenkwirtes, sondern wie wenn er einige Jahre jünger und sehr wohl erzogen wäre, und es war beinahe komisch, wie er nur immer sein feines lustiges Vrenchen ansah, voll Zärtlichkeit, Sorgfalt und Achtung. Denn die armen Leutchen mußten an diesem einen Tage, der ihnen vergönnt war, alle Manieren und Stimmungen der Liebe durchleben und sowohl die verlorenen Tage der zarteren Zeit nachholen als das leidenschaftliche Ende vorausnehmen mit der Hingabe ihres Lebens.

were alone by themselves in the world, and thus they soon drifted back into that train of thought. But they did not long remain by themselves, since this attractive forest road began to be alive with groups and couples out for a bracing walk in the cool shade, most of them returning from service in church, and nearly all of these were singing gay worldly tunes, trifling and joking with each other. For in these parts it so happens that the rustics have their customary walks and promenades as well as the city dwellers, to which they resort at leisure, only with this great difference that their pleasure grounds cost nothing to maintain and that these are finer in every way, since Nature alone has made them. Not alone do they stroll about on Sundays through fields and meadows and woods with a peculiar sense of freedom and recreation, taking stock of their ripening crops and the prospects of the harvest to come, but they also choose with unerring taste excursions along the edge of forest or meadow, hill or dale, sit down for a brief rest on the summit of a height, whence they enjoy a fine view, or sing in chorus at another suitable spot, and certainly obtain fully as much, if not more, pleasure out of all this as town folk do. And since they do all this, not as labor but diversion, one must conclude that these rustics, despite of what has often been claimed to the contrary, are lovers of nature, aside from the strictly utilitarian view of it. And always they break off something green and living, young and old, even weak and decrepit women, when they revisit the scenes of long ago, and the same spirit is seen in the habit that these country people have, including sedate men of business, of cutting for themselves a slender rod of hazel, or a snappy cane, whenever they walk through woods or forest, and these they will peel all but a small bunch of green leaves at the point. Such rods or twigs they will bear as though it were a sceptre, and when they enter an office or public place they will put them in a corner of the room, and never forget to get them again, even after the most serious and important matters have been discussed, and to take them along with them home. And it is then only the privilege of the youngest of their boys to seize it, break it, play with it, in fine, destroy it. When Sali and Vreni noticed these many couples out for a holiday stroll, they laughed to themselves, and rejoiced that they, too, were such a happy pair; they lost themselves on side paths that led away from every noise, and there they felt protected by the green solitude. They remained where they liked, went on or rested again for a spell, and in unison with the sky overhead which was cloudless, no carking care came to disturb their serenity. This state of perfect, unalloyed bliss lasted for them for hours, and they for the time forgot wholly whence they came and whither they were

So liefen sie sich wieder hungrig und waren erfreut, von der Höhe eines schattenreichen Berges ein glänzendes Dorf vor sich zu sehen, wo sie Mittag halten wollten. Sie stiegen rasch hinunter, betraten dann aber ebenso sittsam diesen Ort, wie sie den vorigen verlassen. Es war niemand um den Weg, der sie erkannt hätte; denn besonders Vrenchen war die letzten Jahre hindurch gar nicht unter die Leute und noch weniger in andere Dörfer gekommen. Deshalb stellten sie ein wohlgefälliges ehrsames Pärchen vor, das irgendeinen angelegentlichen Gang tut. Sie gingen ins erste Wirtshaus des Dorfes, wo Sali ein erkleckliches Mahl bestellte; ein eigener Tisch wurde ihnen sonntäglich gedeckt, und sie saßen wieder still und bescheiden daran und beguckten die schön getäfelten Wände von gebohntem Nußbaumholz, das ländliche, aber glänzende und wohlbestellte Buffet von gleichem Holze und die klaren weißen Fenstervorhänge. Die Wirtin trat zutulich herzu und setzte ein Geschirr voll frischer Blumen auf den Tisch. »Bis die Suppe kommt«, sagte sie, »könnt ihr, wenn es euch gefällig ist, einstweilen die Augen sättigen an dem Strauße. Allem Anschein nach, wenn es erlaubt ist zu fragen, seid ihr ein junges Brautpaar, das gewiß nach der Stadt geht, um sich morgen kopulieren zu lassen?« Vrenchen wurde rot und wagte nicht aufzusehen, Sali sagte auch nichts, und die Wirtin fuhr fort: »Nun, ihr seid freilich beide noch wohl jung, aber jung geheiratet lebt lang, sagt man zuweilen, und ihr seht wenigstens hübsch und brav aus und braucht euch nicht zu verbergen. Ordentliche Leute können etwas zuwege bringen, wenn sie so jung zusammenkommen

going, and behaved with such a degree of decorum that Vreni's little posy actually remained as fresh and intact as it had been early in the morning, and her plain Sunday dress showed neither crease nor stain. As to Sali, he behaved all this time not like a youthful rustic of less than twenty, nor like the son of a broken-down tavern keeper, but rather like a youth a couple of years younger and quite innocent, withal of the best education. It was almost comical to observe his conduct towards his merry Vreni, looking at her with a touching mixture of tenderness, respect and care. For these two lovers, so unsophisticated and so entirely without guile, somehow understood how to run in the course of this one day of perfect joy vouchsafed them through all the gamut of love, and to make up not alone for the earlier and more poetic stages of it but also to taste its bitter and ultimate end with its passionate sacrifice of life itself.

Thus they thoroughly tired themselves running about part of the day, and hunger had come a second time that day when, from the crest of a shady mountain, they at last perceived, far down at their feet, a village of some size lying there in the glow of the westering sun. Rapidly they made the descent, and entered the village just as decorously as they had done the other earlier in the day. Nobody was about that knew them even by sight, for Vreni particularly had scarcely at all mingled with people during the last few years, nor had she been off on visits to other villages. Therefore they presented entirely the appearance of a decent young couple out on an errand of importance. They went to the best inn of the place, and there Sali at once ordered a good and substantial meal. A table was specially reserved for them, and everything needful was there laid out and they sat down again demurely in the corner and eyed the trappings and furniture of the handsome room, with its wainscoted walls of polished walnut, the well-appointed sideboard of the same wood, and the filmy window curtains of white lace. The hostess stepped up to them in a sociable manner, and set a vase full of fresh flowers on the table. "Until the soup is ready," she said pleasantly, "you may like to feast your eyes on these flowers from our garden. From all appearance, if you don't mind my curiosity, you are a young couple on their way to town to get married tomorrow?" Vreni blushed furiously, and did not dare raise her head. Nor did Sali say anything in reply, and the hostess continued: "Well, of course, you are both still very young. But young love, long life, as the saying is, and at least you are both good-looking enough and need not hide yourselves from people. If you will but work and strive together like sensible folk, you may succeed in life before you know it, for youth is a good thing, and so are diligence and faith in one another. But that, of

und fleißig und treu sind. Aber das muß man freilich sein, denn die Zeit ist kurz und doch lang, und es kommen viele Tage, viele Tage! Je nun, schön genug sind sie und amüsant dazu, wenn man gut haushält damit! Nichts für ungut, aber es freut mich, euch anzusehen, so ein schmuckes Pärchen seid ihr!« Die Kellnerin brachte die Suppe, und da sie einen Teil dieser Worte noch gehört und lieber selbst geheiratet hätte, so sah sie Vrenchen mit scheelen Augen an, welches nach ihrer Meinung so gedeihliche Wege ging. In der Nebenstube ließ die unliebliche Person ihren Unmut frei und sagte zur Wirtin, welche dort zu schaffen hatte, so laut, daß man es hören konnte: »Das ist wieder ein rechtes Hudelvölkchen, das, wie es geht und steht, nach der Stadt läuft und sich kopulieren läßt, ohne einen Pfennig, ohne Freunde, ohne Aussteuer und ohne Aussicht als auf Armut und Bettelei! Wo soll das noch hinaus, wenn solche Dinger heiraten, die die Jüppe noch nicht allein anziehen und keine Suppe kochen können? Ach der hübsche junge Mensch kann mich nur dauern, der ist schön petschiert mit seiner jungen Gungeline!« – »Bscht! willst du wohl schweigen, du hässiges Ding!« sagte die Wirtin, »denen lasse ich nichts geschehen! Das sind gewiß zwei recht ordentliche Leutlein aus den Bergen, wo die Fabriken sind; dürftig sind sie gekleidet, aber sauber, und wenn sie sich nur gern haben und arbeitsam sind, so werden sie weiterkommen als du mit deinem bösen Maul! Du kannst freilich noch lang warten, bis dich einer abholt, wenn du nicht freundlicher bist, du Essighafen!«

So genoß Vrenchen alle Wonnen einer Braut, die zur Hochzeit reiset die wohlwollende Ansprache und Aufmunterung einer sehr vernünftigen Frau, den Neid einer heiratslustigen bösen Person, welche aus Arger den Geliebten lobte und bedauerte, und ein leckeres Mittagsmahl an der Seite eben dieses Geliebten. Es glühte im Gesicht wie eine rote Nelke, das Herz klopfte ihm, aber es aß und trank nichtsdestominder mit gutem Appetit und war mit der aufwartenden Kellnerin nur um so artiger, konnte aber nicht unterlassen, dabei den Sali zärtlich anzusehen und mit ihm zu lispeln, so daß es diesem auch ganz kraus im Gemüt wurde. Sie saßen indessen lang und gemächlich am Tische, wie wenn sie zögerten und sich scheuten, aus der holden Täuschung herauszugehen. Die Wirtin brachte zum Nachtisch süßes Backwerk, und Sali bestellte feinern und

course, is necessary, for there will come also days you will not like, many days, many days. But after all, life is pleasant enough, if one but understands how to make a proper use of it. And don't mind my chatter, you young people, but it does me good to look at you two, so handsome and young." Just then the waitress brought in the soup, and since she had overheard the concluding phrases, and would herself have liked to get married, she regarded Vreni with envious eyes, for she begrudged her what she assumed was so soon in store for this young girl. She retired precipitately into the adjoining room, and there she let her tongue go clacking. To the hostess who was busy there with some household task, she said, so loud as to be distinctly heard by the young people: "Yes, these are indeed the right kind of people to go to town and hurry up marrying, without a penny, without friends, without dowry, and with nothing in view but misery and beggary! What in the world is to become of such people if the girl is still so young that she does not even know how to put on her frock or jacket, nor how to cook a plate of soup! Oh, what fools! But I feel sorry for the young fellow, such a good-looking fellow he is, and then to get a little ignorant doll like that!" "Sh-sh-- will you keep your mouth shut, you evil-mouthed slut," broke in the indignant hostess. "Don't you dare say anything against them. I am pretty sure that is a deserving young couple, and I will not hear them wronged. Probably they are from the mountains where the factories are, and while they are not dressed richly they look neat and cleanly, and if only they are fond of each other and not afraid of work, they will get along better than you with your bitter tongue. And that I will tell you--you'll have to wait a long while before anybody will take you, unless you change considerably, you vinegary old thing!"

Thus it was that Vreni tasted all the delights of a bride on her wedding trip: the well-meaning conversation of an experienced and sensible woman, the jealousy of a wicked and man-crazy person, one who from anger at the bride praises and sympathizes with the lover, and an appetizing meal at the side of this same lover. She glowed in the face like a carnation, her heart beat like a trip hammer, but she ate and drank nevertheless with a perfectly normal appetite, and was all the more amiable with the waitress who served them, but could not help on such occasions looking tenderly at Sali, and whispering to him, so that he also began to feel rather amorous. However, they sat a long time over their meal, delaying its end, as though they were both unwilling to destroy the lovely deception. The hostess came and brought them for dessert all sorts of sweet cakes and other dainties, and Sali ordered rarer and more fiery wine, so that the choice liquor ran through Vreni's veins like a flame, albeit

stärkern Wein dazu, welcher Vrenchen feurig durch die Adern rollte, als es ein wenig davon trank; aber es nahm sich in acht, nippte bloß zuweilen und saß so züchtig und verschämt da wie eine wirkliche Braut. Halb spielte es aus Schalkheit diese Rolle und aus Lust, zu versuchen, wie es tue, halb war es ihm in der Tat so zu Mut, und vor Bangigkeit und heißer Liebe wollte ihm das Herz brechen, so daß es ihm zu eng ward innerhalb der vier Wände und es zu gehen begehrte. Es war, als ob sie sich scheuten, auf dem Wege wieder so abseits und allein zu sein; denn sie gingen unverabredet auf der Hauptstraße weiter, mitten durch die Leute, und sahen weder rechts noch links. Als sie aber aus dem Dorfe waren und auf das nächstgelegene zugingen, wo Kirchweih war, hing sich Vrenchen an Salis Arm und flüsterte mit zitternden Worten: »Sali! warum sollen wir uns nicht haben und glücklich sein?« – »Ich weiß auch nicht warum!« erwiderte er und heftete seine Augen an den milden Herbstsonnenschein, der auf den Auen webte, und er mußte sich bezwingen und das Gesicht ganz sonderbar verziehen. Sie standen still, um sich, zu küssen; aber es zeigten sich Leute, und sie unterließen es und zogen weiter. Das große Kirchdorf, in dem Kirchweih war, belebte sich schon von der Lust des Volkes; aus dem stattlichen Gasthofe tönte eine pomphafte Tanzmusik, da die jungen Dörfler bereits um Mittag den Tanz angehoben, und auf dem Platz vor dem Wirtshause war ein kleiner Markt aufgeschlagen, bestehend aus einigen Tischen mit Süßigkeiten und Backwerk und ein paar Buden mit Flitterstaat, um welche sich die Kinder und dasjenige Volk drängten, welches sich einstweilen mehr mit Zusehen begnügte. Sali und Vrenchen traten auch zu den Herrlichkeiten und ließen ihre Augen darüber fliegen; denn beide hatten zugleich die Hand in der Tasche, und jedes wünschte dem andern etwas zu schenken, da sie zum ersten und einzigen Male miteinander zu Markt waren; Sali kaufte ein großes Haus von Lebkuchen, das mit Zuckerguß freundlich geweißt war, mit einem grünen Dach, auf welchem weiße Tauben saßen und aus dessen Schornstein ein Amörchen guckte als Kaminfeger; an den offenen Fenstern umarmten sich pausbäckige Leutchen mit winzig kleinen roten Mündchen, die sich recht eigentlich küßten, da der flüchtige praktische Maler mit einem Kleckschen gleich zwei Mündchen gemahlt, die so ineinander verflossen. Schwarze

she was cautious and sipped it but sparingly and kept up the semblance of a chaste and prudent young bride. Half of this was natural cunning on her part; but as for the other half, she felt indeed as if the rôle were reality, and what with anxiety and what with ardent love for Sali she thought her little heart would burst, so that the walls seemed to her too narrow, and she begged him to go. And they went off. It was now as if they were afraid to turn aside from the main road and into side paths, where they would be by themselves, for they continued on the highway, right through the throng of pleasure seekers, not looking to right or left. But when they had left the village behind them and were on their way towards the next, where kermess was being celebrated, Vreni linked her arm in his and whispered: "Sali, why not belong altogether one to the other and be happy!" And Sali answered, fastening his dreamy eyes upon the sun-flooded valley below where the meadows showed like a purple carpet of wildflowers, "Ah, why not?" And they instantly stopped in the road, and wanted to kiss each other. But suddenly a group of passers-by broke out of the near woods, and then they felt shy and desisted. On they went towards the big village in which the bustle of kermess was already noticeable from afar. The lanes were crowded, and before the most considerable tavern of the place a multitude of noisy, shouting people were assembled. From inside the tavern the strains of a lively, gay tune were heard. For the young villagers had begun dancing shortly after the noon hour, and on an open square in front of the tavern a market had been established where all sorts of sweets were for sale, and in another couple of booths could be seen flimsy bits of finery, ornaments, silk kerchiefs and the like, and around these were to be seen children and some others who for the moment were content to be mere observers. Sali and Vreni also stepped up to these booths, and they let their eyes travel over all these things. For both had instantly put their hands in their pockets and each wanted to present the other with a little gift, since that was the first and only time they had been together at a fair. Sali, therefore, bought a big house of gingerbread, the walls of which were calsomined with a mixture of butter and melted sugar, and on the green roof of which were perching snow-white pigeons, while from the chimney a small cupid was peeping forth clad as a chimney sweep. At the open windows of this wonderful house plump-cheeked persons with diminutive red mouths were embracing each other most affectionately, the kissing process being represented by the gingerbread artist by a sort of double mouth, or twins, one melting into the other. Black points meant eyes, and on the pinky-red housedoor there could be read the following touching stanzas:

Pünktchen stellten muntere Äuglein vor. Auf der rosenroten Haustür aber waren diese Verse zu lesen:

> Tritt in mein Haus, o Liebste!
> Doch sei Dir unverhehlt:
> Drin wird allein nach Küssen
> Gerechnet und gezählt.
>
> Die Liebste sprach: »O Liebster,
> Mich schrecket nichts zurück!
> Hab alles wohl erwogen
> In Dir nur lebt mein Glück!
>
> Und wenn ich's recht bedenke,
> Kam ich deswegen auch!«
> Nun denn, spazier mit Segen
> Herein und üb den Brauch!

Ein Herr in einem blauen Frack und eine Dame mit einem sehr hohen Busen komplimentierten sich diesen Versen gemäß in das Haus hinein, links und rechts an die Mauer gemalt. Vrenchen schenkte Sali dagegen ein Herz, auf dessen einer Seite ein Zettelchen klebte mit den Worten:

> Ein süßer Mandelkern steckt in dem Herze hier,
> Doch süßer als der Mandelkern ist meine Lieb zu Dir!

Und auf der anderen Seite:

> Wenn Du dies Herz gegessen, vergiß dies Sprüchlein nicht:
> Viel eh'r als meine Liebe mein braunes Auge bricht!

Sie lasen eifrig die Sprüche, und nie ist etwas Gereimtes und Gedrucktes schöner befunden und tiefer empfunden worden als diese Pfefferkuchensprüche; sie hielten, was sie lasen, in besonderer Absicht auf sich gemacht, so gut schien es ihnen zu passen. »Ach«, seufzte Vrenchen, »du schenkst mir ein Haus! Ich habe dir auch eines und erst das wahre geschenkt; denn unser Herz ist jetzt unser Haus, darin wir wohnen, und wir tragen so unsere Wohnung mit uns, wie die Schnecken! Andere haben wir nicht!« – »Dann sind wir aber zwei Schnecken, von denen jede das Häuschen der andern trägt!« sagte Sali, und Vrenchen erwiderte: »Desto weniger dürfen wir

Enter my house, beloved,
Yet do not thou forget
That all the coin accepted
Is kisses sweet, you bet.

His sweetheart said: "Oh, dear one,
This threat does not deter!
My love for thee is greater
Than any kind of fare.

"And come to think it over,
'Twas kisses I did seek."
Well, then, step in, my lady,
And let thy lips now speak.

A gentleman in a blue frock coat and a lady with an expansive bosom thus complimented each other by these rhymes into the house; both were painted to right and left of the wall. Vreni on her part presented Sali with a gingerbread heart, on which on either side these verses were pasted:

A sweet, sweet almond pierces my heart, as you see,

But sweeter far than almonds is my love for thee.

When thou my heart hast eaten,

Oh, let me not disguise

That sooner than my love can break Will break my nutbrown eyes.

Both of them eagerly read these verses, and never had rhymes, never had any kind of poetry, been more deeply felt and appreciated than were these gingerbread stanzas. They could not help fancying that they had been specially written for them, for they fitted so marvelously their requirements. "Ah, you give me a house," sighed Vreni. "But I have first made thee a gift of one myself, and of the real one. For our hearts are now our sole dwellings, and within them we live, and we carry our houses about with us wherever we may go, just like the snail. Other abode we have none left now." "But then we are snails really, of which each carries the house of the other," replied Sali. "Then we must never leave each other, for fear that we lose the other's house," answered Vreni. They

voneinander gehen, damit jedes seiner Wohnung nah bleibt!« Doch wußten sie nicht, daß sie in ihren Reden ebensolche Witze machten, als auf den vielfach geformten Lebkuchen zu lesen waren, und fahren fort, diese säße einfache Liebesliteratur zu studieren, die da ausgebreitet lag und besonders auf vielfach verzierte kleine und große Herzen geklebt war. Alles dünkte sie schön und einzig zutreffend; als Vrenchen auf einem vergoldeten Herzen, das wie eine Lyra mit Saiten bespannt war, las: »Mein Herz ist wie ein Zitherspiel, rührt man es viel, so tönt es viel!« ward ihm so musikalisch zu Mut, daß es glaubte, sein eigenes Herz klingen zu hören. Ein Napoleonsbild war da, welches aber auch der Träger eines verliebten Spruches sein mußte, denn es stand darunter geschrieben: »Groß war der Held Napoleon, sein Schwert von Stahl, sein Herz von Ton; meine Liebe trägt ein Röslein frei, doch ist ihr Herz wie Stahl so treu!« – Während sie aber beiderseitig in das Lesen vertieft schienen, nahm jedes die Gelegenheit wahr, einen heimlichen Einkauf zu machen. Sali kaufte für Vrenchen ein vergoldetes Ringelchen mit einem grünen Glassteinchen, und Vrenchen einen Ring von schwarzem Gemshorn, auf welchem ein goldenes Vergißmeinnicht eingelegt war. Wahrscheinlich hatten sie den gleichen Gedanken, sich diese armen Zeichen bei der Trennung zu geben.

Während sie in diese Dinge sich versenkten, waren sie so vergessen, daß sie nicht bemerkten, wie nach und nach ein weiter Ring sich um sie gebildet hatte von Leuten, die sie aufmerksam und neugierig betrachteten. Denn da viele junge Bursche und Mädchen aus ihrem Dorfe hier waren, so waren sie erkannt worden, und alles stand jetzt in einiger Entfernung um sie herum und sah mit Verwunderung auf das wohlgeputzte Paar, welches in andächtiger Innigkeit die Welt um sich her zu vergessen schien. »Ei seht!« hieß es, »das ist ja wahrhaftig das Vrenchen Marti und der Sali aus der Stadt! Die haben sich ja säuberlich gefunden und verbunden! Und welche Zärtlichkeit und Freundschaft, seht doch, seht! Wo die wohl hinaus wollen?« Die Verwunderung dieser Zuschauer war ganz seltsam gemischt aus Mitleid mit dem Unglück, aus Verachtung der Verkommenheit und Schlechtigkeit der Eltern und aus Neid gegen das Glück und die Einigkeit des Paares, welches auf eine ganz ungewöhnliche und fast vornehme Weise verliebt und aufgeregt war und in dieser rückhaltlosen Hingebung und

did not notice that they themselves were perpetrating the same species of humor as was spread out on the printed pasters of the gingerbread literature. So they continued to study the latter with deep interest. The most pathetic sentiments, both agreed, were found on the heartshaped cakes, whereof there was a great choice, both plain and ornamental, small and large. All the verses they read seemed to them wonderfully apt and appropriate to the occasion. When Vreni read on a gilt heart which like a lyre bore strings: My heart is like a fiddlestring, Touch gently it and it will sing, she could not refrain from remarking: "How true that is! Why, I can hear my own heart making music!" An image of Napoleon in gingerbread was also there, and even this, instead of speaking in heroic measure, symbolized a love-smitten swain, for it declared in wretched rhyme: Terrific was Napoleon's might, His sword of steel, his heart was light; My love is sweet like any rose, Yet is she faithful, goodness knows. But while both seemed busy sounding all the depths of these appeals to the muses, they secretly made a purchase. Sali bought for Vreni a small gift ring, with a stone of green glass, and Vreni a ring fashioned out of chamois horn, in which a gold forget-me-not was cleverly inlaid. Probably both were moved with the same idea, that of a farewell gift.

However, while they thus were entirely engrossed with these things they had not remarked that a wide ring was forming gradually around them made up of people who watched them closely and curiously. For as quite a number of lads and lasses from their own village had come to the kermess, they had been recognized, and these all now stood at some little distance away from them, regarding with astonishment this neatly dressed couple that in their intense preoccupation had eyes for nothing else in the world. "Just look," the murmuring went round; "why, that is Vreni Marti and Sali from town. They surely have met and made up. And what tenderness, what friendship for one another! Only notice!" The amazement of these onlookers was strangely mingled of pity with the ill-fortune of the young couple, of disdain for the wickedness and poverty of their parents, and of envy for the happiness and deep affection of these two. For it struck these coarse materialistic rustics that the couple were fond of each other in a manner most unusual in their own circles, excited to an uncommon degree and so taken up with one another and indifferent to all else, as to make them almost appear to belong to a more aristocratic sphere, so that altogether they seemed singular

Selbstvergessenheit dem rohen Völkchen ebenso fremd erschien wie in seiner Verlassenheit und Armut. Als sie daher endlich aufwachten und um sich sahen, erschauten sie nichts als gaffende Gesichter von allen Seiten; niemand grüßte sie, und sie wußten nicht, sollten sie jemand grüßen, und diese Verfremdung und Unfreundlichkeit war von beiden Seiten mehr Verlegenheit als Absicht. Es wurde Vrenchen bang und heiß, es wurde bleich und rot, Sali nahm es aber bei der Hand und führte das arme Wesen hinweg, das ihm mit seinem Haus in der Hand willig folgte, obgleich die Trompeten im Wirtshause lustig schmetterten und Vrenchen so gern tanzen wollte. »Hier können wir nicht tanzen!« sagte Sali, als sie sich etwas entfernt hatten, »wir würden hier wenig Freude haben, wie es scheint!« – »Jedenfalls«, sagte Vrenchen traurig, »es wird auch am besten sein, wir lassen es ganz bleiben und ich sehe, wo ich ein Unterkommen finde!« – »Nein«, rief Sali, »du sollst einmal tanzen, ich habe dir darum Schuhe gebracht! Wir wollen gehen, wo das arme Volk sich lustig macht, zu dem wir jetzt auch gehören, da werden sie uns nicht verachten; im Paradiesgärtchen wird jedesmal auch getanzt, wenn hier Kirchweih ist, da es in die Kirchgemeinde gehört, und dorthin wollen wir gehen, dort kannst du zur Not auch übernachten.« Vrenchen schauerte zusammen bei dem Gedanken, nun zum ersten Mal an einem unbekannten Ort zu schlafen; doch folgte es willenlos seinem Führer, der jetzt alles war, was es in der Welt hatte. Das Paradiesgärtlein war ein schöngelegenes Wirtshaus an einer einsamen Berghalde, das weit über das Land wegsah, in welchem aber an solchen Vergnügungstagen nur das ärmere Volk, die Kinder der ganz kleinen Bauern und Tagelöhner und sogar mancherlei fahrendes Gesinde verkehrte. Vor hundert Jahren war es als ein kleines Landhaus von einem reichen Sonderling gebaut worden, nach welchem niemand mehr da wohnen mochte, und da der Platz sonst zu nichts zu gebrauchen war, so geriet der wunderliche Landsitz in Verfall und zuletzt in die Hände eines Wirtes, der da sein Wesen trieb. Der Name und die demselben entsprechende Bauart waren aber dem Hause geblieben. Es bestand nur aus einem Erdgeschoß, über welchem ein offener Estrich gebaut war, dessen Dach an den vier Ecken von Bildern aus Sandstein getragen wurde, so die vier Erzengel vorstellten und gänzlich verwittert waren. Auf dem Gesimse des Daches

and strange to these gross villagers. When therefore Sali and Vreni finally awoke from their dreams and threw a glance around, they saw nothing but staring faces. Nobody greeted them; and they themselves knew not whether to salute anyone of these former acquaintances, whose show of unfriendliness was, just the same, not so much design as astonishment. Vreni became afraid and blushed from sheer embarrassment, but Sali took her hand and led her away. And the poor girl followed him willingly, bearing in her hand the huge gingerbread cottage, although the trumpets and horns from inside the inn sounded so invitingly, and although she was most anxious and eager to dance. "We cannot dance here," said Sali, when they had been going some little distance aside, "for there would not be any amusement in it under the circumstances." "You are right," Vreni said sadly, "and I really think now we had better drop the whole idea and I will try and find a place for me to stay overnight." "No," Sali cried, "you must have a chance to dance for once. For that, too, I brought you the shoes. Let us go where the poor folks are having a good time, since we, too, belong to them. They will not look down on us. At every kermess here there is also dancing at the Paradise Garden, since it belongs to this parish, and we are going there, and you can, if it comes to the worst, also find a bed to sleep there." Vreni shuddered at the thought of having to sleep for the first time of her young life in a place where nobody knew her. But she followed without a murmur where Sali led her. Was he not everything in the world to her now? The so-called Paradise Garden was a house of entertainment situated in a beautiful spot, lying all by itself at the side of a mountain from which one had a view far over the whole country. But on holidays like this only the poorer classes, the children of small farmers and of day laborers, even vagrants, used to resort to it. A hundred years before a wealthy man of queer habits had built it as a summer villa for himself, and nobody had succeeded him as tenant, and since the house could not be used for anything else, the whole place after a while began to decay, and so finally it got into the hands of an innkeeper who managed it in his own peculiar way. The name alone and the style of architecture had remained. The house itself consisted of but one story, and on top of that an open loggia had been erected, the roof of which was borne on the four corners by statues of sandstone. These were meant for the four archangels and were wholly defaced. At the edge of the roof could be seen all about small angels carved of the same material and all of them playing some musical instrument, the angels themselves showing monstrous heads and big paunches, fiddling, touching the triangle, blowing the flute, striking the cymbal or the tambourine; these

saßen ringsherum kleine musizierende Engel mit dicken Köpfen und Bäuchen, den Triangel, die Geige, die Flöte, Zimbel und Tamburin spielend, ebenfalls aus Sandstein, und die Instrumente waren ursprünglich vergoldet gewesen. Die Decke inwendig sowie die Brustwehr des Estrichs und das übrige Gemäuer des Hauses waren mit verwaschenen Freskomalereien bedeckt, welche lustige Engelscharen sowie singende und tanzende Heilige darstellten. Aber alles war verwischt und undeutlich wie ein Traum und überdies reichlich mit Weinreben übersponnen, und blaue reifende Trauben hingen überall in dem Laube. Um das Haus herum standen verwilderte Kastanienbäume, und knorrige starke Rosenbüsche, auf eigene Hand fortlebend, wuchsen da und dort so wild herum wie anderswo die Holunderbäume. Der Estrich diente zum Tanzsaal; als Sali mit Vrenchen daherkam, sahen sie schon von weitem die Paare unter dem offenen Dache sich drehen, und rund um das Haus zechten und lärmten eine Menge lustiger Gäste. Vrenchen, welches andächtig und wehmütig sein Liebeshaus trug, glich einer heiligen Kirchenpatronin auf alten Bildern, welche das Modell eines Domes oder Klosters auf der Hand hält, so sie gestiftet; aber aus der frommen Stiftung, die ihm im Sinne lag, konnte nichts werden. Als es aber die wilde Musik hörte, welche vom Estrich ertönte, vergaß es sein Leid und verlangte endlich nichts, als mit Sali zu tanzen. Sie drängten sich durch die Gäste, die vor dem Hause saßen und in der Stube, verlumpte Leute aus Seldwyla, die eine billige Landpartie machten, armes Volk von allen Enden, und stiegen die Treppe hinauf, und sogleich drehten sie sich im Walzer herum, keinen Blick voneinander abwendend. Erst als der Walzer zu Ende, sahen sie sich um; Vrenchen hatte sein Haus zerdrückt und zerbrochen und wollte eben betrübt darüber werden, als es noch mehr erschrak über den schwarzen Geiger, in dessen Nähe sie standen. Er saß auf einer Bank, die auf einem Tische stand, und sah so schwarz aus wie gewöhnlich; nur hatte er heute einen grünen Tannenbusch auf sein Hütchen gesteckt, zu seinen Füßen hatte er eine Flasche Rotwein und ein Glas stehen, welche er nie umstieß, obgleich er fortwährend mit den Beinen strampelte, wenn er geigte, und so eine Art von Eiertanz damit vollbrachte. Neben ihm saß noch ein schöner, aber trauriger junger Mensch mit einem Waldhorn, und ein Buckliger stand an einer Baßgeige. Sali erschrak

instruments had originally been gilt. The ceiling inside and the low sidewalls, as well as all the rest of the house were still covered with rather dingy fresco paintings, and these represented dancing and singing saints. But all of it had suffered from the weather and the rain, and was now as indistinct and chaotic as a dream itself. And besides, all over the walls clambered grapevines, and at this time of year purplish ripening grapes peeped forth from between the foliage. All about the house itself there stood chestnut trees, and gnarled big rosebushes, growing wildly after a fashion of their own, just as lilac bushes would grow elsewhere. The loggia served as dance hall, and as Vreni and Sali came in sight of the building they could notice the dancing couples turning around and around under the open roof, and outside, under the trees, drinking, shouting and noisy men and women were disporting themselves. It was a merry throng. Vreni, who was carrying in her hand, demurely and almost piously, her wonderful gingerbread palace, resembled one of those ancient and sainted church patronesses sometimes seen in missals, with a model of the cathedral or other devout foundation displayed which would earn her the Church's benediction. But as soon as she heard the wild music that came down in a tumbling stream from the loggia, the poor thing forgot her grief. Suddenly all alive she demanded rapturously that Sali should dance with her. They pushed their way through all these people that were crowding the environs of the house and the lower floor, these being mostly ragged people from Seldwyla, with some who had been making a cheap excursion into the country, and all sorts of homeless vagrants. Then they ascended the stairs and at once after arriving on top they seized each other and were whirling away in a lively waltz. Not an eye did they give to their surroundings until the music came to a temporary halt. Then they stopped and turned around. Vreni had crushed her gingerbread house, and was just going to shed a few tears on that account when she noticed the black fiddler, and now felt a veritable terror. He was seated near them, upon a bench which itself stood upon a big table, and he looked just as black and tawny as ever. But to-day he wore a bunch of green holly and pine in his funny little hat, and at his feet there stood a big bottle of claret and a tumbler, and he did not in the least touch either of these with his feet, although he was forever kicking up his legs to keep the tune while fiddling. Next to him sat a handsome young man with a French horn, but the young man looked melancholy, and a hunchback there also was, standing next a bass viol. Sali also had a fright in seeing the black fiddler, but the latter greeted them both in the friendliest manner and called out to them: "You see I knew that some day I should play to your

auch, als er den Geiger erblickte; dieser grüßte sie aber auf das freundlichste und rief: »Ich habe doch gewußt, daß ich euch noch einmal aufspielen werde! So macht euch nur recht lustig, ihr Schätzchen, und tut mir Bescheid!« Er bot Sali das volle Glas, und Sali trank und tat ihm Bescheid. Als der Geiger sah, wie erschrocken Vrenchen war, suchte er ihm freundlich zuzureden und machte einige fast anmutige Scherze, die es zum Lachen brachten. Es ermunterte sich wieder, und nun waren sie froh, hier einen Bekannten zu haben und gewissermaßen unter dem besondern Schatze des Geigers zu stehen. Sie tanzten nun ohne Unterlaß, sich und die Welt vergessend in dem Drehen, Singen und Lärmen, welches in und außer dem Hause rumorte und vom Berge weit in die Gegend hinausschallte, welche sich allmählich in den silbernen Duft des Herbstabends hüllte. Sie tanzten, bis es dunkelte und der größere Teil der lustigen Gäste sich schwankend und johlend nach allen Seiten entfernte. Was noch zurückblieb, war das eigentliche Hudelvölkchen, welches nirgends zu Hause war und sich zum guten Tag auch noch eine gute Nacht machen wollte. Unter diesen waren einige, welche mit dem Geiger gut bekannt schienen und fremdartig aussahen in ihrer zusammengewürfelten Tracht. Besonders ein junger Bursche fiel auf, der eine grüne Manchesterjacke trug und einen zerknitterten Strohhut, um den er einen Kranz von Ebereschen oder Vogelbeerbüscheln gebunden hatte. Dieser führte eine wilde Person mit sich, die einen Rock von kirschrotem weißgetüpfeltem Kattun trug und sich einen Reifen von Rebenschossen um den Kopf gebunden, so daß an jeder Schläfe eine blaue Traube hing. Dies Paar war das ausgelassenste von allen, tanzte und sang unermüdlich und war in allen Ecken zugleich. Dann war noch ein schlankes hübsches Mädchen da, welches ein schwarzseidenes abgeschossenes Kleid trug und ein weißes Tuch um den Kopf, daß der Zipfel über den Rücken fiel. Das Tuch zeigte rote, eingewobene Streifen und war eine gute leinene Handzwehle oder Serviette. Darunter leuchteten aber ein Paar veilchenblaue Augen hervor. Um den Hals und auf der Brust hing eine sechsfache Kette von Vogelbeeren auf einen Faden gezogen und ersetzte die schönste Korallenschnur. Diese Gestalt tanzte fortwährend allein mit sich selbst und verweigerte hartnäckig, mit einem der Gesellen zu tanzen. Nichtsdestominder bewegte sie sich anmutig und leicht her-

dancing, just as I said when I last met you. And now, you darlings, I trust you'll have a good time, and take a drink with me." He offered the full glass to Sali, who accepted it, emptied it and thanked the fiddler. And when he saw that Vreni was badly scared at seeing him, he did his best to reassure her, and jested with her in a rather nice way, until he had made her laugh. Thereupon Vreni recovered her courage, and both of them felt rather glad that they had an acquaintance there and were in a certain sense standing under the special protection of the black fellow. Then they danced steadily, forgetting themselves and the whole world in the constant twirling, singing, shouting and general noise, a noise which rolled down the hill and over the whole landscape which gradually began to be shrouded in a silvery autumn haze. They danced until twilight, when most of the merry guests disappeared, unsteady on their feet and shouting at the top of their voices. Those still remaining were the vagrants and stragglers, houseless and strongly inclined to turn night into day. Amongst these there were some who seemed on very friendly terms with the black fiddler and who for the most part looked outlandish because of oddities of costume. There was, for instance, a young man in a green corduroy jacket and a tattered straw hat, who wore around the crown of the latter a wreath of wild scarlet berries. He again had with him a savage sort of female who wore a skirt of cherry-red chintz and had a hoop made of young grapevine tied around her temples, so that at each side of her face hung a bunch of grapes. This couple was the jolliest of all, to be met with everywhere, and was dancing and singing without a stop. Then there was a slender, graceful girl there, wearing a thin silk dress and a white cloth on her head, the ends of which fell on her shoulders. The cloth had evidently once been a napkin or towel. But below this doubtful cloth there glowed a pair of magnificent eyes of deep violet hue. Around her neck this extravagant person wore a sixfold chain of the same autumnal berries, and this ornament suited her complexion marvelously well. This strange woman was dancing perpetually with none but herself, whirling almost unintermittently, with great grace and a very light step, refusing every partner that offered himself. Every time she passed in her dancing the sad hornblower she smiled, and the musician turned away his head. Some other gay women or girls there were, together with their escorts, all of them poorly or fantastically clad, but with all that they assuredly enjoyed themselves greatly, and there seemed to be perfect accord among them all. When it had turned completely dark the host refused to furnish light for illumination, since the wind would blow the candles out anyway, and besides the full-moon would be out in a short spell, and for the

um und lächelte jedesmal, wenn sie sich an dem traurigen Waldhornbläser vorüberdrehte, wozu dieser immer den Kopf abwandte. Noch einige andere vergnügte Frauensleute waren da mit ihren Beschützern, alle von dürftigem Aussehen, aber sie waren um so lustiger und in bester Eintracht untereinander. Als es gänzlich dunkel war, wollte der Wirt keine Lichter anzünden, da er behauptete, der Wind lösche sie aus, auch ginge der Vollmond sogleich auf und für das, was ihm diese Herrschaften einbrächten, sei das Mondlicht gut genug. Diese Eröffnung wurde mit großem Wohlgefallen aufgenommen; die ganze Gesellschaft stellte sich an die Brüstung des luftigen Saales und sah dem Aufgange des Gestirnes entgegen, dessen Röte schon am Horizonte stand; und sobald der Mond aufging und sein Licht quer durch den Estrich des Paradiesgärtels warf, tanzten sie im Mondschein weiter, und zwar so still, artig und seelenvergnügt, als ob sie im Glanze von hundert Wachskerzen tanzten. Das seltsame Licht machte alle vertrauter, und so konnten Sali und Vrenchen nicht umhin, sich unter die gemeinsame Lustbarkeit zu mischen und auch mit andern zu tanzen. Aber jedesmal, wenn sie ein Weilchen getrennt gewesen, flogen sie zusammen und feierten ein Wiedersehen, als ob sie sich jahrelang gesucht und endlich gefunden. Sali machte ein trauriges und unmutiges Gesicht, wenn er mit einer anderen tanzte, und drehte fortwährend das Gesicht nach Vrenchen hin, welches ihn nicht ansah, wenn es vorüberschwebte, glühte wie eine Purpurrose und überglücklich schien, mit wem es auch tanzte. »Bist du eifersüchtig, Sali?« fragte es ihn, als die Musikanten müde waren und aufhörten. »Gott bewahre!« sagte er, »ich wüßte nicht, wie ich es anfangen sollte!« – »Warum bist du denn so bös, wenn ich mit andern tanze?« – »Ich bin nicht darüber bös, sondern weil ich mit andern tanzen muß! Ich kann kein anderes Mädchen ausstehen, es ist mir, als wenn ich ein Stück Holz im Arm habe, wenn du es nicht bist! Und du? wie geht es dir?« – »Oh, ich bin immer wie im Himmel, wenn ich nur tanze und weiß, daß du zugegen bist! Aber ich glaube, ich würde sogleich tot umfallen, wenn du weggingest und mich dalißest!« Sie waren hinabgegangen und standen vor dem Hause; Vrenchen umschloß ihn mit beiden Armen, schmiegte seinen schlanken zitternden Leib an ihn, drückte seine glühende Wange, die von heißen Tränen feucht war, an sein Gesicht und

present company, he claimed, the moonlight was ample. This declaration, instead of being opposed, caused general satisfaction among this mongrel crowd; they all stood up at the open sides of the dance hall and watched the moon rise in her full splendor, and when the new golden light flooded the wide hall, dancing was resumed with great earnestness. And so quiet, good-natured and well-mannered was it done as if they were turning under the light of a hundred wax candles. This singular light, too, made them all more intimately acquainted with each other, as though they had known them for years, and thus it was that Sali and Vreni could not very well avoid mingling with the rest and dancing with other partners. But whenever they had been separated for just a short while they flew and rejoined the other without delay, and felt delighted thereat. Sali made a sad face at this, and when dancing with another person would turn toward Vreni. But she would not notice that, but would glide along like a fairy, her features transfigured with pleasure, and her whole soul enraptured with the swaying motions of the dance, no matter who her partner. "Are you jealous, Sali?" she asked smilingly, when the musicians took a longer rest. "Not the least," he replied. "Then why are you so angry when I'm dancing with somebody else?" she wanted to know. "I am not angry because of that," he said, "but only because I am forced to dance with another person but you. I cannot feel pleasant towards another girl. In fact, I feel just as though I had a block of wood in my arms if it is anybody but you. And you? How do you feel about that?" "Oh, I feel as though I were in heaven so long as I merely can dance and know that you are present," replied Vreni. "But I believe I should at once fall down dead if you went and left me here by myself." They had gone down from the dance hall and were now standing in the grounds before the house. Vreni put both her arms around his neck, pressed her slender trembling body against him, and put her burning cheek, wet from hot tears, to his, sobbing out: "We cannot marry, and yet I cannot leave you, not for a moment, not for a minute." Sali embraced the girl, pressed her ardently against his heart, and covered her with kisses. His confused thoughts were struggling for some way out of the labyrinth that encompassed them both, but he saw none. Even if the blot of his family misery and his neglected education were not weighing against him, his extreme youth and his ardent passion would have prevented a long period of patience and self-denial, and then there would still have been his misfortune in having injured Vreni's father for life. The consciousness that happiness for himself and her was, after all, to be found only in a union honest, blameless and approved by the whole world, was just as much alive in

sagte schluchzend: »Wir können nicht zusammen sein, und doch kann ich nicht von dir lassen, nicht einen Augenblick mehr, nicht eine Minute!« Sali umarmte und drückte das Mädchen heftig an sich und bedeckte es mit Küssen. Seine verwirrten Gedanken rangen nach einem Ausweg, aber er sah keinen. Wenn auch das Elend und die Hoffnungslosigkeit seiner Herkunft zu überwinden gewesen wären, so war seine Jugend und unerfahrene Leidenschaft nicht beschaffen, sich eine lange Zeit der Prüfung und Entsagung vorzunehmen und zu überstehen, und dann wäre erst noch Vrenchens Vater dagewesen, welchen er zeitlebens elend gemacht. Das Gefühl, in der bürgerlichen Welt nur in einer ganz ehrlichen und gewissenfreien Ehe glücklich sein zu können, war in ihm ebenso lebendig wie in Vrenchen, und in beiden verlassenen Wesen war es die letzte Flamme der Ehre, die in früheren Zeiten in ihren Häusern geglüht hatte und welche die sich sicher fühlenden Väter durch einen unscheinbaren Mißgriff ausgeblasen und zerstört hatten, als sie, eben diese Ehre zu äufnen wähnend durch Vermehrung ihres Eigentums, so gedankenlos sich das Gut eines Verschollenen aneigneten, ganz gefahrlos, wie sie meinten. Das geschieht nun freilich alle Tage; aber zuweilen stellt das Schicksal ein Exempel auf und läßt zwei solche Äufner ihrer Hausehre und ihres Gutes zusammentreffen, die sich dann unfehlbar aufreiben und auffressen wie zwei wilde Tiere. Denn die Mehrer des Reiches verrechnen sich nicht nur auf den Thronen, sondern zuweilen auch in den niedersten Hütten und langen ganz am entgegengesetzten Ende an, als wohin sie zu kommen trachteten, und der Schild der Ehre ist im Umsehen eine Tafel der Schande. Sali und Vrenchen hatten aber noch die Ehre ihres Hauses gesehen in zarten Kinderjahren und erinnerten sich wie wohlgepflegte Kinderchen sie gewesen und daß ihre Väter ausgesehen wie andere Männer, geachtet und sicher. Dann waren sie auf lange getrennt worden, und als sie sich wiederfanden, sahen sie in sich zugleich das verschwundene Glück des Hauses, und beider Neigung klammerte sich nur um so heftiger ineinander. Sie mochten so gern fröhlich und glücklich sein, aber nur auf einem guten Grund und Boden, und dieser schien ihnen unerreichbar, während ihr wallendes Blut am liebsten gleich zusammengeströmt wäre. »Nun ist es Nacht«, rief Vrenchen, »und wir sollen uns trennen!« – »Ich soll nach Hause gehen und dich

him as in Vreni. In her case as in his, two beings ostracized by all, these reflections were like the last flaring up of their lost family honor, an honor that had been blazing for centuries in their respectable houses like a living flame, and which their fathers had involuntarily extinguished and destroyed by a misdeed which at the time had been committed more in thoughtlessness than with malice aforethought. For when they, in the attempt to enlarge their holdings by a piece of dishonesty that seemed at the time wholly without risk and not likely to entail serious consequences, had been guilty of a wrong to a person that had been universally given up as lost, they had done something which many of their otherwise correct neighbors would, under the same circumstances, likewise have done. Such wrongs as that are indeed perpetrated every day in the year, on a large or a small scale. But once in a while Fate furnishes an example of how two such transgressors against the honor of their houses and against the property of another may oppose each other, and then these will unfailingly fight to the death and devour one the other like two savage beasts. For those who furtively or forcibly increase their estate may commit such fateful blunders not only when they are seated on thrones and then apply a high-sounding name to their lust and their misdeed, but the same in substance is often done as well in the humblest hut, and both categories of sinners frequently accomplish the very reverse of what they aimed at, and their shield of honor then becomes overnight a tablet of shame. But Sali and Vreni had both of them, when still children, seen and cherished the honor of their families, and well remembered how well they themselves were taken care of and how respected and highly considered their fathers had been in those days. Later they had been separated for long years, and when they met again they saw in each other also the lost honor and luck of their houses, and that instinctive feeling had helped to make them cling to each other all the more tenaciously. They longed indeed, both of them, for happiness and joy, but only if it might be done legitimately and in the sight of all; yet at the same time their ardent affection for each other could not be suppressed and their senses, their bounding blood, called loudly for the consummation of their desires. "Now it is night," said Vreni in a low tone of voice, "and we will have to part." "What, I am to go home now and leave you alone?" retorted Sali. "No, that can never be." "But what then?" said Vreni, plaintively. "Tomorrow morning by daylight things will look no better."

allein lassen?« rief Sali, »nein, das kann ich nicht!« – »Dann wird es Tag werden und nicht besser um uns stehen!«

»Ich will euch einen Rat geben, ihr närrischen Dinger!« tönte eine schrille Stimme hinter ihnen, und der Geiger trat vor sie hin. »Da steht ihr«, sagte er, »wißt nicht wo hinaus und hättet euch gern. Ich rate euch, nehmt euch, wie ihr seid, und säumet nicht. Kommt mit mir und meinen guten Freunden in die Berge, da brauchet ihr keinen Pfarrer, kein Geld, keine Schriften, keine Ehre, kein Bett, nichts als euern guten Willen! Es ist gar nicht so übel bei uns, gesunde Luft und genug zu essen, wenn man tätig ist; die grünen Wälder sind unser Haus, wo wir uns liebhaben, wie es uns gefällt, und im Winter machen wir uns die wärmsten Schlupfwinkel oder kriegen den Bauern ins warme Heu. Also kurz entschlossen, haltet gleich hier Hochzeit und kommt mit uns, dann seid ihr aller Sorgen los und habt euch für immer und ewiglich, solange es euch gefällt wenigstens; denn alt werdet ihr bei unserm freien Leben, das könnt ihr glauben! Denkt nicht etwa, daß ich euch nachtragen will, was eure Alten an mir getan! Nein! es macht mir zwar Vergnügen, euch da angekommen zu sehen, wo ihr seid; allein damit bin ich zufrieden und werde euch behilflich und dienstfertig sein, wenn ihr mir folgt.« Er sagte das wirklich in einem aufrichtigen und gemütlichen Tone. »Nun, besinnt euch ein bißchen, aber folget mir, wenn ich euch gut zum Rat bin! Laßt fahren die Welt und nehmet euch und fraget niemandem was nach! Denkt an das lustige Hochzeitbett im tiefen Wald oder auf einem Heustock, wenn es euch zu kalt ist!« Damit ging er ins Haus. Vrenchen zitterte in Salis Armen, und dieser sagte: »Was meinst du dazu? Mich dünkt, es wäre nicht übel, die ganze Welt in den Wind zu schlagen und uns dafür zu lieben ohne Hindernis und Schranken!« Er sagte es aber mehr als einen verzweifelten Scherz denn im Ernst. Vrenchen aber erwiderte ganz treuherzig und küßte ihn. »Nein, dahin möchte ich nicht gehen, denn da geht es auch nicht nach meinem Sinne zu. Der junge Mensch mit dem Waldhorn und das Mädchen in dem seidenen Rock gehören auch so zueinander und sollen sehr verliebt gewesen sein. Nun sei letzte Woche die Person ihm zum ersten Mal untreu geworden, was ihm nicht in den Kopf wolle, und deshalb sei er so traurig und schmolle mit ihr und mit den andern, die

"Let me give you a piece of advice," a shrill voice suddenly was heard behind them. It was the black fiddler, who now came up to them. "You foolish young things! There you are now, and you know not what to do with yourselves, although you are fond of each other. Yet nothing easier than that. I advise you to delay no more. Let one take the other, just as you are. Come along with me and my good friends here, right into the mountains, for there you need no priest, no money, no documents, no honor, no dowry, no bed and no wedding--nothing but your mutual good will. Don't get frightened. Things are not at all so bad with us. Pure air and enough to eat, provided one is not afraid to work. The green woods are our home, and there we love and keep house just as we wish. During the winter we lie snug in some warm, cosy den of our own contriving, or else we creep into the warm hay of the peasants. Therefore, lose no time. Keep your wedding right now and here, and then come along with us, and you are rid of all your cares, and may belong to each other forever and aye, or at least as long as you want to. For have no fear--you'll grow old with us; our style of life procures good strong health, you may well believe me. And don't think, you silly young folk, that I am bearing you a grudge because of what your fathers have done to me. No indeed. Of course, it gives me pleasure to see you arrived there where you now are. But with that I rest content, and I promise you to help and aid you in all sorts of ways if you will only be guided by me." He said all this in a sincere and well-meaning tone. "Well, think it over, if you wish, for a spell," he encouraged them still further, "but follow my counsel if you are wise. Let the world go, and belong to each other and ask nobody's consent. Think of the gay bridal bed in the deep forest glade, and of the comfortable hay barn in winter." And saying which he disappeared again in the house. But Vreni was trembling like aspen in Sali's arms, and he asked her: "What do you think of all that? To me it seems indeed it would be best to let the whole world go hang, and to love each other without hindrance and fear." But Sali said this more jokingly than in earnest. Vreni, on the other hand, took it all seriously, kissed him and replied: "No, I should not like that. These people do not act according to my notions. That young man with the French horn, for instance, and the girl in the silk skirt also belong together in that way, and are said to have been very much in love. But last week, it seems, she has been, for the first time, unfaithful to her lover, and he grieves greatly on that account, and he is angry at her and at the others, but they merely ridicule him.

ihn auslachen. Sie aber tut eine mutwillige Buße, indem sie allein tanzt und mit niemandem spricht, und lacht ihn auch nur aus damit. Dem armen Musikanten sieht man es jedoch an, daß er sich noch heute mit ihr versöhnen wird. Wo es aber so hergeht, möchte ich nicht sein, denn nie möcht ich dir untreu werden, wenn ich auch sonst noch alles ertragen würde, um dich zu besitzen!« Indessen aber fieberte das arme Vrenchen immer heftiger an Salis Brust; denn schon seit dem Mittag, wo jene Wirtin es für eine Braut gehalten und es eine solche ohne Widerrede vorgestellt, lohte ihm das Brautwesen im Blute, und je hoffnungsloser es war, um so wilder und unbezwinglicher. Dem Sali erging es ebenso schlimm, da die Reden des Geigers, sowenig er ihnen folgen mochte, dennoch seinen Kopf verwirrten, und er sagte mit ratlos stockender Stimme: »Komm herein, wir müssen wenigstens noch was essen und trinken.« Sie gingen in die Gaststube, wo niemand mehr war als die kleine Gesellschaft der Heimatlosen, welche bereits um einen Tisch saß und eine spärliche Mahlzeit hielt. »Da kommt unser Hochzeitpaar!« rief der Geiger, »jetzt seid lustig und fröhlich und laßt euch zusammengeben!« Sie wurden an den Tisch genötigt und flüchteten sich vor sich selbst an denselben hin; sie waren froh, nur für den Augenblick unter Leuten zu sein. Sali bestellte Wein und reichlichere Speisen, und es begann eine große Fröhlichkeit. Der Schmollende hatte sich mit der Untreuen versöhnt, und das Paar liebkoste sich in begieriger Seligkeit; das andere wilde Paar sang und trank und ließ es ebenfalls nicht an Liebesbezeugungen fehlen, und der Geiger nebst dem buckligen Baßgeiger lärmten ins Blaue hinein. Sali und Vrenchen waren still und hielten sich umschlungen; auf einmal gebot der Geiger Stille und führte eine spaßhafte Zeremonie auf, welche eine Trauung vorstellen sollte. Sie mußten sich die Hände geben, und die Gesellschaft stand auf und trat der Reihe nach zu ihnen, um sie zu beglückwünschen und in ihrer Verbrüderung willkommen zu heißen. Sie ließen es geschehen, ohne ein Wort zu sagen, und betrachteten es als einen Spaß, während es sie doch kalt und heiß durchschauerte.

Die kleine Versammlung wurde jetzt immer lauter und aufgeregter, angefeuert durch den stärkern Wein, bis plötzlich der Geiger zum

And she is imposing a kind of self-inflicted and ludicrous penance on herself by dancing all alone, without any partner, and without speaking to anyone, but that, too, is only making a fool of him. However, one may see that the poor musician is going to make up with her this very night. But I must say, I should not like to be with a company where such doings are common, for I never could be unfaithful to you, although I would not mind undergoing all else for the sake of possessing you." For all that, poor Vreni, being held in Sali's arms, became more and more feverish, for ever since noon when that hostess at the inn had mistaken her for a bride, and she herself had not contradicted, this alluring prospect had been burning in her veins, and the less hopeful things seemed to turn for a realization of this idea, the more relentlessly her pulses were hammering with expectation and desire. And Sali was experiencing similar hallucinations, since the fiddler's enticing remarks, while he meant not to listen to them, had also been fuel to his passion. So he said in embarrassment to Vreni: "Let us go inside for a spell. At least we must eat and drink something." They were greeted in entering the guest room where nobody had remained but the fiddler's friends, the vagrants, which latter were seated about a poor meal at table, by a merry chorus: "There comes our bridal pair!" "Yes," added the fiddler, "now be friendly and comfortable, and we will see you married." Urged to join the company the two young lovers did so rather shamefacedly. But after a moment they began to brighten, and were glad to be at least rid for the moment of the darker problem that was yet to be solved. Sali ordered wine and some choicer dishes, and soon general merriment spread among them all. The heretofore implacable lover had become reconciled to his unfaithful one, and the couple now fondled and caressed each other in reestablished ecstasy, while the giddy other pair ceaselessly yodled, sang and guzzled, but they also did not forget to give plain evidences of their amatory disposition. The fiddler and the hunchback accompanied all this with a great deal of cheerful noise. Sali and Vreni kept very close to each other, tightly holding hands, and all at once the fiddler bade all the company be quiet, and a jocular ceremony was performed signifying the union of the two young people. They had to clasp hands, and the whole audience rose and, one by one, stepped up to congratulate them and to bid them welcome within their fraternity. They placidly submitted to it all, but said never a word, and regarded the whole as a jest, while all the while a shudder of voluptuous feeling ran through them.

The merry company now became louder and more excited, the fiery wine spurring them on, until at last the black fiddler urged departure. "We have a long way be-

Aufbruch mahnte. »Wir haben weit«, rief er, »und Mitternacht ist vorüber! Auf! wir wollen dem Brautpaar das Geleit geben, und ich will vorausgeigen, daß es eine Art hat!« Da die ratlosen Verlassenen nichts Besseres wußten und überhaupt ganz verwirrt waren, ließen sie abermals geschehen, daß man sie voranstellte und die übrigen zwei Paare einen Zug hinter ihnen formierten, welchen der Bucklige abschloß mit seiner Baßgeige über der Schulter. Der Schwarze zog voraus und spielte auf seiner Geige wie besessen den Berg hinunter, und die andern lachten, sangen und sprangen hintendrein. So strich der tolle nächtliche Zug durch die stillen Felder und durch das Heimatdorf Salis und Vrenchens, dessen Bewohner längst schliefen.

Als sie durch die stillen Gassen kamen und an ihren verlorenen Vaterhäusern vorüber, ergriff sie eine schmerzhaft wilde Laune, und sie tanzten mit den andern um die Wette hinter dem Geiger her, küßten sich, lachten und weinten. Sie tanzten auch den Hügel hinauf, über welchen der Geiger sie führte, wo die drei Äcker lagen, und oben strich der schwärzliche Kerl die Geige noch einmal so wild, sprang und hüpfte wie ein Gespenst, und seine Gefährten blieben nicht zurück in der Ausgelassenheit, so daß es ein wahrer Blocksberg war auf der stillen Höhe; selbst der Bucklige sprang keuchend mit seiner Last herum, und keines schien mehr das andere zu sehen. Sali faßte Vrenchen fester in den Arm und zwang es stillzustehen; denn er war zuerst zu sich gekommen. Er küßte es, damit es schweige, heftig auf den Mund, da es sich ganz vergessen hatte und laut sang. Es verstand ihn endlich, und sie standen still und lauschend, bis ihr tobendes Hochzeitgeleite das Feld entlanggerast war und, ohne sie zu vermissen, am Ufer des Stromes hinauf sich verzog. Die Geige, das Gelächter der Mädchen und die Jauchzer der Bursche tönten aber noch eine gute Zeit durch die Nacht, bis zuletzt alles verklang und still wurde.

»Diesen sind wir entflohen«, sagte Sali, »aber wie entfliehen wir uns selbst? Wie meiden wir uns?«

Vrenchen war nicht imstande zu antworten und lag hochaufatmend an seinem Halse. »Soll ich dich nicht lieber ins Dorf zurückbringen und Leute wecken, daß sie dich aufnehmen? Morgen kannst du ja dann deines Weges ziehen, und ge-

fore us," he cried, "and it is past midnight. Up, all of you! Let us solemnly escort the young bridal couple, and I myself will open the procession. You will hear me fiddling as never before." Since Sali and Vreni felt perfectly dazed, and scarcely knew what they were doing in this hurly-burly around them, they did not protest when they were made to head the file, the other two couples following, and the hunchback, with his huge bass viol on his shoulder, being at its tail end. The black fiddler, though, strode in advance, playing like a man possessed, skipping down the steep hill path like a chamois, and the others laughed, singing in chorus, and jumping from rock to rock. Thus this nocturnal procession hastened on and on, through the quiet fields and at last through the home village of Sali and Vreni, now sunk in deep slumber.

When they two came through the still lanes and past their abandoned homes, a painfully savage mood seized them, and they danced and whirled along with the others behind the fiddler, kissed, laughed and wept. They also danced up the hill with the three fields that had tempted their fathers to their ruin, the fiddler all the time leading, and on its crest the dusky fiddler fell into a frenzy of fantastic melody, and his train of followers jumped about like veritable demons. Even the poor hunchback acted like demented. This quiet hill resounded with the infernal noise of the whole crew, and it was a perfect witches' Sabbath for a short while. The hunchback breathed hard and in a muffled voice squeaked with delight, swinging his heavy instrument like a baton. In their paroxysm none saw or heard the next. But Sali seized Vreni and thus forced her to halt. He imprinted a kiss on her mouth, thus stopping her shouts of joy. At last she gathered his meaning, and ceased struggling. They stood there, right on the spot where they first had encountered the black fiddler, listening to the wild music and to the singing and shrieking of the demoniac cortège, as the sounds gradually swept onwards down the hill towards the river below. Nobody evidently had missed them in the midst of the whole spook. The shrill tones of the fiddle, the laughter of the girls, and the yodels of the men resounded for another spell through the night, fainter and fainter, until at last the noise died away down by the shores of the river.

"We have escaped those," now said Sali, "but how are we going to escape from ourselves? How shall we separate, and how keep apart?"

Vreni was not able to answer him. Breathing hard she lay on his breast. "Had I not better take you back to the village, and wake some family in order to make them take you in for the night? To-morrow you can leave and look for some work. You'll be able to get along anywhe-

wiß wird es dir wohl gehen, du kommst überall fort!«

»Fortkommen, ohne dich!«

»Du mußt mich vergessen!«

»Das werde ich nie! Könntest denn du es tun?«

»Darauf kommt's nicht an, mein Herz!« sagte Sali und streichelte ihm die heißen Wangen, je nachdem es sie leidenschaftlich an seiner Brust herumwarf, »es handelt sich jetzt nur um dich; du bist noch so ganz jung, und es kann dir noch auf allen Wegen gut gehen!«

»Und dir nicht auch, du alter Mann?«

»Komm!« sagte Sali und zog es fort. Aber sie gingen nur einige Schritte und standen wieder still, um sich bequemer zu umschlingen und zu herzen. Die Stille der Welt sang und musizierte ihnen durch die Seelen, man hörte nur den Fluß unten sacht und lieblich rauschen im langsamen Ziehen.

»Wie schön ist es da rings herum! Hörst du nicht etwas tönen, wie ein schöner Gesang oder ein Geläute?«

»Es ist das Wasser, das rauscht! Sonst ist alles still.«

»Nein, es ist noch etwas anderes, hier, dort hinaus, überall tönt's!«

»Ich glaube, wir hören unser eigenes Blut in unsern Ohren rauschen!«

Sie horchten ein Weilchen auf diese eingebildeten oder wirklichen Töne, welche von der großen Stille herrührten oder welche sie mit den magischen Wirkungen des Mondlichtes verwechselten, welches nah und fern über die weißen Herbstnebel wallte, welche tief auf den Gründen lagen. Plötzlich fiel Vrenchen etwas ein; es suchte in seinem Brustgewand und sagte: »Ich habe dir noch ein Andenken gekauft, das ich dir geben wollte!« Und es gab ihm den einfachen Ring und steckte ihm denselben selbst an den Finger. Sali nahm sein Ringlein auch hervor und steckte ihn an Vrenchens Hand, indem er sagte: »So haben wir die gleichen Gedanken gehabt!« Vrenchen hielt seine Hand in das bleiche Silberlicht und betrachtete den Ring. »Ei, wie ein feiner Ring!« sagte es lachend; »nun sind wir aber doch verlobt und versprochen, du bist mein Mann und ich deine Frau, wir wollen es einmal einen Augenblick lang denken, nur bis jener Nebelstreif am Mond vorüber ist oder bis wir zwölf gezählt ha-re."

"But without you? Get along without you?" said the girl.

"You must forget me."

"Never," she murmured sadly. "Never in my life." And she added, glancing sternly at him: "Could you do that?"

"That is not the point, dear heart," answered Sali, slow and distinct. He caressed her feverish cheeks, while she kept pressing herself against his bosom. "Let us only consider your own case. You, Vreni, are still so very young, and quite likely you will fare well enough after a short while."

"And you also--you ancient man," she said, smiling wistfully.

"Come!" now said Sali, and dragged her along. But they only went on a few steps, and then they halted once more, the better to embrace and kiss. The deep quiet of the world ran like music through their souls, and the only sound to be heard around them was the gentle rush and swish of the waves as they slowly went on further down the valley below.

"How beautiful it is around here! Listen! It seems to me there is somebody far away singing in a low voice."

"No, sweetheart; it is only the water softly flowing."

"And yet it seems there is some music--way out there, everywhere."

"I think it is our own blood coursing that is deceiving our ears."

But though they hearkened again and again, the solemn stillness remained unbroken. The magic effect of the light of a resplendent full moon was visible in the whole landscape, as the autumnal veil of fog that rose in semi-transparent layers from the river shore mingled with the silvery sheen, waving in grayish or bluish bands. Suddenly Vreni recalled something, and said: "Here, I have bought you something to remember me by." And she gave him the plain little ring, and placed it on his finger. Sali, too, found the little ring he had meant for her, and while he put it on her hand, he said: "Thus we have had the same thought, you and I." Vreni held up her hand into the silvery light of the moon and examined the little token curiously. "Oh, what a fine ring," she then said, laughing. "Now we are both betrothed and wedded. You are my husband, and I'm your wife. Let us imagine so, just long enough until that small cloud has passed the moon, or else until we have counted twelve. You must kiss me twelve times."

ben! Küsse mich zwölfmal!«

Sali liebte gewiß ebenso stark als Vrenchen, aber die Heiratsfrage war in ihm doch nicht so leidenschaftlich lebendig als ein bestimmtes Entweder – Oder, als ein unmittelbares Sein oder Nichtsein, wie in Vrenchen, welches nur das Eine zu fühlen fähig war und mit leidenschaftlicher Entschiedenheit unmittelbar Tod oder Leben darin sah. Aber jetzt ging ihm endlich ein Licht auf, und das weibliche Gefühl des jungen Mädchens ward in ihm auf der Stelle zu einem wilden und heißen Verlangen, und eine glühende Klarheit erhellte ihm die Sinne. So heftig er Vrenchen schon umarmt und liebkost hatte, tat er es jetzt doch, ganz anders und stürmischer und übersäete es mit Küssen. Vrenchen fühlte trotz aller eigenen Leidenschaft auf der Stelle diesen Wechsel, und ein heftiges Zittern durchfuhr sein ganzes Wesen, aber ehe jener Nebelstreif am Monde vorüber war, war es auch davon ergriffen. Im heftigen Schmeicheln und Ringen begegneten sich ihre ringgeschmückten Hände und faßten sich fest, wie von selbst eine Trauung vollziehend, ohne den Befehl eines Willens. Salis Herz klopfte bald wie mit Hämmern, bald stand es still, er atmete schwer und sagte leise: »Es gibt eines für uns, Vrenchen, wir halten Hochzeit zu dieser Stunde und gehen dann aus der Welt – dort ist das tiefe Wasser – dort scheidet uns niemand mehr, und wir sind zusammen gewesen – ob kurz oder lang, das kann uns dann gleich sein. –«

Vrenchen sagte sogleich: »Sali – was du da sagst, habe ich schon lang bei mir gedacht und ausgemacht, nämlich daß wir sterben könnten und dann alles vorbei wäre – so schwör mir es, daß du es mit mir tun willst!«

»Es ist schon so gut wie getan, es nimmt dich niemand mehr aus meiner Hand als der Tod!« rief Sali außer sich. Vrenchen aber atmete hoch auf, Tränen der Freude entströmten seinen Augen; es raffte sich auf und sprang leicht wie ein Vogel über das Feld gegen den Fluß hinunter. Sali eilte ihm nach; denn er glaubte, es wolle ihm entfliehen, und Vrenchen glaubte, er wolle es zurückhalten. So sprangen sie einander nach, und Vrenchen lachte wie ein Kind, welches sich nicht will fangen lassen. »Bereust du es schon?« rief

Sali was surely fully as much in love as was Vreni, but the marriage problem was, after all, not of such intense interest to him, not such a question of Either--Or, of an immediate To Be or Not To Be, as it was in the case of the girl. For Vreni could feel just then only that one problem, saw in it with passionate energy life or death itself. But now at last he began to see clearly into the very soul of his companion, and the feminine desire in her became instantly with him a wild and ardent longing, and his senses reeled under its potency. And while he had previously caressed and embraced her with the strength and fervor of a devoted lover, he did so now with an incomparably greater abandonment to his passion. He held Vreni tightly to his beating heart, and fairly overwhelmed her with endearments. In spite of her own love fever, the girl with true feminine instinct at once became aware of this change, and she began to tremble as with fear of the unknown. But this feeling passed almost in a moment, and before even the cloud had flitted over the moon's face her whole being was seized by the whirlwind of his ardor, and engulfed in its depths. While both struggled with and at the same time fondled the other, their beringed hands met and seized the other as though at that supreme moment their union was consummated without the consent of their will power. Sali's heart knocked against its prison door like a living being; anon it stood still, and he breathed with difficulty and said slow and in a whisper: "There is one thing, only one thing, we can do, Vreni; we keep our wedding this hour, and then we leave this world forever--there below is the deep water--there is everlasting peace and fulfilment of all our hopes--there nobody will divorce us again--and we have had our dearest wish--have lived and died together--whether for long, whether for short--we need not care--we are rid of all care--"

And Vreni instantly responded. "Yes, Sali--what you say I also have thought to myself--not once but constantly these days--I have dreamed of it with my whole soul--we can die together, and then all this torment is over--Swear to me, Sali, that you will do it with me!"

"Yes, dearest, it is as good as done--nobody shall take you from me now but Death alone!" Thus the young man in his exaltation. But Vreni's breath came quick and as if freed from an intolerable burden. Tears of sweetest joy came to her eyes, and she rose with spontaneous alacrity and, light as a bird, flew down towards the river side. Sali followed her, thinking for a moment she wanted to escape him, while she fancied he would wish to prevent her. Thus they both sprang down the steep path, and Vreni laughed happily like a child that will not allow her playmate to catch her. "Are you sorry for it already?"

eines zum andern, als sie am Flusse angekommen waren und sich ergriffen; »nein! es freut mich immer mehr!« erwiderte ein jedes. Aller Sorgen ledig, gingen sie am Ufer hinunter und überholten die eilenden Wasser, so hastig suchten sie eine Stätte, um sich nieder zu lassen; denn ihre Leidenschaft sah jetzt nur den Rausch der Seligkeit, der in ihrer Vereinigung lag, und der ganze Wert und Inhalt des übrigen Lebens drängte sich in diesem zusammen; was danach kam, Tod und Untergang, war ihnen ein Hauch, ein Nichts, und sie dachten weniger daran, als ein Leichtsinniger denkt, wie er den andern Tag leben will, wenn er seine letzte Habe verzehrt.

»Meine Blumen gehen mir voraus«, rief Vrenchen, »sieh, sie sind ganz dahin und verwelkt!« Es nahm sie von der Brust, warf sie ins Wasser und sang laut dazu: »Doch süßer als ein Mandelkern ist meine Lieb zu dir!«

»Halt!« rief Sali, »hier ist dein Brautbett!«

Sie waren an einen Fahrweg gekommen, der vom Dorfe her an den Fluß führte, und hier war eine Landungsstelle, wo ein großes Schiff, hoch mit Heu beladen, angebunden lag. In wilder Laune begann er unverweilt die starken Seile loszubinden. Vrenchen fiel ihm lachend in den Arm und rief: »Was willst du tun? Wollen wir den Bauern ihr Heuschiff stehlen zu guter Letzt?« – »Das soll die Aussteuer sein, die sie uns geben, eine schwimmende Bettstelle und ein Bett, wie noch keine Braut gehabt! Sie werden überdies ihr Eigentum unten wiederfinden, wo es ja doch hin soll, und werden nicht wissen, was damit geschehen ist. Sieh, schon schwankt es und will hinaus!«

Das Schiff lag einige Schritte vom Ufer entfernt im tiefern Wasser. Sali hob Vrenchen mit seinen Armen hoch empor und schritt durch das Wasser gegen das Schiff; aber es liebkoste ihn so heftig ungebärdig und zappelte wie ein Fisch, daß er im ziehenden Wasser keinen Stand halten konnte. Es strebte Gesicht und Hände ins Wasser zu tauchen und rief: »Ich will auch das kühle Wasser versuchen! Weißt du noch, wie kalt und naß unsere Hände waren, als wir sie uns zum ersten Mal gaben? Fische fingen wir damals, jetzt werden wir selber Fische sein und zwei schöne große!« – »Sei ruhig, du lieber Teufel!« sagte Sali, der Mühe hatte, zwischen dem tobenden Liebchen und den Wellen sich aufrecht zu halten, »es zieht mich, sonst fort!« Er hob seine Last in

Thus they both apostrophized the other, as they in a twinkling had reached the river shore and seized hold of each other. And both answered: "No, indeed, how can you think so?" And carefree they now walked briskly along the river bank, and they outdistanced the hastening waves, for thus keenly they sought a spot where they could stay for a while. For in the trance of their enthusiasm they knew of nothing but the bliss awaiting them in the full possession of each other. The whole worth and meaning of their lives just then condensed itself into that one supreme desire. What was to follow it, death, eternal oblivion, was to them a mere nothing, a puff of air, and they thought less of it than does the spendthrift think of the morrow when wasting his last substance.

"My flowers shall precede me," cried Vreni, "only look! They are quite withered and dusty!" And she plucked them from her bosom, cast them into the water, and sang aloud: "But sweeter far than almonds is my love for thee!"

"Stop!" called out Sali. "Here is our bridal chamber!"

They had reached a road for vehicles which led from the village to the river, and here there was a landing, and a big boat, laden high with hay, was tied to an iron ring in the bank. In a reckless mood Sali instantly set to freeing the ship from the strong ropes that held it to the landing. But Vreni grasped his arm, and she shouted laughing: "What are you about? Are we to wind up by stealing from the peasants their haycock?" "That is to be the dowry they give us," replied Sali with humor. "See! A swimming bedstead and a couch softer than any royal couple ever had. Besides, they will recover their property unharmed somewhere near the goal whither it was to travel anyway, and they will hardly trouble their hard heads with the question how it got there. Do you notice, dear, how the boat is swaying and rocking? It is impatient to start on the journey."

The ship lay a few paces off the shore in deeper water. Sali lifted Vreni in his arms high up, and began to wade through the water towards the boat. But she caressed him so fervently and wriggled like a fish on the angle, that Sali was losing his footing in the rather strong current. She strained her hands and arms in order to plunge them in the water, crying: "I also want to try the cool water. Do you remember how cold and moist our hands were when we first met? That time we had been catching fish. Now we ourselves will be fish, and two big and handsome ones to boot." "Keep still, you wriggling darling," said Sali, scarcely able to stand up in the water, with his sweetheart tossing in his arms and the current pulling at him, "or it will drag me under!" But now he lifted his pretty burden into the boat, and scrambled up its side himself. Then he hoisted her up to the hay,

das Schiff und schwang sich nach; er hob sie auf die hochgebettete weiche und duftende Ladung und schwang sich auch hinauf, und als sie oben saßen, trieb das Schiff allmählich in die Mitte des Stromes hinaus und schwamm dann, sich langsam drehend, zu Tal.

Der Fluß zog bald durch hohe dunkle Wälder, die ihn überschatteten, bald durch offenes Land; bald auf stillen Dörfern vorbei, bald an einzelnen Hütten; hier geriet er in eine Stille, daß er einem ruhigen See glich und das Schiff beinah stillhielt, dort strömte er um Felsen und ließ die schlafenden Ufer schnell hinter sich; und als die Morgenröte aufstieg, tauchte zugleich eine Stadt mit ihren Türmen aus dem silbergrauen Strome. Der untergehende Mond, rot wie Gold, legte eine glänzende Bahn den Strom hinauf, und auf dieser kam das Schliff langsam überquer gefahren. Als es sich der Stadt näherte, glitten im Froste des Herbstmorgens zwei bleiche Gestalten, die sich fest umwanden, von der dunklen Masse herunter in die kalten Fluten.

Das Schiff legte sich eine Weile nachher unbeschädigt an eine Brücke und blieb da stehen. Als man später unterhalb der Stadt die Leichen fand und ihre Herkunft ausgemittelt hatte, war in den Zeitungen zu lesen, zwei junge Leute, die Kinder zweier blutarmen zugrunde gegangenen Familien, welche in unversöhnlicher Feindschaft lebten, hätten im Wasser den Tod gesucht, nachdem sie einen ganzen Nachmittag herzlich miteinander getanzt und sich belustigt auf einer Kirchweih. Es sei dies Ereignis vermutlich in Verbindung zu bringen mit einem Heuschiff aus jener Gegend, welches ohne Schiffleute in der Stadt gelandet sei, und man nehme an, die jungen Leute haben das Schiff entwendet, um darauf ihre verzweifelte und gottverlassene Hochzeit zu halten, abermals ein Zeichen von der um sich greifenden Entsittlichung und Verwilderung der Leidenschaften.

packed in orderly fashion in the middle, sweet-scented and downy like a vast pillow, and next he swung himself up to her. When they both were thus enthroned on their bridal bed the ship drifted gently into the middle of the stream, and then, turning slowly, it headed sluggishly in an easterly direction.

The river flowed through dark woods, shadowing it; it flowed through the fruitful plain, past quiet villages and hamlets and single homesteads; there it broadened out like a still lake and the ship moved but slightly downwards, and here it turned tall rocks and left the slumbering landscape quickly behind. And when dawn broke there was in sight at some distance a town rising with its age-worn towers and steeples above the silver-gray river. The setting moon, red as gold, cast a quivering track of light upstream towards the dim outlines of the ancient city, and into this luminous bed the ship finally turned its prow. When the houses of the town at last approached closely two pale shapes, locked in a tight embrace, glided in the autumnal frost of early morn from off the dark mass of the ship into the silent waters.

The ship itself shortly after fetched up near a bridge, unharmed, and remained there. When sometime later the two bodies, still locked in each others' arms, were found, and details about the young man and his sweetheart were learned, one might have read in the newspapers that these two, the children of two ruined and impoverished families that had lived in bitter enmity, had sought death in the water together after dancing with great animation at a kermess. This event probably was connected with the other fact that a boat laden with hay had landed in town without anyone on board. It was supposed that the young couple had cut loose the boat somewhere in order to hold their godforsaken wedding on it. "Once again a proof of the spread of lawless and impious passion among the lower classes." That was the concluding paragraph in the newspaper report.

Lightning Source UK Ltd.
Milton Keynes UK
UKHW051541220123
415778UK00014B/219